CAl

Call of the Herald
Book One of The Dawning of Power trilogy
Brian Rathbone

The Godfist

Prologue

Within his cabin, General Dempsy adjusted his uniform, making certain every medal was straight and every button oriented properly. Moving automatically to counter the movements of the ship was normally as natural to him as breathing, but he felt unsteady on his feet, as if his years of sailing had suddenly been forgotten. It was not a feeling he was accustomed to. At sea or just about anywhere on Godsland, his power was undeniable, his orders obeyed without question. There was one place, however, where his power was surpassed, and even a man of his accomplishments must exercise great caution: Adderhold, seat of the Zjhon empire. It was from there that Archmaster Belegra ruled with an unforgiving will, and it was to there that General Dempsy was destined.

He had no reason to expect anything but a warm welcome, given his success, but there was an uneasy feeling in his gut. Again, automatically, he adjusted his uniform, as if a single stitch out of place could decide his fate. The general cursed himself for such weakness, yet he jumped when there came a knock at his cabin door. After cursing himself again, he answered in his usual commanding tone: "Come."

Mate Pibbs presented himself and saluted. "Adderhold is within sight, sir. We've been cleared by the sentry ships, and there is a slip reserved for us. Do you wish to be on deck when we land, sir?"

General Dempsy nodded, and Mate Pibbs saluted again before turning on his heel. To some the salute is a source of great pride and a feeling of power, and most times General Dempsy felt much the same, but on this day it felt like mockery. After a final check of his uniform, he made his way to the prow. From there, he watched Adderhold grow larger and more intimidating with every passing moment. It was a feeling that should have passed long before, but the builders of Adderhold had done their job well. The place looked as if it could swallow his entire fleet in a single strike.

When they reached the docks, General Dempsy was unsure of what to think. There was no fanfare; no throng awaited the returning army, and there was not so much as a victory dinner to celebrate their conquest of an entire continent. The Greatland was theirs to rule, yet Adderhold bustled with preparations for war. Barges surrounded the island, and they sat low in the water, piled high with grain and supplies, ready to transport the goods to the waiting armada. These were not the usual preparations for an assault on a coastal province. The scale of their provisions foretold a lengthy sea voyage, and the taste of victory turned to bile.

General Dempsy knew, long before the page arrived with his new orders, that the Church had declared holy war. He tried to convince himself otherwise, but what he saw could only mean an invasion of the Godfist, a preemptive strike intended to stave off the prophecy. He thought it was sheer madness. Archmaster Belegra would ruin everything by sending them on a fool's quest. This was a hunt for some fantasized adversary, one not only destined to destroy the entire Zjhon nation, but also one that might herald the return of a goddess Archmaster Belegra and the devotees of the Zjhon Church had both dreamed of and feared. The devout believed that Istra would imbue them with miraculous gifts but that her presence would also mark the return of their greatest adversary.

In the face of such fanaticism, General Dempsy struggled to maintain his equilibrium. To him, the Zjhon beliefs made little sense. Though he had played his role in many ceremonies, he believed none of it; he simply did what the Church asked of him because it furthered his own goals. His military genius had only served to strengthen the Zjhon and their beliefs, and though it had granted him the power he desired, he suddenly wondered if it had been a mistake--a grave and deadly mistake. To say his army was unprepared for an assault on the Godfist was a gross understatement. Two-thirds of his men came from lands that had only recently been conquered; few were well trained, and fewer still were loyal. With his experienced and trusted men spread throughout the regiments, he was barely able to maintain control. He knew it was a suicide mission and that it would

4

be years before they were ready to undertake a long-distance campaign.

Orders to get his army ready for the invasion confirmed the insanity, and when he saw them, he requested an immediate audience with Archmaster Belegra under the pretense of misunderstanding the mission. It was highly unusual for any member of the armies to meet with the archmaster in person, but General Dempsy felt he was entitled. He and his men had offered up their lives for the empire, and they deserved to know why they were being thrown away.

Days passed before he was granted the audience, and that gave him time to ponder every word he might use to implore the archmaster to change his mind. When a page finally arrived with his summons, the uncertainty was festering in his belly. Archmaster Belegra was the only person with enough power to have him executed, and his every instinct warned that the wrong choice of words could send him to the headsman's block.

A slight figure in dark robes greeted General Dempsy with little more than a slight bow. Though his features were concealed within a deep hood, the general knew of him. He was the nameless boy whose insolence had cost him his tongue. As he led General Dempsy to a private hall, he served as a silent warning. This had the potential to be a very dangerous encounter.

When he entered the hall, General Dempsy saw Archmaster Belegra swathed in thick robes and huddled in an ornate chair that was pulled up close to the fire. Though the years had barely grayed his hair, he looked like a feeble old man. As austere as ever, he did not acknowledge General Dempsy in any way, as if he were oblivious to his presence.

"A humble servant of the Zjhon requests the consideration of the Church," General Dempsy said in a polite tone, trying to sound unassuming, but he feared it came out sounding forced and insincere. Archmaster Belegra did not look at him, nor did he speak; he simply extended his right hand and waited. The general did not hesitate in moving to the archmaster's side, taking his hand, and kissing the signet ring, wishing to dispense with protocol as quickly as possible.

"The Church recognizes her child and will suffer you to speak."

"With all due respect, Your Eminence, I must ask you to reconsider this course of action. Launching an attack on such a distant nation, when we've barely secured the lands surrounding us, will put everything we've achieved at risk." General Dempsy was more direct than was advisable, but he was determined and pushed on. "It's not that I don't believe the prophecies, but sending two-thirds of our strength on a--" Archmaster Belegra raised an eyebrow, and Dempsy stopped. He knew he was treading in dangerous waters, and he preferred to keep his head.

"The prophecies are quite clear on this matter, General, but I will refresh your memory if I must. Vestra, God of the Sun, has ruled Godsland's skies for nearly three thousand years, but he will not always reign alone. Istra, Goddess of the Night, shall return to preside over the night skies. A harbinger shall be born of her hand and will be revealed by the power they wield. Thus, the advent of Istra shall be heralded. Faithful of the Church, beware, for the Herald of Istra shall desire your destruction and will endeavor to undo all you have wrought."

General Dempsy despaired. The prophecies were impossible to argue since no proof could be offered to discredit them. They were sacred and above reproach.

"It is your responsibility to protect this nation and all the inhabitants of the Greatland. The Herald of Istra poses an imminent threat to the Church and the entire Zjhon empire. The holy documents have rewarded us with clues regarding the timing of Istra's return, and we must use these divine gifts to our full advantage. To do otherwise would be sacrilege and blasphemy. Is that clear?"

General Dempsy nodded, mute. He struggled to find words that would drive away the madness, but they remained beyond his grasp.

"You have your orders, General. You know your duty; the army is to set sail for the Godfist by the new moon and is not to return without the Herald of Istra. Go forth with the blessings of the Zjhon Church."

Chapter 1

Life is the greatest of all mysteries, and though I seek to solve its many riddles, my deepest fear is that I will succeed.
--CiCi Bajur, philosopher

* * *

Immersed in its primordial glow, a comet soared through space with incredible speed. Three thousand years had passed since it last shed its light upon the tiny blue planet known to its inhabitants as Godsland, and the effects had been cataclysmic. A mighty host of comets followed the same elliptical orbit as the first as they returned from the farthest reaches of the solar system. Their light had already charged the atmosphere of Godsland, and the comets themselves would soon be visible to the naked eye.

The cycle of power would begin anew. Radiant energy, though still faint, raced toward Godsland, bearing the power of change.

As the force angled over the natural harbor where the fishing vessels were moored for the night, it soared beyond them over the Pinook Valley, and nothing barred its path. Beyond a small town, amid foothills dotted with farmsteads, it raced toward a barn where a young woman dutifully swept the floor. A slight tingle and a brief twitch of her eyebrows caused Catrin to stop a moment, just as a chance wind cast the pile of dirt and straw back across the floor. It was not the first thing to go wrong that morning, and she doubted it would be the last.

She was late for school. Again.

Education was not a birthright; it was a privilege--something Master Edling repeatedly made more than clear. Those of station and power attended his lessons to gain refinement and polish, but for those from the countryside, the purpose was only to stave off the epidemic of ignorance.

His sentiments had always rankled, and Catrin wondered if the education was worth the degradation she had to endure. She had already mastered reading and writing, and she was more adept at mathematics than most, but those were skills taught to the younger students by Master Jarvis, who was a kind, personable teacher. Catrin missed his lessons. Those approaching maturity were subjected to Master Edling's oppressive views and bland historical teachings. It seemed to her that she learned things of far more relevance when she worked on the farm, and the school lessons seemed a waste of time.

Master Edling detested tardiness, and Catrin was in no mood to endure another of his lectures. His anger was only a small part of her worries on that day, though. The day was important, different. Something was going to happen-- something big; she could feel it.

The townies, as Catrin and her friends called those who placed themselves above everyone else, seemed to feed on the teacher's disdainful attitude. They adopted his derogatory manner, which often deteriorated into pranks and, lately, violence. Though she was rarely a target, Catrin hated to see her friends treated so poorly. They deserved better.

Peten Ross was the primary source of their problems; it was his lead the others followed. He seemed to take pleasure in creating misery for others, as if their hardships somehow made him more powerful. Perhaps he acted that way to impress Roset and the other pretty girls from town, with their flowing dresses and lace-bound hair. Either way, the friction was intensifying, and Catrin feared it would escalate beyond control.

Anyone from the countryside was a target, but it was her friend Osbourne Macano, son of a pig farmer, who bore the brunt of their abuses. The low regard in which his family profession was held and his unassuming manner made him an easy target. He had never fought back, and still the attacks continued. Chase, Catrin's beloved cousin, felt they should stand up for themselves since passive resistance had proven fruitless. What choice did they have?

Catrin understood his motives, but to her, the problem seemed unsolvable. Surely retaliation would not end the struggle, but neither had inaction, which left her in a quandary. Chase seemed to think they needed only to scare the townies once to make them realize such treatment would not be tolerated. That, he said, was the only way to gain their respect, if not their friendship. She could see his logic, but she also saw other, less appealing possibilities, such as a swift and violent response or even expulsion from the school lessons. Too many things could go wrong.

Chase was determined, though, and she would support him and Osbourne in their fight, if that was their choice. But she did not have to like it.

From bribing a woman who had once worked as Peten's nursemaid, Chase learned that Peten had a terrible fear of snakes--any snake, not just the venomous varieties. Chase planned to catch a snake and sneak it into the hall during lessons, though he admitted he had no plan for getting it near Peten without being seen. Just thinking about it, Catrin began to feel queasy, and she concentrated even more on her work. As she slid the heavy barn door closed to keep out the wind, she was submerged in darkness and had to resweep the floor by the light of her lantern.

Her father and Benjin, his close friend, were returning from the pastures with a pair of weanlings just as she lugged her saddle into Salty's stall. She watched the skittish colt and filly enter the barn wide eyed, but they gave the experienced men little trouble and would soon become accustomed to frequent handling. The lamplight cast a glow on Benjin's dark features. Bits of gray showed in his neatly trimmed beard, and his ebon hair was pulled back in a braid, giving him the look of a wise but formidable man.

Salty, Catrin's six-year-old chestnut gelding, must have sensed she was in a rush, for he chose to make her life even more difficult. He danced away from her as she tossed the saddle over his back, and when she grabbed him by the halter and looked him in the eye, he just snorted and stepped on her toes. After pushing him off her foot, she prepared to tighten the girth, and Salty drew in a deep breath, making himself as big as possible. Catrin knew his tricks and had no desire to find herself in a loose saddle. Kneeing him in the ribs just enough to make him exhale, she cinched the strap to the wear marks. Salty nipped her on the shoulder, letting her know he didn't appreciate her spoiling his joke.

Dawn backlit the mountains, and heavy cloud cover rode in with the wind. A light spray was falling as Catrin walked Salty from the low-ceilinged barn into the barnyard. Salty danced and spun as she mounted, but she got one foot in the stirrup and a hand on the saddle horn, which was enough to pull herself up even as he pranced. His antics were harmless, but Catrin had no time for them, and she drove her heels into his flanks with a chirrup to urge him forward.

In that, at least, he did not disappoint as he leaped to a fast trot. She would have given him his head and let him gallop, but the wagon trail was growing muddy and slick in the steady rain. Cattleman Gerard appeared in the haze ahead, his oxcart leaving churned mud in its wake. Trees lined the narrow trail, and Catrin had to slow Salty to a walk until they cleared the woods. When they reached a clearing, she passed Gerard at a trot, waving as she rode by, and he gave her a quick wave in return.

Fierce gusts drove stinging rain into her eyes, and she could barely see the Masterhouse huddled against the mountains; in the distance, only its massive outline was visible. Harborton materialized from the deluge, and as she approached, the rain dwindled. The cobbled streets were barely damp, and the townsfolk who milled about were not even wet. In contrast, Catrin was bespattered and soaked, looking as if she had been wallowing in mud, and she received many disapproving looks as she trotted Salty through town.

The aroma of fresh-baked bread wafting from the bakery made her stomach grumble, and the smell of bacon from the Watering Hole was alluring. In her rush, she had forgotten to eat, and she hoped her stomach would not be talkative during the lessons, a sure way to irritate Master Edling.

She passed the watchtower and the large iron ring that served as a fire bell, and she spotted her uncle, Jensen, as he dropped off Chase on his way to the sawmill. He waved and smiled as she approached, and she blew him a kiss. Chase climbed from the wagon, looking impish, and Catrin's appetite fled. She had hoped he would fail in his snake hunt, but his demeanor indicated that he had not, and when the leather bag on his belt moved, any doubts she had left her.

How he had concealed the snake from her uncle was a mystery, but that was Chase, the boy who could do what no one else would dare attempt.

His mother and hers had died fifteen years before on the same day and under mysterious circumstances; no one understood what killed them. Since then, Chase seemed determined to prove that he wasn't afraid of anything or anyone.

Catrin pulled Salty up alongside him, and they entered the stables together. Once clear of the gate, she turned to the right, hoping to slip into her usual stall unnoticed, but instead she saw another insult. All the stalls were taken, despite there being plenty for those students who rode. Many of the townies, including Peten, rode to the lessons even though they were within walking distance. In a parade of wealth and arrogance, they flaunted their finely made saddles with gilded trim. It seemed they now felt they needed pages to attend to their mounts, and they, too, must ride. It was the pages' horses that had caused the shortage of stalls. Catrin stopped Salty and just stared, trying to decide what to do.

"What's going on, Cat?" Chase bellowed. "Have the townies gotten so fat they need two horses to carry each of them?"

"Hush, I don't want any trouble," she said with a pointed glance at his writhing bag. "I'll stable Salty at the Watering Hole."

"Strom may let you stable him there, but certainly not for free. Where does it stop, Cat? How much abuse do they think we'll tolerate?" he asked, sounding more incensed with each word.

"I don't have time for this now. I'll see you at the lesson," she said, turning Salty. Chirruping, she gave him a bit of her heels, trotted him around the block, and slowed only when she neared Baker Hollis, who was busy sweeping the walk. He gave her a sidelong glance and shuffled into the bakery. Inside, Catrin saw his daughter, Trinda, who stared with haunted eyes. She rarely left the bakery, and it was said she spoke even less often. Most thought she was daft, but

Catrin suspected something entirely different, something much more sinister.

As she turned into the alley behind the Watering Hole, she whistled for Strom, who emerged from the stable looking tired and irritable.

"Cripes, it's early, Cat. What brings you here?" he asked, rubbing his eyes. He had once attended the lessons and had been friends with Catrin and Chase. After his father died, though, he had gone to work as a stable boy for Miss Mariss to help support his mother. He was shunned by most. His humble circumstances and departure from the lessons marked him as undesirable in the eyes of many, but Catrin enjoyed his company and considered him a good friend.

"I'm sorry to wake you, but I really need to stable Salty here today. The stable at the academy is full, and I'm already late. Please let me keep him here--just for today," she asked with her most appealing look.

"If Miss Mariss finds out, she'll have my hide for a carpet. I can only stable a horse if the owner patronizes the inn and pays a copper for the stall," he said.

Digging into her coin purse, Catrin pulled out a worn silver half she'd been saving for an emergency. She tossed it to Strom. "Buy yourself something to eat and take good care of Salty for me. I have to go," she said as she grabbed her wax pad from her saddlebags.

Strom rolled the coin across his knuckles as she sprinted away. "I hate to take your money, Cat, but I assure you it won't go to waste!" he shouted.

Catrin raced back to the academy, turning toward the lesson hall at a full run. Master Beron shouted for her to slow down, but she was nearly there. She reached the door and opened it as quietly as she could, but the hinge betrayed her, squeaking loudly. Everyone in the room turned to see who would be the target of Master Edling's ire, and Catrin felt her face flush.

She entered with mumbled apologies and quickly sought a vacant desk. The townies gave her nasty looks and placed their wax tablets on the empty chairs near them, clearly indicating she was not welcome. In her rush to reach the desk next to Chase, her wet boots slipped on the polished floor, leaving her suspended in air for an instant before she hit with a crash. The air rushed from her lungs with a whoosh, and the room erupted in laughter.

As soon as she regained her breath, she immediately held it, seeing Chase take advantage of the distraction. He slinked behind Peten and slid the leather pouch under his chair. The drawstrings were untied and the top lay open, but nothing emerged. Catrin stood and quickly took the seat between Chase and Osbourne, still blushing furiously.

"This isn't going to go well for you, Cat. Edling looks boiled," Osbourne whispered, but Master Edling interrupted in a loud voice.

"Now that Miss Volker has seen fit to join us, perhaps she will allow us to commence. What say you, Miss Volker? Shall we begin, or do you need more leisure time?" he asked, looking down his nose, and several of the townies sniggered, casting her knowing glances. Catrin just mumbled and nodded. She was grateful when Master Edling began his lecture on the holy war; at least he was no longer adding to her embarrassment by making a bigger fool of her.

"When Istra last graced the skies," he began, "the Zjhon and Varic nations waged a holy war that lasted hundreds of years. They fought over conflicting interpretations of religious documents, none of which could be proved or disproved. Meanwhile, the Elsic nation remained neutral, often acting as a mediator during peace talks. Many times peace was made only to be broken again upon the first provocation.

"Then there came a new Elsic leader, Von of the Elsics. He ascended the throne after killing his uncle, King Venes. Von had been clever and murdered his uncle during the harvest festival, when there were hundreds of people in attendance who might have wanted the king dead. No one could identify the killer, and a veil of suspicion hung over the court. Elaborate conspiracy theories were rampant, and Von encouraged them since they served his purposes well. Those who believed treachery was afoot were much less likely to speak out for fear of being the next mysterious death."

The teacher droned on. "Von believed his nation's historical neutrality in the war was folly and that it would be better to conquer both nations while they were weakened by the prolonged war. The Elsics did not condone the use of Istra's powers, claiming it was blasphemous, and none of their scholars were skilled in arcana. Von had no large army at his disposal either, so he concluded that Istra's power was the only way he could defeat both nations. He would use the very powers that were flaunted by the Zjhon and the Varics as the agents of their destruction.

"He staged clandestine raids against each nation, disguising his men as soldiers from the opposing nation. His instructions were clear: he wanted people captured, not killed, because he wanted slaves. Those captured were transported in secret to the Knell Downs, which we believe to be high in the Pinook Mountains. Camps were built, and the slaves were forced to experiment with creating powerful weapons using Istra's power.

"There were many failures, as most of those captured had no experience in such things, but after countless attempts, a slave named Imeteri made a deadly discovery. Weakened from working in stuffy quarters, he convinced his captors to let him work outside whenever the sun shone. His efforts were fruitless for many weeks, and many of his experiments lay about in disarray, unfinished or forgotten completely, except for the details in his copious notes. Most of them consisted of various compounds of elements he placed in clay mugs, which he sealed with mud. One day, while working on his experiments, an explosion knocked him off his feet, and he knew one of his concoctions had worked. It took many more efforts for him to duplicate his success.

"One major problem was that his explosive needed to charge in the light of both Istra and Vestra before it would detonate. As it became saturated with energy, it would begin to glow, gradually getting brighter and brighter until it would eventually explode.

"Von was pleased by Imeteri's discovery, and after several refinements and small-scale demonstrations, he declared it the success he had been looking for. Imeteri was raised to the highest status of slave, barely less than a free man. Von ordered the other slaves to build enormous statues

15

in the likeness of Istra and Vestra sharing a loving embrace. These great behemoths became known as the Statues of Terhilian, and packed with the new explosive, they were sent to the various Zjhon and Varic cities. Appearing to be tokens of peace, they were readily accepted and revered. The wars had drained the Zjhon and Varic nations, and lacking the resources to fight, they were relieved to receive the gifts.

"It was an abominable tactic and one I hope is never eclipsed. Drawn to the statues like moths to a flame, the faithful and war-weary congregated in enormous numbers around the likenesses of their gods. All but a few of the statues detonated, resulting in cataclysmic explosions that leveled entire cities, killing countless souls. The toxic aftermath debilitated those not killed by the initial blasts, and most died soon thereafter. And so began mankind's darkest age, a time known as the Purge," Master Edling continued, his unvarying cadence threatening to put Catrin, and most of the other students, into a deep sleep.

The snake, which Catrin now saw was an olive-green tree snake, was lured from Chase's pouch by the stillness, its slender head and neck poked from the pouch, looking like a bean pod with eyes. Catrin held her breath as it slithered forward and coiled itself around the chair leg. Peten noticed Catrin's sideways glances and gave her a snide look, tossing his long, blond hair over his shoulders.

With his muscular build, strong jaw, and piercing blue eyes, he cast a striking figure, but his attitude and ego made him the least attractive person Catrin had ever met. She felt little pity for him as the snake continued to follow its instinct, which was to climb. Peten was oblivious to its presence and continued to look bored, casting his own glances to get the attention of Roset Gildsmith.

The snake slithered up the slats on the back of his chair; it brushed against his curls, and still he remained unaware. He shifted in his seat, as if sensing the stares of Catrin, Chase, and Osbourne, and turned his head to glare at them. As he did, his eyes met those of the snake, and he shrieked. His high-pitched scream and sudden movement alarmed the snake, and it struck, biting him on his nose. Catrin knew the snake was not venomous, but Peten obviously knew nothing of the sort.

He leaped from his chair, sending his desk and the snake flying. Charging from the hall, he knocked Roset and another girl from their chairs. He showed no concern for anyone in the hall, and it was obvious his only care was for his own safety.

Master Edling stormed to the back of the hall, fuming, and snatched the agitated snake from the ruins of Peten's chair. After releasing it at the base of a tree in the courtyard, he returned, pushing Peten before him, forcing the shaken young man to return the desks to order.

Chase's eyes danced with glee, and Osbourne let a giggle slip. The townies and Master Edling glared at them with eyes like daggers. Catrin sat quietly, hoping the situation would somehow improve, but instead it worsened.

"Peten Ross, you are a coward and a boor," Roset said with a haughty look. "Do not aspire to speak to me again." She turned smugly away, her jaw stuck out in defiance.

Chase seemed to think things were going very well, but Catrin could see Peten's fury rising, his embarrassment fueling his desire for retribution. How Chase could not see mounting danger was a mystery to Catrin. Perhaps he was simply caught up in his own thirst for revenge.

Master Edling concluded his lecture and dismissed the class curtly. Catrin was just glad to have the lesson over and tried to flow out with the rest of the crowd, but Master Edling barred her path.

"Miss Volker, I would have a word with you," he said, and he clearly did not wish to compliment her.

"Yes sir, Master Edling, sir," Catrin replied softly. "I'm sorry I was late, sir."

"I'll have no excuses from you. It is your responsibility to arrive before the appointed time. If you cannot do so, then I recommend you do not attend at all. Since you wasted my time at the beginning of class, it is only fair I waste your time now. Be seated," he said, and Catrin slumped into the chair nearest the door, anxiously waiting for her punishment to be concluded.

Outside the lesson hall, Chase ducked into a darkened recess and waited for Osbourne. Roset came first, and she cast him a haughty glance, but he was grateful that she said nothing. Using the darkness for cover, he held his breath as Peten stormed by, followed by a mob of agitated townies. Minda and Celise walked by, and Osbourne seemed to be trying to hide behind them. Hoping no one noticed, Chase grabbed Osbourne by the shirt and dragged him into the alcove. Osbourne let out a small yelp before he realized it was Chase who had grabbed him, and he looked over his shoulder more than once.

"Looks like Edling held Catrin after class," Chase said.

"I told you he looked boiled," Osbourne said, but there was a tremble in his voice, and he looked nervously over his shoulder. "Are you going to wait around for Cat?"

"I can't. I promised my dad I'd help with the afternoon deliveries."

"I can't either," Osbourne said. "I've chores to do, and I should probably study for the test we have coming up."

"Bah, who needs to study?" Chase asked with a grin. "Just remember everything Edling says; that's all."

Osbourne shook his head. "That may work for you, but my father'll tan my hide if I bring home bad marks. I'd better get Patches saddled and get going, or I'm going to run out of light."

Chase peeked around the corner before walking back into the light, half expecting to find Peten and the rest of the townies waiting for him, but the stables were eerily quiet. Only Patches remained in her stall, and Chase stayed with Osbourne while he got her saddled.

"Never seen everyone clear out so quickly," Chase said.

"I'm starting to think the snake was a bad idea," Osbourne said as he tightened the girth. "Feels like I've got squirrels in my guts. You don't think they'll do anything to Cat, do you?"

"You worry too much," Chase said, but he secretly wondered if Osbourne was right. It seemed strange that Peten and the others had left so quickly, and letting

Osbourne and Catrin travel home alone suddenly seemed like a very bad idea. There was nothing he could do about it, though, no way to take back what was already done, and he tried to drive the worry from his mind. "I'm sure everything will be fine."

"I hope you're right," Osbourne said as he mounted. Patches, who was a well-mannered mare, must have sensed Osbourne's nervousness, for she danced around the stable, her ears twitching as she spun. Osbourne soothed her with a hand on her neck, and she trotted away with her tail tucked. "I'll see you tomorrow," Osbourne said with a wave.

"Be careful," Chase said, betraying his own fears, and Osbourne rode away looking more nervous than ever.

Checking around every corner as he went, Chase made his way to the mill. At each turn he expected to find the townies waiting, and their absence only increased his anxiety. "I wish they would just get on with it," he mumbled to himself as he passed the market.

When he saw his father waiting with the wagon already loaded, though, he forgot his fears. They had enough work to keep them until nightfall, and he would have time to think of little else.

* * *

After sitting far longer than needed to make up the time she had missed, Catrin began to wonder if Master Edling had forgotten she was there. He was completely engrossed in his text, and she was hesitant to interrupt. She tried to be patient, but she desperately wanted to talk to Chase, and she shifted in her seat constantly.

"You are dismissed," he said suddenly without looking up.

"Thank you, Master Edling; it won't happen again, sir," Catrin said as she rose to leave.

"It had better not. And do not think for a moment that I'm unaware of your involvement in today's disruption; you can pass that along to your cousin as well," he said, and Catrin did not bother to deny it, knowing it would do no good.

19

She walked quickly to the Watering Hole, arriving to find Strom busy with the mounts of two nobles. She waited in the shadows, not wanting the nobles to complain about riffraff hanging around the stables; it had happened before, and she didn't want to impose on Strom. Once the nobles made their instructions abundantly clear, they strolled into the Watering Hole, and Catrin emerged from her hiding place.

"Thanks for keeping out of sight," Strom said. "Salty's in the last stall. You can saddle him yourself, can't you?" he asked with a smirk.

"I think I can manage, though the task is beneath me," Catrin replied, and her sarcasm brought a chuckle from Strom. Her tack had been cleaned and hung neatly outside the stall; he had treated her horse and gear as if they were his own, and she appreciated the gesture. Salty gave her no trouble, being aware he was on his way home, where his feed bucket waited. Strom was still attending to the nobles' horses and tack when she mounted.

"Thank you, Strom. I appreciate your help," she said, waving as she left.

"Don't mention it, Cat; just try not to make a habit of it," he replied with a wink and returned to his work.

Salty needed little prompting, and he broke into a trot as soon as they left town. Catrin turned him onto the wagon trail that meandered toward her home, hoping Chase would meet her there. She had expected to find him waiting at the Watering Hole, and his absence concerned her. She was tempted to push Salty to a gallop but resisted the urge. The trail was muddy and slick, and speed would only put her and Salty at risk. Her father and Benjin had warned her about such behavior, and she heeded their advice.

Engrossed in her thoughts, she let Salty cover the familiar distance without her input, but as she approached the woods, she heard someone cry out. Urging Salty forward, she scanned the trees for signs of trouble. Through the foliage, she saw flashes of movement in a clearing, and harsh laughter echoed around her. When she saw Patches, Osbourne's mare, wandering through the trees, still saddled and bridled, she nearly panicked. Osbourne would never leave his horse in such a state, and she knew he was in trouble.

After jumping from the saddle, she tied Salty to a nearby tree and approached Patches, who recognized her and cooperated as Catrin tied her to another tree. Meanwhile, she heard more muffled cries. Running as fast as she could toward the nearby sound, she burst into the clearing. Osbourne was near the center on his hands and knees. Blood flowed freely from his nose and mouth, and he clutched his side. Peten Ross, Carter Bessin, and Chad Macub were on horseback and appeared to have be taking turns riding past Osbourne, beating him with their wooden staves.

"Stop this madness!" Catrin shouted as she ran to Osbourne's side. She crouched over his body, hoping to protect him yet knowing she could not; she was overmatched. He whimpered beneath her, spitting blood through his ruptured lips.

"Out of the way, farm girl, or you'll share this one's fate. He needs a lesson in showing respect to his betters," Peten said as he spurred his horse. As he swept past, he swung his staff in a powerful arc, landing a solid blow on Catrin's shoulder. She barely had time to recover from his attack before Carter approached. His mount was blowing hard from the workout, sweat frothing around saddle and bridle alike.

His staff swung wide, striking her on her hip, but she barely felt the pain. As Peten wheeled his horse and dug in his heels, his eyes were those of a madman. He seemed intent on killing her and Osbourne, and Catrin became convinced her death approached. Peten was a well-muscled athlete who had trained in the jousts for as long as he could ride. He would not miss his target again, and her defiance clearly enraged him, leaving little chance of mercy.

Time slowed, and as she cried out in fear, her voice sounded hollow and strange in her ears. Still Peten came, aiming his mount so close that she feared they would be trampled. He did not run them down, though; instead he brought his horse just close enough to provide a clear shot at Catrin. She watched in horror as his staff swung directly at her head, and she saw her own terrified reflection in its highly polished surface as it blocked out the rest of the world. Intense sadness overwhelmed her as she prepared to die. Though she hoped Osbourne would survive the encounter, it seemed unlikely.

In the next instant, Catrin's world was forever changed. Her body shuddered, and a sound louder than thunder ripped through the clearing. She tried to make sense of what she saw as the world seemed to fly away from her. Everything took on a yellowish tint, which faded to blackness as she crumbled to the ground.

* * *

Nat Dersinger turned his nose to the wind and inhaled deeply. The wind carried the smell of misfortune, and he had learned better than to ignore his instincts. Despite the fact that he'd caught no fish, he pulled in his nets. Looking out at the clear skies, broken by only fluffy white clouds that seemed frozen in time, he wondered if he was just being silly, but the ill feeling persisted and grew more intense with every passing moment.

With a sense of urgency, he raised his sails and guided his small craft back to the harbor. Along the way he passed other fishing vessels, but no one waved or shouted out in greeting, as they did with other fishermen. Most just cast Nat suspicious glances, others glared at him until they were lost from sight. Nat tried not to let any of it bother him, but he soon realized he was grinding his teeth and his hands were clenched into fists. Too many times he'd been treated as an outcast, as if he were not even human. With a long sigh, he released his frustration and concentrated on avoiding the scores of hidden rock formations that flanked the harbor entrance.

At the docks, he received more strange looks--partly because he was back long before most of the other fishermen would return, and partly because he brought no fish to the cleaning tables, but mostly it was because he was Nat Dersinger, son of a madman. Most would rather see him dead or exiled; others simply tolerated him. There were few people he trusted and fewer still who trusted him. It was a lonely and unforgiving existence, but he had to believe it was all for a purpose, some grand design beyond his ability to perceive or understand. He let his mind be consumed by the possibilities, and he entered an almost dreamlike state; nothing around him seemed real, as if he walked in a place somewhere between this life and the great unknowable that lay beyond.

Unaware of where he was going, he let his feet follow a path of their own choosing, permitting his unconscious mind--rather than his conscious mind--to guide the way. It was one of the few lessons his father had taught him: sometimes the spirit knows things the mind cannot; never ignore the urgings of your spirit.

When he reached the woods outside of town, he barely recalled the walk. His feet continued to carry him into the countryside, and he wondered--as he often did--if he was simply fooling himself, assigning himself otherworldly powers rather than admitting he shared his father's illness. In truth, that was the crux of his life. Most seek answers to a myriad of questions, but Nat was consumed by one question alone: Had his father been a true prophet or a madman? As he found himself suddenly climbing over a hedge of bramble, he was inclined to believe the latter, but then the ground trembled and the air was split by a mighty thunderclap. Leaping over the hedge, Nat moved with confidence and purpose, suddenly trusting his instincts more than his senses. For the first time in a very long time, he believed not only in his father, but also in himself.

* * *

As the sun was sinking behind the mountains, casting long shadows across the land, Catrin woke. She sat up slowly, dizzy and disoriented, and put one hand out toward the ground to steady herself; it found Osbourne's chest. He was unconscious, his breathing shallow, but at least he looked no worse than he had when she'd arrived. She hoped he was not seriously injured. Her body ached as she moved,

23

and she closed her eyes. Drawing a deep breath, she tried to calm herself.

Moans broke the eerie silence, and Catrin heard someone behind her gasp. She turned to see who it was, and only then did she behold the devastation that surrounded her. The clearing was a good bit larger than when she'd entered it; every blade of grass, bush, and tree within a hundred paces had been leveled. She stood, unsteadily, at the center of a nearly perfect circle of destruction. All the debris pointed away from her, as if she had felled it with a giant sickle.

Turning around slowly, she took in the awful details. Supple stalks of grass had been so violently struck that they were broken cleanly in half. In all her seventeen summers, Catrin had never witnessed such a terrifying sight. Behind her stood Nat Dersinger, a local fisherman who was thought to be mentally unstable. He leaned on his ever-present staff, his jaw slack, and made no move. The staff was taller than he was, half its length shod in iron, which formed a sharp point. His wild, graying hair stuck out in all directions, and his eyes were wide, making him look every bit the madman some thought him to be. Though he was of an age with Catrin's father, the lines on his face made him appear much older.

Peten's horse lay, unmoving, in a tangle of downed trees. Horrified, Catrin saw Peten's boots sticking out from under the animal, and she feared him dead, but she could not make herself move.

"Help, my leg is broken!" she heard Carter shout, and she turned to see him struggling to get out from under his own dead horse. Chad wandered aimlessly, followed by his faithful mount, which limped badly.

"Gods have mercy. I bear witness to the coming of the Herald. The prophecy has been fulfilled, and Istra shall return to the world of men." The words poured out of Nat and struck fear into those who heard them.

Townsfolk and farmers had begun to arrive, having heard the blast and been guided by the shouting. They tended the wounded, and word was sent to the Masters as well as the parents of the students involved. People scrambled to help Peten and the others, and many cast frightened glances at Catrin as they passed. Osbourne regained consciousness, and a kindly old man helped him to the edge of the clearing to await the Masters.

Few folk had the courage to speak to Catrin, but those who did all asked the same question: "What happened?"

"I don't know," was the only honest answer Catrin could give, but no one seemed to believe her. When her father arrived, he ran to where she stood, tears filling his eyes. Overwhelmed, she collapsed into his embrace. He hugged her and tried to comfort her, but he seemed unable to find the right words. Instead, he tied Salty to his saddle and pulled Catrin atop his roan mare, and they rode home in cautious silence.

* * *

A pool of molten wax and a dwindling wick were all that remained of Wendel Volker's candle, and he let it burn. His eyes, swollen with tears, were focused beyond the blank wall he faced. Raising Catrin alone had never been in his plans. He had done the best he could without Elsa, but in Wendel's mind it never seemed enough. If not for Benjin, he wasn't sure they would have survived. All along, they had struggled, but now they faced a danger far too great. The chill of fear crept up his neck--fear, not for himself, but for his beloved daughter.

Remembering the damage in the clearing, Wendel felt goose bumps rise on his skin. More disturbing than the damage was the look in Catrin's eyes. She felt responsible and guilty; that much was clear. Wendel tried to figure out what might have happened, but he found no answers. Instead, he accepted the fact that he might never know. What mattered was that people would be angry, confused, and afraid; all of which put Catrin in danger. Stronger and deeper than his greatest personal desire was the need to protect his daughter. So powerful was this urge that he went to where she slept and stood over her, watching her breathe.

"Help me be strong for her, my dearest Elsa," he said under his breath. He wept quietly. "If ever you've heard me, hear me now. I can't do this alone. I need you. Catrin needs

25

you." Then he stiffened his jaw and firmed his resolve. "Watch over her, my love, and keep her safe."

* * *

As darkness claimed the sky, Nat Dersinger stood at the center of the clearing. All the others had long since gone to their homes and were probably discussing the day's events over their evening meals, but Nat tried to push that vision from his mind. Such thoughts brought him only pain and misery, and this was not a time he needed to be reminded of his loss. What he needed was guidance on what to do next. The prophecies warned of disastrous events, but they gave no indication of anything that could be done to prevent the foretold dangers. There must be something he could do, Nat thought, but he came to the same realization he had come to in the past: It would take more than just him. Somehow, he would have to convince those who had enough power to make a difference. Given his past failures, he found it difficult to be optimistic. Bending down, he pulled a blade of grass from the ground and marveled at how cleanly it had been broken. He let his mind wander for a time until something tugged at his awareness and demanded his attention. A familiar yet indefinable smell drifted on the breeze, and Nat's eyes were drawn to the heavens. As a sailor, he knew the stars as friends and followed their guidance, but on this night, they seemed almost insignificant, as if their power were about to be usurped, their beauty eclipsed. Nat had nothing more than his feelings to guide him, and his thoughts ran in a familiar pattern. So many times his instincts and gut feelings had caused him nothing but trouble. He would spill his heart to save those who showed him only hostility. "Why?" he asked himself for what seemed the thousandth time. But then his familiar pattern changed, irrevocably, as he looked at the blade of grass and the tangled mass of downed trees that lined the clearing. It was proof. No one could argue it or claim that it was a creation of his deranged mind. This was real and undeniable. For the first time in more than a decade, he did not question himself.

When he looked back to the sky, he believed completely. His father had been right all along. There was little consolation in this knowledge, for it foretold a difficult and perilous future for all, but it was vindicating for Nat nonetheless. As his thoughts wandered, he felt himself drifting into a different state of awareness, his eyes fixed on the sky yet focused on nothing. He felt himself being drawn upward, lifted to the heavens. His eyes felt as if they would be pulled from their sockets, so strongly did the sky seem to reach for them, longingly and insistent. The vision began more as a feeling than images in his mind; he felt small and afraid in the face of a coming storm. Lightning flashed across his consciousness, and thunder rattled his soul. From the skies came a rain of fire and blood, and the land was rent beneath his feet. A single, silhouetted figure stood between him and the approaching inferno. Nat reached out, his hands clawing toward salvation, but his only hope faded along with the vision.

Lying faceup at the center of the grove, just as Catrin had found herself, Nat drew a ragged breath. Sweat ran into his eyes, and his heart beat so fast and hard that he thought it might burst. He realized then that it might be better if he were truly mad.

Chapter 2

If peace cannot be made, then peace shall be seized.
--Von of the Elsics

* * *

As daylight streamed in through the open window, Catrin woke from a restless sleep, and she struggled to bring herself fully awake. Nightmarish visions plagued her slumber. Twisted dreams were so vivid that she had trouble distinguishing which events were real and which were nightmares. She pulled herself from her sweat-soaked linens, hoping the attack on Osbourne had been nothing but a dream. Sleep still filled her eyes and muddled her thoughts as she padded into the small common room she shared with her father.

He had left water in the washbasin for her, but that had been some time ago, and the water was no longer warm. Catrin tried to wash away the sweat from her fevered dreams, wishing that she could scrub away the horrors she felt closing around her, waiting to strike. The cold water helped clear the haze from her mind, allowing her to separate fantasy from reality. Her aching body brought her to a chilling realization.

It was real. The attack, the explosion, the strange way she was treated were all real!

On shaking legs, she dressed in her leathers and homespun, tears welling in her eyes as she imagined the consequences. Her life would be forever changed, and depression overwhelmed her. In an effort to feel normal, she got ready to do her chores. She donned her heavy boots and worn leather jacket, which had been left by the fire to dry. The jacket was covered in creosote stains and had a host of minor rips and tears, but she insisted on wearing it until it fell apart completely. Like a cherished companion, it had been with her on many an adventure, and she was loath to abandon it.

After she strapped on her belt knife, she gathered her laundry, a washboard, and some bits of soap. If she wished to have something comfortable to sleep in, she would need to get her things hung to dry. Not even raising her head as she stepped from the cottage into the barnyard, she let her feet carry her across the familiar distance. It was a short walk to the river, and she had a well-worn path to follow.

Turbulent thoughts rattled her mind, and when she reached the river's edge, she did not recall most of the walk. Kneeling on the shore, she dipped her nightclothes into the clear, frigid water, which numbed her fingers. She applied a bit of soap to the garments and scrubbed them vigorously on the washboard, but then she heard shouts coming from the barn. Throwing her garments into the dirt, she sprinted to the barn, fearing someone was hurt. The sound of several voices shouting carried across the distance, which alarmed her even more since her father and Benjin were normally the only ones about.

She stopped short when a familiar-looking man backed out of the barn, waving his arms in front of him, and he came close to falling over backward. Two more men followed, both in similar states of retreat, and Catrin was shocked to the core of her being when her father charged out next, looking like a man in a murderous rage. Benjin swarmed out at his side, his pitchfork leveled at the retreating men.

"You expect us to live with that abomination in our midst?" one man shouted as he backpedaled. "That hussy damn near killed m'boy. He might die yet from what she did to 'im."

"You've no proof of that, Petram, nor do you, Burl, nor you, Rolph. You'll take yourselves off my property this instant, or so help me . . ." he said through clenched teeth; then he actually growled at them. A threatening step forward sent the other men scrambling back. Benjin had not said a word, but the look in his eyes made it clear he would not hesitate to stick them with his pitchfork if they persisted, and it appeared as though the men might leave before any blood was shed.

Massive waves of fear, embarrassment, and guilt washed over Catrin, freezing her in place. She wanted to flee or scream but could do neither. Instead she stood still as a stone and watched the events unfold, hoping to remain unseen, but it was not to be. The men spotted her and glared.

"What are you staring at, you boiling little witch?" one man shouted, and Catrin recognized him as Peten's father, Petram. She also recognized the fathers of the other boys. As they scowled at her, she quailed; the hatred in their eyes made her feel small and dirty.

"You will burn for this, Catrin Volker!" Burl shouted over his shoulder, but his speech was cut short when Benjin swung the pitchfork handle at his head, and the three men fled.

"The council will hear of this!" Petram shouted.

Then they were gone, leaving Catrin to consider their words. Her father turned to her, and the look on his face softened. She stood silent, tears streaming down her cheeks, unchecked, and her lip quivered as she struggled to maintain her composure.

"Ah, Cat. I wish none of this were happening. You've certainly done nothing to deserve what those sons of jackals just said. Don't take their words into your heart, dear one. They are just scared, confused, and looking for someone to blame. I'll take care of them; don't you worry. Come along now. We've horses to tend, and I need to make a trip to the cold caves this afternoon," he said as he guided her into the barn.

Catrin's father had inherited the cold caves from his father, Marix. A popular barroom tale said her grandfather had won the caves in a wager with Headmaster Edem. They said Edem had been drinking with Marix at the Watering Hole after the Summer Games. Edem's son had won the cross-country horse race, and he celebrated with Marix, who had trained the horse, and they both got too far into their drink. Edem bet Marix he could not get the innkeeper, Miss Olsa, to show them her wares. Miss Olsa was an older woman at the time, though not unattractive, and she had a reputation for being a shrewd businesswoman.

Marix called her to his table and whispered into her ear for a long time. When he pulled his cupped hand away, Miss Olsa turned to the drunken headmaster, pulled up her blouse, and boldly revealed herself. Then she ran into the kitchen, giggling like a young girl. No one knew what Marix said, but the locals swore no one ever duplicated the feat, which made her grandfather a bit of a town hero. Catrin suspected he said something regarding the free cold cave storage still enjoyed by Olsa's daughter, Miss Mariss, long after Olsa's passing.

Benjin had followed the men off the property to make sure they caused no more trouble, and he returned just as Catrin entered the barn.

"Don't let those fools bother you, li'l miss. They haven't got the sense the gods gave 'em," he said, hefting his pitchfork in mock combat. On his way back to the stall he'd been cleaning, he stopped and patted Catrin on the shoulder with his over-large, calloused hand. His simple act of kindness shattered Catrin's fragile composure, and with each step, more tears flowed down her cheeks. Sobs wracked her, and she stood before her father, trembling, her shoulders hunched forward. She could not bring herself to look him in the eye, and she stared at the ground instead.

Her father never let the tribulations of the day disturb his routine, which gave Catrin comfort. He brought Charger, his roan mare, from her stall and put her on cross-ties. He ran a currycomb over her muddy coat with one hand and smoothed the freshly brushed coat with his other. Charger was accustomed to his ministrations and promptly fell asleep, letting the cross-ties hold up her head.

"What happened in the woods yesterday?" her father asked without looking up from his task.

"Peten was angry at Chase and Osbourne for playing a trick on him, and the townies attacked Osbourne on his way home. I tried to protect him, and they attacked me. I thought I was going to die, but right before Peten hit me, the world exploded. It's hard to explain; it was so strange and so very horrible," she said, and she tried to continue, but her sobs would not be suppressed.

She hugged herself in an effort to maintain control while her father deftly unhooked the cross-ties and returned Charger to her stall. After closing the stall gate, he went to Catrin and awkwardly put his arms around her. It was a rare

31

gesture, which neither of them was truly comfortable with, but it meant a lot to her nonetheless.

"You certainly have your mother's knack for turning the world on its side, my little Cat. It'd be easier if she were here; I'm sure she would know what to do, but we'll get through this together, you and I. Don't you worry yourself sick. It's not so bad as it seems," he said with a forced laugh as he tousled her hair. "Now you run along and take the rest of the day for yourself. You've more than earned it with all of the hard work and long days you put in this winter," he continued. Catrin tried to argue, but he insisted. "Benjin and I can handle things around here."

"Off you go now, li'l miss. Maybe you could catch us some nice bass for dinner, eh?" Benjin said with a wink, and her father shot him a good-natured scowl.

"I give my daughter the day off, and you want her to catch your dinner?" Wendel said, shaking his head.

Laughter released some of Catrin's anxiety, and she left to fetch the laundry she had abandoned by the river. After she finished the washing, she took it to the cottage to hang it up to dry. When she was done, she took a piece of waxed cheese, some dried fruit, and a few strips of smoked beef for her breakfast. On her way back out of the cottage, she grabbed her bow, two fishing arrows, and her fishing pole. There was more than one way to catch a fish, and she was determined to bring back dinner.

Following the path back down to the riverbank, she turned north onto the trail that ran alongside the river, feeling as if every step took her farther from society and away from the source of her fears. She climbed past the shoals and falls, where the path was often steep and rocky. Along the way, she turned over rocks and collected the bloodworms that had been hiding in the darkness. By the time she reached the lake at the top of the falls, she had an ample supply of bait. Along the shores the water was shallow and slow, and the fishing was generally quite good. When she reached one of her favorite places, she laid out her gear.

Dark red blood oozed over her delicate fingers as she slid a bloodworm onto her hook, and she wiped it on her jacket, adding yet another stain. Her fishing line was far too coarse for her liking, but good fishing wire was expensive; she would have to make do with what she had. After checking the knot that held her lightwood bobber in place, she cast her line near a downed tree, which was partially submerged in the dark water, forming a perfect hiding place for the fish.

A towering elm gave her shade, and its moss-covered trunk provided a comfortable seat. She leaned against the tree and waited for the fish to bite. The stillness of the lake stood out in stark contrast to the maelstrom of thoughts that cluttered her mind. She attempted to review the events of the previous day, but she could not focus; when she tried to concentrate on one thought, another would demand her attention then another and another. Frustrated, she tried to put it all from her mind.

Her pole jerked in her hands, and the lightwood bobber jumped back to the surface. With a hurried yank, she set the hook and pulled the fish in, relieved it had not gotten away with her bait. The large-mouth bass put up a good fight, and when it emerged from the water, she was pleased to see it was longer than her forearm--not enough to feed three but a good start.

After baiting her hook again, she cast it near where she'd caught the first fish, but she got no more bites for the rest of the afternoon. The dark shadows of large fish moved below the surface, taunting her, and as the sun began to sink, she decided to try her luck with the bow. Normally, fishing arrows were used only when the carp were spawning since they made easy targets as they congregated in the shallows. Bass would be much harder to hit, but she had been practicing her archery skills, and she hoped the effort would pay off.

After securing her long string to the fishing arrow, she tied the other end off on an elm branch. Not wanting to lose her arrow, she double-checked her knots. Confident they were secure, she located a likely target and took aim. Ripples in the lake surface distorted her depth perception, and her first few shots missed their marks. Determined, she did her best to compensate for the distortion, and her next shot was true, catching another bass in the tail and pinning it to the bottom.

"Nice shot," Chase shouted from behind her, and she nearly leaped from her skin.

"Don't you know it's not nice to sneak up on people?" she said, truly glad to see him. He just grinned in response. She gave a tug on her string, but her arrow was firmly wedged, and she removed her boots, preparing to go in after it.

"Let me get that for you," Chase offered.

"I can get it; I'm not crippled," she retorted angrily and instantly regretted it. She had no reason to be angry with Chase, but she felt helpless--a feeling she despised--and she needed to lash out at someone. Chase took it in stride, though, and simply sat on the shore while she waded out to the flailing fish. She freed the arrow quickly and grabbed the fish by the tail; it was slightly smaller than the first, but it would be enough.

The bruises on her hip and shoulder ached as she climbed from the water, her muscles stiff from the time spent sitting beneath the tree. Chase grabbed the other fish and Catrin's bow while she retrieved her pole and her other fishing arrow. She was grateful for his help; without it, she would have had a difficult time carrying it all home. Chase was quiet for the first part of their walk, and Catrin allowed the silence to hang between them.

"I visited the infirmary this morning," he said after a while, and when Catrin made no reply, he continued. "Osbourne is doing much better and should recover quickly. He has a broken nose, a couple of badly bruised ribs, and a score of bumps and bruises, but he was awake this morning. He told everyone that you saved his life." Catrin grunted but said nothing.

"Carter has a broken leg, but otherwise he's fine. Chad has a head wound and can't remember much of anything; heck, he didn't even know who I was. The Masters said his memory should return in a few days, but his mother is hysterical. She just keeps shouting that her baby has been mortally wounded. Peten's hurt bad. The Masters won't say if he will live or die, but he did wake up for a while this morning. I think he'll recover myself; he didn't look nearly as bad as most were making him out to be." He stopped, and Catrin turned to look him in the eye. Her lip quivered, but otherwise she maintained her composure.

"I didn't do anything, Chase. I don't know what happened," she said, and Chase remained silent. "The last thing I remember was Peten bearing down on us and swinging his staff at my head. I saw my reflection in his staff, Chase. It was coming right at my face. How could I not have a mark on my head?" she asked, not anticipating a response. "At the very moment I expected his staff to crush my skull, there was a loud bang--like thunder but without the lightning. Just before I passed out, it looked like the world was flying away from me, and when I woke, it was like being in a nightmare."

"I believe you, Cat. Besides, even if it was something you did, you were just saving Osbourne from those boiling townies," he said.

She didn't like the insinuation that it could have been something she did, but she couldn't blame him. What evidence was there to prove otherwise? She began to doubt herself, but for the moment, she clung to what she knew to be true.

"They were going to kill poor Osbourne; I just know it. They probably would've gotten away with it too. I'm sure they would have just made up some story about him trying to rob them or some other rubbish, and that is just the kind of thing the Masters would believe of us farm folk," she said.

"They'll believe worse than that. The main reason I came was to warn you: rumors are spreading. Some say you are a witch or monster, and others have even claimed you are a Sleepless One. There have been some who have spoken up for you, but several suffered beatings as a result. I don't think it's safe for you to go into town right now; too many people have lost their senses, and they are starting to believe some of the crazy things people are making up," he said sadly.

Catrin sniffed and wiped her eyes but made no other sound.

"I'm truly sorry, Cat. I feel like this is my fault; if I hadn't brought that snake in, none of this would've happened. I'll do anything I can to help you, and I'll always stand up for you--"

"No," Catrin interrupted. "I don't want you getting hurt because of me. Keep your thoughts private. You'll be more help to me if you just listen and let me know what people are saying. Perhaps you could bring me my lessons," she said, but her voice cracked, and she could not get the rest out.

"Don't worry. I'll bring your lessons to you, and I won't do anything stupid, but I'm not going to let them get away with telling lies about you either."

"Thank you," was all she could manage to say without sobbing, and they walked back to the farm in silence.

As they approached, her father and Benjin waved, and they held up the bass in silent greeting. Benjin let out a whoop of glee on seeing the fish, and her father just shook his head. Benjin met them halfway.

"Nice catch ya got there, li'l miss. Here, let me take those. I'll get started on the cleaning," he said with a smile. Catrin started to object, but Benjin grabbed the fish and looked quite happy carrying them off to be cleaned and filleted.

"You go get washed up for dinner!" he shouted over his shoulder, and Catrin was happy to oblige; she was wet, dirty, and in need of a good scrubbing. After she and Chase washed up, they joined Benjin and her father in the cottage and were greeted by the smell of vegetable stew.

"I knew you wouldn't come home empty handed, li'l miss. I'll just boil the fish and add it to the stew; we'll eat like kings," Benjin said as he stoked the fire.

* * *

Chase pulled the rough but warm blanket around his shoulders as he curled up in front of the fire. Everyone else slept, but he could not. His thoughts would not allow it. He had been ready to face the repercussions of his actions, but he had not been prepared for Osbourne and Catrin to pay the price in his stead. He decided he didn't like the taste of guilt and remorse.

Catrin was gentle and fragile, and he was supposed to protect her. He had promised Uncle Wendel that he would always look after her, but when she and Osbourne had needed him most, he had failed them. Running his thumb over the locket that hung around his neck, he vowed to do better. Somehow he would shield her from the harshness of this world.

* * *

Wendel sat upright as he woke with a start. Darkness covered the land, and the wind made the rafters creak. But he was accustomed to hearing those noises; something else had disturbed his sleep, but he no idea what. Straining his hearing, he listened for anything out of the ordinary but heard nothing distinct, only brief hints that someone was moving outside the cottage. Creeping through the darkness, with the precision of intimate familiarity, he dressed and reached beneath his bed to retrieve Elsa's sword. Touching it normally brought tears to his eyes, but this was the first time in more than a decade that he unsheathed it with the intent of using it, and he moved with purpose.

Using skills he had long since abandoned, Wendel crept without a sound to where Catrin slept. Her chest rose and fell, and her eyelids twitched as they do only when one dreams. Seeing her safe relieved much of his anxiety, but Wendel was not yet satisfied. Perhaps the noises he'd heard were made solely by the wind, but he knew he would never be able to sleep without checking.

The predawn air carried a chill, and dense fog hovered above the ground. As Wendel emerged, the air grew still, as if he had somehow intruded on the wind and chased it away. The world seemed more like the place of dreams, and Wendel wondered if he could still be asleep. The snap of a branch in the distance startled him, but he could see nothing from where the noise had come. Could it have been a deer?

After checking around the cottage, he checked the barns, careful not to let the horses hear him, lest they give him away. Shadows shifted and moved, and the fog constantly changed the landscape, but Wendel found no signs of anyone about. Still his anxiety persisted, and he waited for what seemed an eternity for the coming of the false dawn. Across the barnyard, a shadow moved, and Wendel froze. Shifting himself from a sitting position to a more aggressive stance, he watched and waited. Again he saw movement, and he moved in to intercept. Out of the night came a blade to match his own, but before the blades met, he knew whom he faced. "Was that you I heard sneaking around the cottage?" he asked.

"You woke me while you were out here stomping around," Benjin said with a lopsided smile.

"We're getting old," Wendel said.

"I may be fat, lazy, and out of practice," Benjin said, "but watch who you're calling old."

"Catrin will be up soon. I don't want her to know we were both out here like a couple of worried hens."

"She won't hear it from me," Benjin said, and with a wave over his shoulder, he wandered back to his cabin.

Catrin was still asleep when Wendel returned to his bed, but it seemed only moments later that she began to stir.

Chapter 3

Anything worth having is worth working for. Anything you love is worth fighting for.
--Jed Willis, turkey farmer

* * *

Catrin woke, feeling oddly refreshed, happy to have slept well, and ready to face the day with more optimism than she would have thought possible. After dressing, she stirred the stew, which hung over the banked coals of the fire. More flavorful than it was the night before, it made for a good morning meal.

She stoked the fire and hung a pot of water over the flames, warming it for her father, who said washing with cold water made his bones ache. Benjin wandered in from outside, looking barely awake but smiling appreciatively as Catrin handed him a mug of stew. While he ate his breakfast, Catrin ladled a mug for her father, who had begun to stir. She knew he would be hungry when he emerged. He grunted in acknowledgment as he accepted the food, and she left them to their meal.

Lighting her lantern, Catrin left the warmth of the cottage and walked into the damp coolness of the early morning air. Millie, a gray and white tabby cat, greeted her at the door, weaving in and out of her legs. By the time she reached the feed stall, a mob of cats surrounded her, demanding attention and, more emphatically, food. Catrin kept a supply of dried meat scrap and grain in an old basin, and she used a bowl to scoop out enough for all of them.

A parade of scampering felines following in her wake, Catrin put the food outside the barn. The cats fell on it, each wanting their share and more, and they were soon begging again. Catrin stopped and looked at the cats trailing her. "Now listen to me. If I feed you any more, you'll get fat and lazy and not catch any mice," she said, shaking her finger and smiling. The cats looked at her and dispersed to various hay bales and horse blankets, content to preen or nap for the moment.

39

Catrin mixed oats and sweet grain into neatly organized buckets. Some horses required special herb mixtures in their feed, and Catrin took great care to be certain the mixtures went into the correct buckets. Giving an animal the wrong herbs could have dire consequences, and it was not a mistake she wished to repeat. A week of cleaning Salty's stall after giving him oil of the posetta by mistake had left a lasting impression on her.

Growing impatient, the horses banged their water buckets and pawed the floor to let her know they wanted their food immediately. Benjin came into the barn and started dumping the small buckets into the larger buckets that hung in the stalls. He knew the order; this was a dance they had performed many times.

"How much wikkits root did you put in Salty's feed, li'l miss?"

"Two small spoons of wikkits and a large spoon of molasses," Catrin replied, and Benjin chuckled.

"You did good; looks like you mixed it in fine. Never thought I'd see a horse eat around a powder, but he'll eat the grain and leave a pile of powder in the bucket. I'm telling ya, he does it just to spite me," he said, walking into Salty's stall. He gave the gelding a light pinch on the belly. Salty squealed and stomped and grabbed Benjin's jacket in his teeth, giving it a good shake. Without missing a beat, Benjin emptied the feed into the bucket and patted Salty on the forehead.

"Nice horsy," he said, and Catrin had to laugh. "Ah, there is that smile, li'l miss. It's good to see it again," he said with a wink.

She made no reply, unsure of what to say, and returned to her work. As she opened a bale of hay, mold dust clouded the air. They had lost too much hay to mold this year, and she knew not to feed the horses moldy hay. There was not much more they could have done to prevent the problem, though. The weather had turned bad at harvest time, and they had not been able to get the hay fully dry before bailing it. Forced to store the hay damp, they salted it to reduce moisture, stave off mold, and help prevent fire. Mold claimed much of the hay nonetheless, but at least it had not caught fire.

40

Her grandfather had lost a barn to a fire caused by wet hay. When hay dries, it goes through a process called a sweat, where it sheds water and produces heat. If packed too tightly, intense heat can build up and cause spontaneous combustion. The lesson had been passed to her father then down to Catrin. It was something she planned to teach her own children someday.

The moldy bale of hay she threw to the steer, which could eat just about anything, and she grabbed another bale for the horses. After giving each horse two slices of hay, she collected the water buckets, carrying them to the well her father and Benjin had dug long ago. It was something the men took great pride in, and Catrin was glad to have it. Her father often said it was not deep enough for his liking, and he feared it would run dry during droughts, but it had yet to fail them.

He once explained to Catrin that they were at the upper edge of an artesian basin. Water became trapped between layers of rock and was subjected to immense pressure. If you were to penetrate the rock anywhere along the basin, water would rise on its own, possibly forming a small fountain. Some places in Harborton had such wells, which had been allowing water to escape for hundreds of years.

After dumping out the dirty water, she gave the buckets a good scrubbing before refilling them; then she and Benjin hung them in the stalls. Afterward, they took hay and water to the horses that were out to pasture. The routine soothed Catrin; the rhythm of life on the farm was predictable and comforting. The tasks were familiar, and she could perform them skillfully, which gave her great pride. She liked nothing better than to do something well; doing a mediocre job was one of her greatest fears.

Finding herself thirsty, she walked over to the well for a drink and was disturbed to see a shiny black carriage under the trees. A squire tended a fine black mare, and Catrin was dumbfounded to see Master Edling speaking with her father. He was garbed in formal black robes, the blue embroidery as bright as a bluebird. He seemed out of place on the farm, a place of sweat and dirt, far from the pristine halls of the

41

Masterhouse. Her father did not look happy, but neither did he appear to be angry, at least not with Master Edling.

Frozen in anxious suspense, Catrin stood very still, hoping no one would notice her and fighting the urge to flee. Benjin came to her side, carrying a spare water bucket.

"Don't let them get the best of you, li'l miss. They are no better than the rest of us, no matter how prettily they dress or how clean they keep their fingernails," he said, filling the bucket. He pushed her toward her father as he carried the bucket to the squire. Her father shot her a steely glance and pointed to the cottage, an unspoken command. Catrin followed the two men into the cottage, cowed.

Her father offered Master Edling a seat and served summerwine and cheese. After a respectful interval, he turned to Catrin.

"Master Edling has come for two reasons. First, he is here to represent the Council of Masters. They've decided, due to the serious nature of the 'incident,' it would be best if you did not attend the public lessons--at least until this has all been sorted out," he said.

Catrin heard his words, and she understood what the council meant. *We don't think you should appear in public again-- ever,* she thought, shrinking in on herself.

"Second, Master Edling has volunteered to act as your tutor. He must still instruct the public lesson days, but he will come here on the off days to give you lessons. Quite kind of him, I'd say," he said with a nod to Master Edling. "I should be getting back to work, so I'll leave you to your lesson. If you'll excuse me, Master Edling."

"Yes, yes, indeed," Master Edling said, absently waving him from the room.

Catrin felt trapped, forced into isolation. Master Edling's visit was just the beginning. Keeping her away from town would only make her appear guilty of some crime. People would start to believe the crazy stories about her. She would be shunned for the rest of her life. Master Edling was not there to tutor her, she thought; he'd come only to see if she had grown horns or sprouted wings. Her mood dropped from fear into anger then to frustration. Her rage was building, seeking release, and it took great effort not to lash out. She had committed no crime. She had only tried to save her friend. As thanks, they would ruin her life, and it made her want to scream.

"Miss Volker?" Master Edling said, interrupting her mental torment. "I think that will do for today," he said, giving her one of his most disgusted looks. "I do not believe you heard a single word I said, did you? I could give you the same lesson on the morrow, and you would know no difference," he added in disgust. Catrin could not argue with him; she had not even realized he had begun his lecture, but his attitude only fueled her anger.

Master Edling stood and left without another word, his robes billowing around him. Catrin doubted he would return; he had seen what he had come to see. She was no monster or evil murderer, just a rude farm girl who had ignored and insulted him. His departure was bittersweet; while Catrin was not sorry to see him go, his leaving was like the death knell for her friendships. She wondered if she were destined to live as a hermit because of one freak incident.

Her father came back into the cottage, looking concerned. "Is your lesson over so quickly?" he asked. "Master Edling barely spoke a word as he left." His movements made it clear he was not pleased.

Catrin could not look him in the eye. She stared at the floor, stifling her tears. "I'm so sorry, Father. I was angry and confused, and I was thinking about everything and what it all meant and--" Her voice cracked, and she knew she was going to cry.

"Slow down, Cat. Don't get too upset on me. Let's just talk about this," he said gently, and Catrin did her best to steel herself and try to keep her emotions under control.

"I don't think Master Edling believes I am a worthy student."

"Are you?"

"No, sir, I don't think I am," she replied sadly.

"Now, Cat, you must stop this. Master Edling came here to help you, and you ignored him. He may never return. I can't send you back to the public lessons. Even if I could convince the council, it would be asking for trouble. Talk in town has grown a bit wild of late. Nat Dersinger has

43

convinced some people that you are the Herald and that Istra will return to the skies of Godsland soon," he said then stopped, fearing he had gone too far and frightened his daughter.

"Now most sane people don't believe a word of it, Cat. Everyone that knows you loves you. They know you as the spirited young athlete who competes in the Summer Games and as the hardworking girl that doesn't hesitate to help at a barn building. Your friends and family won't give up on you just because something unexplainable happened," he said, pulling up a chair. "I'm disappointed in you for insulting Master Edling today, but I can understand your distraction. I'll have a word with him on your behalf. Your best hope is that he has it in him to forgive you."

"Yes, sir," Catrin replied, looking downcast.

"There's no sense dwelling on it; we'll just have to see what tomorrow brings. For now, I want you to look after a few more things around the farm."

* * *

In the darkness of the bakery attic, where the heat was more than most could bear, Trinda watched, just as she always did. Always careful to remain undetected, she watched and waited, looking for anything that might please the dark men. It seemed all her life had been lived in fear of the strange men who came in the night, and here every waking hour was devoted to keeping them pleased. As long as she gave them what they wanted, they would never hurt her again. The memories still seared and burned as if they were new. The dark men were coming again; she could feel them getting closer.

When Miss Mariss walked out of the Watering Hole, Trinda jumped and then chastised herself for her carelessness. Of all the people she did not want to know about her spying, it was Miss Mariss. The dark men always asked questions about her; they always wanted to know whom she talked to and what they talked about. Trinda had only some of the answers they wanted, and it was all she

44

could do to come up with enough information to satisfy them.

Holding her breath, Trinda froze until Miss Mariss was lost from view. She was, no doubt, coming to place her order. Without the breads her father baked or the dough she used to make her famous sausage breads, Miss Mariss would surely suffer. The relationship between her and Trinda's father had always been tense and strained, but they were both professionals, and they did not let personal feelings stand in the way of business.

As Trinda stood, ready to climb down and make an appearance by the ovens, she stopped. Someone she didn't recognize was approaching the Watering Hole, and he went neither to the front entrance nor to the stables; instead he walked into the shade provided by an old maple. It seemed a strange thing to do, considering there were no doors on that side of the inn. Knowing her father would scold her for not appearing while Miss Mariss was in the bakery, Trinda stayed, intrigued by this unknown man's mysterious behavior.

For what seemed a long time, he stood in the shadows, only the toes of his boots visible from Trinda's vantage. Then, when the streets were empty, he squatted down and wiggled a loose piece of the inn's wood siding. After sliding what looked like a rolled piece of parchment into the space behind the siding, he quickly adjusted the wood until it looked as it had. Then he melted into the shadows and disappeared.

* * *

"Where is Trinda today?" Miss Mariss asked, trying to make the question sound entirely casual, as she always did, and Baker Hollis looked nervous and fidgety, as he always did.

"Must know there's work to be done," he said. "Any time there's somethin' needin' done, she turns invisible."

"Those her age can be like that," Miss Mariss said, despite not believing any of what he said. "I'll be making double the usual amount of sausage breads, and I'll need

45

triple the usual baked loaves for the Challenges. That won't be a problem will it?"

"No problem at all," Baker Hollis said, and he looked over his shoulder as if expecting to see Trinda. Miss Mariss was as surprised as he that she had not shown herself. It seemed whenever Miss Mariss came to the bakery, Trinda would make a point of making herself seen. "Everyone's sayin' this year'll be better than any before. I suppose we'll have to rise to the challenge," he said.

"I'll send Strom over in the morning for the daily order," Miss Mariss said as she turned to leave. Before she reached the door, though, a small, sweat-soaked head peeked around the corner and briefly met her eyes. Miss Mariss could read nothing from Trinda's expression; it was the same bland and sullen look as always. With a sigh, she left the bakery behind and soon forgot about Trinda as the responsibilities of running her inn once again consumed the majority of her thoughts and time.

* * *

Sitting on a bale of hay with his knees pulled to his chest, Chase kept to the shadows, not wanting to cause any trouble for Strom, who was busy saddling a pair of horses. So many things had changed in such a short period of time that Chase could hardly believe it. He no longer felt safe in places where he'd once felt quite at home. People he had considered friends no longer met his eyes, yet he could feel the stares that lingered on his back as he walked away.

"Sorry about that," Strom said once the customers had ridden around the corner.

Chase just handed him the jug of huckles juice they were sharing. "Do you remember when things used to be normal?"

"I remember," Strom said. "I remember things were sometimes good and sometimes bad, but it always seemed like things would get better. Now . . ."

"I know what you mean," Chase said. "I really made a mess of things."

Strom laughed. "You're still blaming yourself for all of this? You sure do think a great deal of yourself. Are you so powerful that you can control everyone else? I don't think so. You need to face the fact that you're just as helpless as the rest of us. Whatever happens just *happens,* and there's not a thing you can do about it."

"Thanks for the uplifting speech," Chase said. "I feel much better now."

"Don't come to me if you want sunshine and roses. That's not how I see the world. You could go talk to Roset. She still lives in a land of buttercups and faeries; maybe she could make you feel better."

"She won't even talk to me," Chase said, his mood continuing to be dour in the face of Strom's humor.

"You see? You're utterly powerless. Therefore you can't possibly be at fault. Doesn't that make you feel better?"

"If I said yes, would you stop talking about it?" Chase asked.

"Probably not."

* * *

Catrin spent the next few weeks throwing herself into every task her father assigned. Master Edling did not return, despite her father's many requests. Benjin and her father did what they could to teach her, but what they remembered of their own lessons was fragmented and disjointed. Catrin learned other things from the extra time she was spending on the farm. Benjin taught her the basics of shoeing horses along with other farrier skills. She was an apt student and excelled with little practice. It interested her because she loved horses, and they had always been part of her daily life. She had seen it done a hundred times, which helped her to quickly master even the most difficult techniques.

Forge and anvil became outlets for her frustration. She coerced the hot bars into the desired form, shaping them with her will. The song of the hammer and anvil soothed her, and she quickly replenished their supply of horseshoes. Benjin also taught her to make shoeing nails, whose shape was critical. Wide heads prevented the shoe from slipping

47

over the nails, while the tapered edges prevented injuries by forcing the nail to turn outward to the edge of the hoof against the taper.

As long as a farrier is careful not to drive one backward, the nail will always poke back out of the hoof, a finger's width above the shoe. The farrier would clip most of the tip of the nail then crimp the remains against the hoof. The technique provided a secure fit and better protection from sprung shoes.

"A horse will always spring a shoe at the worst possible moment, and it's good to know how to handle it," Benjin said. "You seem to handle the hammer well. Would you like to make a farrier's kit?" he asked. Catrin was delighted with the idea.

The hours she spent at the forge with Benjin were the only times she forgot her worries. Using tools to create new tools enthralled her, and she was immensely proud of her new implements. In a way, they brought her freedom. There were always coppers to be made shoeing horses and trimming hooves at local farms, and the knowledge that she could earn her own way was comforting. She would take pride in whatever work she did with them. Smiling, she tucked them into her saddlebags with care.

The weather was becoming unusually volatile, and intense storms confined Catrin to the barn or the cottage much of the time. Clear skies could quickly turn dark and foreboding, and fierce winds drove the rain. One afternoon, the sky was an eerie shade of green, like nothing she had ever seen before. Hail made her run for cover, each stone growing in size as she ran, some even larger than her fist. Benjin and her father sprinted into the barn just behind her.

Wind howled so fiercely through the valley that it lifted a hay wagon into the air and over a fence, depositing it, unharmed, in a pasture. When the storm passed, they checked for damage. Catrin helped her father and Benjin repair the roofs on the cottage and barn. The chicken coop had also suffered damage, but Benjin mended it quickly.

Abe Waldac, a local cattleman, drove his wagon behind a team of mules to the front of the barn. "Anyone hurt?"

"Luck was with us, Abe. We're fine. Thank you for checking on us, though. It's much appreciated," her father replied.

"You've always been good neighbors. I'm glad to see you all well. A funnel cloud ripped through the lowlands; looks like it made a boiling mess of things. I'm going to see if anyone needs help."

"We'll go with you. I'm sure they could use some extra hands down there. Catrin, you stay here and mind the farm. We'll be back late. Gunder may come for his mare. She's in the second stall," her father said, and the men rode off in Abe's wagon, leaving her alone. She knew someone had to watch the farm, but Catrin could not help feeling ashamed. Her father did not want to be seen in public with her.

* * *

Depression drove Nat back into seclusion. No one wanted to face the truth, even with the proof visible to all. It sickened him. They would rather die than admit he might have been right all along. In the end, he gave up trying to convince anyone else of the danger they faced. There seemed no point in even trying. Miss Mariss, at least, had listened politely, but even she refused to see the truth.

Returning to his normal life seemed almost surreal at first, but the feeling grew faint over time until he no longer noticed it. After days of blue skies and good fishing, he had almost been able to forget about his visions and feelings of impending doom; his life had been almost normal, even tranquil. The storm changed all that. Sudden winds had forced him north, well beyond the waters he normally fished, out to where dangerous currents had been known to carry away craft as small as his boat and pull them into open water.

Despite his efforts, he was pushed farther and farther from shore, and with every passing moment, the chances of his survival diminished. His only hope lay with a change in the wind. Occasionally he felt a shift in the air, as if a crosswind fought against the storm, and Nat prayed it would win.

Lightning splayed across the clouds, illuminating them from within and revealing the intricate structures and formations. Taller than mountains, yet flowing like rivers, the clouds seemed to reach from the sky and attack the sea itself, and Nat shivered. Though he hated the life of a fisherman, longing instead for the life of a scholar, the seas were the giver of life, and he quailed at the sight of waterspouts, which thrashed the waves, tore them asunder, and tossed them into the sky.

As the storm finally passed, the sun began to set. The failing of the light was like a slow death knell for Nat, who was near despair when he saw a sight that chilled his soul. Silhouetted against the orange and purple sky along the edges of the storm was a multimasted warship. Like the image that haunted his dreams, it came to life and gave him reason to fear. Only the sudden shift in the wind gave him any hope.

* * *

Osbourne recovered from his wounds and came with Chase to visit Catrin on several occasions. The boys seemed to feel it was their duty to keep her informed of the happenings in town. Much of the news they brought seemed to have lost all significance in her life. She no longer cared what girls the boys were fighting over or whose father had been thrown into the lockup for being drunk. There were other times, though, when she wished she could achieve the same level of detachment.

"Nat Dersinger came back from fishing the northern coast, and he claims to have seen long ships on the horizon," Chase said. It was not the first time Nat claimed to have seen long ships, only to have them disappear before another ship could verify the sighting. Nat was not the only fisherman to have seen strange ships in the distance, but he was certainly the most vocal about it.

"He said our ancient enemies, the Zjhon, were planning an attack. Waving his staff over his head while he ranted, he really went overboard. He said the Herald would destroy the Zjhon, according to some prophecy. He even said the Zjhon would kill all the inhabitants of the Godfist--just to be sure they kill the Herald. Most folks pay him no heed, but some fools actually believe him."

Osbourne said rumors of unusual occurrences were increasing. A shepherd reported losing half of his flock in a single night without ever hearing a sound, and a western village claimed the community well had run dry for the first time in recorded history. Fishermen complained of dangerous shifts in the currents; fishing was poor for the most part, though some returned with bizarre and unknown fish. They said the strange creatures were caught in warm water currents, unusual for so close to the Godfist because they normally stayed much farther out to sea.

Unsure if the exotic fish were safe to touch or eat, most fishermen threw them back into the sea. Some claimed to have been stung by poisonous fish, and others grew fearful of anything not easily identified. Most simply cut the lines when they brought up something they did not recognize.

"This year's Spring Challenges are going to be the grandest ever," Osbourne said, seemingly trying to lighten the mood. "You should see the new game fields, Cat, and the rows of benches for spectators." Catrin was lost in her own thoughts and barely heard him. Chase elbowed him in the ribs to make him stop.

Catrin had participated in the Challenges since she was old enough to ride, and most years she qualified for the Summer Games, but this year would be different. She knew she would not be allowed to compete, and she had no need to ask because it was understood. The townspeople did not want her. She was unwelcome.

"I was thinking about going on an outing, maybe a hike into the highlands," Chase said. "Telling stories around a campfire would be more fun than the Challenges and a lot less work. Wouldn't you agree, Osbourne?" Chase asked, elbowing him again. He had known Catrin her whole life, and he knew how crushed she must be.

"I can't attend the Challenges, but that doesn't mean the rest of you shouldn't. I know how much both of you like to compete, and I was looking forward to hearing of your victories," she said with a slight catch in her voice, which she had tried to control.

They stood, and Chase announced, "I'm going camping," crossing his arms and inflating his chest.

"So am I," Osbourne said, mimicking Chase, though he didn't look quite as imposing.

"But--" Catrin began. Her words were cut short when Chase tackled her. He and Osbourne coerced her into submission by means of the dreaded tickle torture. It was the first time Catrin had truly laughed in a long while, and she felt better for the release.

Despite her acquiescence, she still needed her father's approval, and she feared he would deny the request. She found him sitting at the table, working his way through a stack of parchment. Catrin sat across from him, waiting for him to finish what he was working on. After a few moments, he looked up from his work and acknowledged her with a strained smile.

"What's on your mind?" he asked in his usual straightforward manner.

"I don't think I should compete in the Challenges this year," she said, and he nodded in silent agreement. "Chase and Osbourne are boycotting the Challenges; they want to spend the time with me instead," she continued, and he raised an eyebrow but remained silent. "I was wondering if we could camp at the lake those days," Catrin asked, finally getting to her point. She was always amazed at how much information her father could get out of her without ever saying a word.

"I tried to talk them out of boycotting, Father, really I did, but the harder I argued, the more they argued back," she said with a smile and actually giggled. "They made me agree by means of tickle torture."

Her father chuckled and smiled briefly. "Tickle torture, you say? That does sound serious. I guess I could let you go for a few days. I wouldn't camp near the lake at this time of year, though. The mosquitoes will suck you dry. It'd be better if you climbed past the lake and continued to the highlands. There is a natural stair near the falls, and a grove of ancient greatoaks is due west of there. It's a fine place to camp, and the land is too rocky and dry for mosquitoes to be much of a problem. It's half a day of walking and climbing, but it would be well worth the effort," he said.

Her father had told her stories of the place, but he had always forbidden her to go that far. The closest she had ever ventured was to the very end of the lake, where a large set of falls drained from the river above. There she had climbed the tallest tree and gazed in all directions but was unable to see the grove. She was genuinely excited about the trip and hugged her father and kissed him on the forehead.

"Thank you," she said, smiling broadly. He patted her on the shoulder and told her to run along. She retired to her bed and dreamed of ancient trees dancing in the light of a campfire.

* * *

Jensen piled the last of the lumber near old man Dedrick's barn and gave a wave as he climbed back into his wagon. With all the deliveries done, he had enough time to stop at the Watering Hole. A mug of ale might help the world look better, and Chase always loved it when he brought home some of Miss Mariss's sausage breads. This time of day was a busy time at the Watering Hole, and the tie-offs were all taken. Jensen guided Shama to the back of the inn.

"G'afternoon to ya, Mr. Volker," Strom said as he walked from the stables, but there was an odd look of fear in his eyes, and his voice trembled slightly. "We're just about full up. You might want to come back another day."

"Just the same," Jensen said, looking Strom in the eye. "Mind if I tie Shama off back here."

"Of course, sir," Strom said.

"Give her a bit of water," Jensen said while removing Shama's bridle. He hooked a lead line to her halter and tied her off to a nearby post.

Strom approached with a bucket of water. "Some of those inside are looking for a fight," he whispered without looking at Jensen. "There's been a lot of talk about Catrin.

53

I'm sorry, sir. I don't believe any of it, and I couldn't let you walk into trouble not knowin' it."

"You're a good man," Jensen said, but he failed to keep the anger from his voice, and Strom backed away. "Unhook the wagon and saddle Shama for me," he added, handing Strom three coppers. "I may need to leave in a hurry."

Strom looked as if he would be sick, but at Jensen's nod, he began unhooking Shama. Jensen walked to the kitchen door and slowly pulled it open. Miss Mariss, ever in control of her inn, noticed him immediately and moved in his direction without actually looking at him. "You ought not be here right now," she said. "Petram is acting like the fool he is, and there's a parade of fools ready to follow 'im. I won't have you all settling this in my common room. You understand me?"

"I understand," Jensen said, but he was undeterred. When he stepped inside, Miss Mariss threw her hands in the air. "I promise you there will be no fighting," he said.

"Men," she said. "Stubborn mules refuse to listen to anyone else." Though her irritation was clear, she did not stand in his way.

As he entered the common room from behind the bar, only those at the bar noticed him, and none of them seemed interested at what Petram Ross was shouting to anyone who'd listen. Jensen nodded to the men at the bar then slipped into the crowd. Some turned and glared at him as he pushed his way closer to Petram, but when they saw who it was and the look on his face, they moved aside without a word. Eventually, Jensen found himself standing in front of Petram, and everyone else seemed to be taking a step backward. Enthralled by the sound of his own voice, it took Petram a moment to notice the change in his audience. At first, he seemed annoyed, but then his eyes landed on Jensen, and he instantly took a step back, only to find himself trapped by the hearth he'd chosen to use as a backdrop.

Jensen stepped forward but said nothing. Instead, he glared at Petram with a look that conveyed a host of threats, most of which came from Petram's imagination, which was just as Jensen wanted it. He wanted this man to fear him more than death. Again he moved forward, and Petram

54

looked as if he wanted to climb up the chimney despite the fire burning in the hearth.

"If you even look at my niece the wrong way," Jensen said softly, all the while raising his hand, which was held like a claw and moving toward Petram's throat. Just a hand's breadth away, he stopped and slowly closed his fingers. Petram's eyes bulged as if he were truly being choked. When Jensen finally lowered his hand to his side, Petram ran from the room, leaving a stunned silence hanging over the common room. All eyes were trained on Jensen, and he searched for words, suddenly unprepared. He thought a moment about the little girl who brightened his life and those of everyone around her. "She's a good girl," was all that he could say through his sudden tears. Those who had been gathered now lowered their heads and dispersed.

"I guess you might as well eat since you chased off all my customers," Miss Mariss said as she brought him a platter of cured meats and cheese. "Fools they may be, but a fool's gold is as good as any other."

* * *

Crouched in the darkness, Benjin listened. Only the sounds of frogs and the barking of a distant dog broke the stillness. Creeping into Wendel's cottage, he checked on Catrin and Wendel. Both slept soundly and neither woke. He left as stealthily as he had come.

Feeling silly, he walked back to his cottage. Only moments before, he had been sleeping soundly, but dreams of terror and loss drove him from his bed, demanding he check on those he loved. Assured of their safety, he returned to his bed, but the dreams returned.

When morning finally came, the harsh sunlight seemed to mock the warnings of his dreams. Still he could not shake the sense of foreboding that pressed in on him, suffocating him. With a deep breath, he stood and prepared himself to face the day.

Chapter 4

The mind can travel farther in a single day than the fastest horse could traverse in a lifetime.
--Trevan Dalls, Master of the Arts

* * *

Dense fog hung over the land, holding Catrin's world in its damp embrace. Days like this never seemed real to her, as if, on rare occasions, she left her usual world and stepped into the world of dreams. Even the calls of the birds and the noises of the farm sounded different, almost magical. Catrin suspected she was not the only one who had such feelings, as her father and Benjin also seemed changed in this other world.

"G'morning, li'l miss," Benjin said.

Her father stood behind him with a lopsided grin. "Go in and get Charger harnessed and bring her out to the wagon," he said. "We're going to make a trip to the cold caves."

Catrin nodded and went into the barn, a feeling of anger and shame building in her gut. Going to the cold caves had always been an adventure for her and Chase. Some of her fondest memories were of them playing there as children. It had been like a world of their own, a place where adventure and magic were real and where they could explore the depths of the underworld. The rooms filled with blocks of ice had always drawn them, despite the lectures her father and uncle had given about avoiding those very places. She and Chase had climbed on top of them and slid across their slick surfaces, which were always wet, as the ice melted slowly yet inexorably. As they grew older, much of their time was spent moving stores in or out of the caves, but there were special times, in the winter, when they would gather fresh snowfall to be stored in the caves. Catrin and Chase had spent wonderful days packing the snow into all kinds of shapes and storing them within the caves.

As she harnessed Charger, tears gathered in her eyes, but she refused to let them fall. By the force of her will, she held them in check, determined to be strong. It was something she had learned from Chase, and it seemed that now it was a skill she would need to master. Only the tremble of her chin escaped her control, and she hoped her father and Benjin didn't notice.

Outside they waited in the preternatural light that gave the world an almost greenish hue. Heavy clouds threatened rain, and it seemed unlikely that the fog would burn off as it did on most days. Catrin held Charger's head as Benjin and her father slid the shafts of the wagon through the loops on the harness. While they secured the breast-collar to the shafts, the power of her will began to fade; tears streamed down her cheeks, and her lip quivered noticeably. She hoped the men would simply climb into the wagon and leave without the need for her to speak, but she doubted it, and she chastised herself for showing such weakness. Staying to mind the farm was not so terrible.

"She's all hooked up," her father said as he climbed into the wagon's passenger seat beside Benjin, leaving room for another. "Get the barn door closed and check the gates. We need to get going."

Catrin wiped her tears and ran to the barn, a smile forming on her face. Perhaps it was the fog. Perhaps her father figured no one would see her through the mist, but she did not care. Not only did he plan to let her go, the driver's seat was still vacant, and Catrin eyed it unsurely.

"Are you going to drive us there or not?" her father asked, his grin like a ray of sunshine.

"Yes, sir," she said as she climbed up. He handed her the lines, and Catrin smacked Charger lightly on the rump with them while making a clucking noise with her tongue. Charger knew her business and moved out at a moderate pace. In the mist, Catrin had to use landmarks to guide her around obstacles, but she knew the path well and had little trouble steering Charger along a clear path where she was not likely to trip.

When they reached the place where the Harborton trail met the upland trail, she turned Charger slowly and deliberately. The upland trail was narrow, and Catrin had never driven a wagon on it before. Parts of the trail were treacherous, and there were places she was hesitant to even ride Salty; driving the wagon was much more challenging.

"Move a little to the right," her father said. "There's an old tree stump on the bend, and you don't want to hit it with the wheels."

Charger never faltered and, in truth, knew the way better than any of them. There were times that she corrected the path for Catrin before her father or Benjin could even warn her of an upcoming obstacle. When they reached Viewline Pass, her father asked her to stop. Catrin pulled back on the lines until Charger stopped then maintained moderate tension on the lines to keep her stopped. Charger was not accustomed to stopping here, and she fidgeted constantly.

When she turned to her father, Catrin's gaze passed over the view that gave the pass its name. Below her, looking like an elaborate child's toy from the heights, was her homeland. The fog continued to blanket the land, making it look like an ocean of white with emerald islands, sailed by buildings that floated like ships. The illusion was difficult to break, but her father demanded her attention.

"When driving through the pass, you must be extra careful. Rocks often fall here, and we have no way to know if there is anything beneath this fog that could injure Charger. You must hold the lines with confidence and authority here. Charger fears the rocks and formations that will flank her through the pass, and she often jumps sideways for reasons only she knows. Let her know that you are in control, and she will follow you instead of her fear. Understand?"

"Yes, sir."

"You can do this, li'l miss," Benjin added. "You just have to know you can do it."

With a strange mixture of pride and trepidation, Catrin urged Charger slowly forward. Small rocks caught under the wagon wheels, but Charger showed her worth and pulled the wagon over the obstacles. It made for a bumpy ride, but there was little to be done about it. As Charger reached the place where rocky peaks flanked her, her ears began to flip forward and back, and when she turned her head, Catrin could see the whites around her eyes.

"Make her follow you. Let her know you're in control."

Her father's words bolstered her confidence, and she held the lines firmly but without fear. Charger still sidestepped and pranced, but Catrin maintained control. Soon they were beyond the pass, and the way became easier again.

"You've done well," Benjin said, and Wendel nodded his agreement. From the two of them, it was high praise and Catrin beamed.

When they reached the cold caves, they found it was among the few places not still mired in fog. The main entrance was invisible until one reached the rock face where it hid. Between two mighty slabs of stone stood a chasm just wide enough for a horse--but nothing larger--to fit through. Benjin tied Charger to a stake they had driven in the stone many years before.

"Benjin and I will load the wagon," Wendel said. "Most of what we're after today is heavy. Go back to our personal stores and get what you would like to have for your camping trip."

Catrin wasted no time. Without another thought, she was bounding through caves, passing through the network of corridors that were like old friends. There were some of the deeper tunnels that Catrin had never really liked, but she had most of the place memorized. When she reached the area her father reserved for their storage, she sifted through and grabbed what she thought the others would enjoy as well.

After loading her supplies in the wagon, she did her best to help her father and Benjin. Despite the hard work and the sweat that ran into her eyes, it was the most fun she'd had in quite some time. Only the strange looks from those to whom they made deliveries threatened to spoil her mood, but most of the people they saw were friends of her father's and none treated her with anything but kindness--albeit awkward kindness. For Catrin, it was good enough. Only at the end of the day, as darkness began to creep back over the land, did her fears return. The hairs on the back of her neck stood as she passed by a thicket of trees bathed in shadows; the feeling of being watched was almost overwhelming.

Catrin was barely able to resist the urge to push Charger for more speed, but she knew the horse had put in a full day's work, and it would be unfair to ask more of her. The ill feelings persisted, and Catrin hoped that Benjin and her father did not sense her fear.

* * *

Miss Mariss heard all the gossip; she knew where in her inn to be if she wanted to hear the conversation at a specific table. Much of the inn had been designed around this purpose, though most would never have guessed it. Simple things, such as a knothole in the common room floor that continued through a bored-out log all the way to the cellar, made her task a great deal easier. Her exceptional hearing gave her the advantage of being able to attend to the work of running her inn, all the while collecting valuable information.

Whether Catrin was the Herald of Istra or not remained to be proven in Miss Mariss's mind, but either way there would be much work to do. Everyone in Harborton was tense and afraid, and that alone had far-reaching effects. If it turned out that incident in the clearing was simply a freak occurrence, she would be just as happy, though she knew Catrin would never escape the stigma. Still, that seemed far better than the alternative--far better indeed.

* * *

Anticipation drove Catrin from her sleep earlier than usual. She had been looking forward to this day, and it was finally upon her. She dressed while reviewing her mental list, making sure she had not overlooked some important detail. Her tinderbox and extra clothes were already packed, and she added some dried fruit, smoked beef, and salted fish to her backpack. A trip to the cold cellar yielded a bottle of springwine and waxed cheese she had brought back from the cold caves. Her bedroll wrapped in her leather ground cloth and secured atop her backpack, she wondered what it was she was forgetting; there had to be something.

Her morning chores needed to be finished before she left, and she had asked the boys to give her until daylight. Still, she was not completely surprised when she heard laughter that sounded like a couple of halfwits trying to be quiet and failing. When she opened the door, she found Chase and Osbourne side by side, grinning like fools, and her father walked up behind her at the same moment.

"Good morning, boys. You're here early," he said over her shoulder while she grinned back at the boys.

"G'morning, Mr. Volker," Osbourne replied.

"Good morning, Uncle Wendel. Sorry we're early, but we thought we could help get Catrin's chores done faster, and then we could get an early start," Chase said, but then he jumped as if someone had pinched him. "Oh, yeah, I almost forgot," he twitched again and laughed, squirming. "We have a surprise for you, Cat. Guess who is coming with us?" he asked as he and Osbourne stepped aside with a dramatic flourish. Strom entered the cottage smiling and bowing.

"I'd wager you weren't expecting to see me here," he said. "G'mornin' to you, Mr. Volker."

"Good morning to you, Strom. It's good to see you again. Now, you grinning scoundrels, get out there. Clean and fill those water buckets. Catrin, you get the horses fed and take care of your cats, and then you can go," Wendel said with a smile. He seemed as excited about their big trip as they were.

The group of exuberant young people gave Wendel a mock salute and, almost in unison, said, "Yes, sir."

They made quick work of the buckets and feeding. Benjin wished them a safe trip and told the boys to behave themselves or he would hunt them down like rabid dogs. He said it with a smile, but the boys nodded seriously and said again in unison, "Yes, sir." Benjin laughed, shook his head, and walked into a stall with his pitchfork.

The excited campers waved good-bye as they shouldered their packs and started their walk down the river trail. The false dawn had not yet shown on the horizon, but the moon was bright enough to light the way. They had little trouble getting to the river; once there, they turned and climbed past the shoals and falls. They had covered half the length of the lake by the time the sun cleared the mountains.

They laughed and talked while they hiked, having a generally good time of things, and Catrin began to feel the distance between her and her troubles. A small clearing, shaded by tall pines, seemed like a good place to rest, and they flopped onto the bed of needles. Catrin dug in her pack for the dried fruit and cheese, but it was Strom who got a whoop of delight from the others when he produced four of Miss Mariss's sausage breads. Each one was twice the size of his fist and wrapped in waxed paper.

Strom cleared his throat and said, in his best imitation of Miss Mariss's voice, "Miss Mariss sends these with her best wishes to some of her favorite patrons. She looks forward to your next visit. Her words, not mine," he added, just to make sure Catrin understood the message was intended for her. The subtle message surprised Catrin, as did the support from Miss Mariss, who had always been stern with her, but she decided she would process that information later. Today she was on a grand adventure, and she wanted nothing more than to enjoy the sausage bread.

Her bottle of springwine was drained all too quickly, and she realized she should have brought more.

"No fears. I came prepared for just such an occasion," Strom said, seeing the concern flicker across Catrin's face, and he produced a bottle of springwine and a bottle of huckles juice from his pack.

"I knew we brought you along for some reason," Chase said, patting him on the back. Strom elbowed him in the ribs as he shouldered his pack.

"Sorry about that, m'friend. I didn't see you there," he said, laughing and pushing his way past Chase and Osbourne.

Catrin watched as the boys jostled and roughhoused along the trail, meandering in the direction of their intended campsite, but as the valley narrowed, they walked single file. The sound of the rushing falls grew as they approached the end of the lake, and when they reached the clearing, Catrin smiled in recognition. There was the tree she had climbed so long ago in hopes of catching a glimpse of the enchanted grove. She needn't wonder any longer; now the grove was her destination.

* * *

In search of the natural stair Catrin's father had mentioned, they approached the base of the falls, the mist rolling over them in clouds. Sunlight danced in the moisture, casting rainbows across the clearing, and they moved quickly, hoping to avoid a thorough soaking.

"There it is," Chase said, and Catrin followed his gaze. Rounded lumps, blanketed with moss and soaked with accumulated moisture, formed the crude base of the stair. The rest of the formation created an illusion, appearing flush with the rock face until the spell broke, and Catrin could see the form plainly. A narrow shelf angled up the rock face, its slope irregular.

Heights had never been a problem for Catrin, but the stair was daunting. There was no room for error; any slip could send her over the sheer drop with nothing to break her fall. As they climbed higher, the stair became dry and, in some places, distinct and well formed. Catrin found them a wonder, as if fate had carved a path for them, and she was thankful for the gift.

The mental image did not last long, though, as they soon came on a crumbled section of stair, which was barely passable. Perhaps fate did not wish to speed her trip after all, Catrin thought, laughing at herself. They managed to negotiate the treacherous section of the stair with a bit of help from each other, but none of them looked forward to climbing back down. The remainder of the climb proved to be fairly easy, and they reached the top of the cliff unscathed.

Moving west, they searched for the trail Catrin's father said they would find. Seeing no obvious breaks in the tree line, they moved along it, peering through the branches. Ahead of them, a buck emerged from the forest, his ears flicking forward and back, as if he sensed them. With a snort, he bounded back into the woods, disappearing from view but aiding them nonetheless. As they neared the spot where he had been, a trail materialized within the outer barrier of leaves.

Catrin led them into the forest, following the narrow trail. The canopy of leaves blocked much of the sunlight, and they moved within a shady world that was filled with life. Deer moved almost silently through the woods, while smaller animals ran through the leaves with wild abandon. Squirrels at play sounded like a herd of beasts crashing through the undergrowth. Colorful birds flitted from branch to branch, their varied warbles filling the air.

Menacing spiders had built elaborate webs that spanned open areas between trees. When Catrin walked into one of the clinging webs, she thought she felt its occupant land in her hair, and she gave the boys a good laugh while she tried to shed the imagined spider. Afterward she armed herself with a long stick, which she waved in front of her like a wand, clearing the webs as she walked.

The sound of the waterfall faded into the distance, and Catrin picked up the hint of a noisy brook. She knew a stream ran near the grove, and she wondered if it was the same one. The incline grew steep, and sweat soaked them as they hiked, their legs aching. Soon, though, they emerged from the forest onto a large plateau, which was carpeted with thick, green grass broken occasionally by weathered outcroppings of obsidian rock. Emerald moss clung to the megaliths, marbling their surface, as the land slowly reclaimed the masses of stone.

Ancient and immense, the greatoaks were unmistakable in the distance, towering above the tallest elm. Unlike any trees they had ever seen, the greatoaks soared into the sky, their tops obscured by low-lying clouds. As the group drew closer, the sheer magnitude of the trees became even more evident. Twenty-four in all, they were evenly spaced and formed a nearly perfect circle, but each one was a force unto itself. The trunks were so massive that twenty people could stand around one, with arms outstretched, and still their hands would not meet. Awed by the magnificence of the place, none of them made a sound, afraid to break the spell.

Magical in its beauty, the grove lured them, but Catrin was drawn by more than just the aesthetics. She could feel the power of the grove, a place in which the very air seemed alive with energy. They walked in slow reverence, as if entering a holy place. Much of the grove was blanketed with lush grasses, but an irregular circle of bare stone dominated the heart of it. There were no writings or symbols, nothing beyond its sheer might to indicate it was sacred, but it felt that way. The black stone was smooth and level with the grass, and Catrin found it strange that no moss or grass had encroached on it. It seemed almost as if the plants kept their distance out of respect for the mighty stone.

"I don't think we should camp in here," Osbourne said into the eerie silence, and yet the spell remained unbroken. "I feel like we're welcome, but I don't want to disturb the beauty of this place."

In quiet agreement, they walked toward the far side of the grove in search of a suitable campsite. The western clearing was much the same as the one in the east, and at about the same distance, the forest began again. Only the area between the two sections of forest was clear of underbrush. As Catrin searched for a place to camp, she concentrated on the sound of running water and moved toward it.

An almost imperceptible waterfall glistened down the valley wall. The water flow was slight, but it fed a small stream that lay hidden in the folds of the land. The stream was narrow but its water cool and clear. Not far from the base of the fall, Catrin spotted a large shelf of rock protruding from the cliff face and knew it would provide some shelter. On further inspection, it was obvious that others had camped there before, though it appeared to have been some time ago. A bare spot looked to have been used as a fire pit, and a few rocks still lay in a circle around it.

Catrin and the others knew without saying a word that they had found their campsite. They dropped their packs and stretched sore muscles. Catrin went in search of stones to complete the fire circle.

"Would you boys gather some wood?" she asked, and they set off for the western forest since no dead trees or branches were to be found in the grove. By the time they returned, Catrin had finished constructing the fire circle and gathered dried grass for kindling. Chase and Osbourne dumped their armloads of wood directly into the circle of stones, and Strom started a woodpile off to one side.

They left Catrin to start the fire while they ventured out for more wood. The wood they left was damp, and she knew she would have a hard time getting it to burn. Strom had left some sticks and leaves along with the larger pieces of wood, and Catrin gathered what was dry, placing it at the center of the fire circle. She retrieved her tinderbox from her pack and pulled out some dry shavings and her flint. She piled the dry shavings neatly at the base of her kindling pile and grabbed some larger pieces of wood, leaning them against one another so they formed a cone above her kindling.

Sparks flew as she struck her stones against one another, but few actually made it to the shavings. After several sparks hit the shavings, going out almost immediately, one took hold, a small flame blooming around it. She cupped her hands and blew gently, and though the tiny flame went out, the shavings glowed red. The flames returned, double their size, and quickly consumed the kindling but barely even dried the damp branches. Piling even the damp kindling atop her small blaze, she sent a cloud of smoke into the air. With a few puffs, though, the flames returned, licking eagerly at the branches.

"Is that little fire the best you could do? I was expecting you to have dinner cooked by now," Chase said, dumping his armload of wood, and he jumped back as Catrin took a swipe at him. He laughed and went to lay out his bedroll. He chose a spot that was near the fire yet still shaded by the rock overhang; Osbourne and Strom threw their bedrolls down near his. By the time they were comfortable, Catrin had a nice fire going. The air above it shimmered, and the light danced over them.

She retrieved her bedroll, only to find all the sheltered spots taken, and the boys pretended not to notice her irritation. She stood with her hands on her hips, glaring at each of them. Chase could no longer keep up the ruse and was the first to start laughing.

He and Osbourne moved their bedrolls closer together, and Strom moved his to the other side, making a spot in the middle for Catrin. She curtsied and pounced on the newly cleared spot, leaving them no chance for reconsideration. Something about being in a strange place together and sitting around a fire made everything seem right with the world.

They rummaged through their packs in search of various goodies, and they feasted on sausage breads, cheeses, and dried fruit. They made sure to leave themselves enough supplies for a few more meals, but what they ate was delicious--it was adventure food, free of restraint and responsibility. There was nothing to clean up when they were done, and they could relax with full bellies. They had no reason to wake in the morning, no chores awaiting them; it was a glorious feeling, only slightly dampened by the knowledge that it was temporary.

Catrin just watched the flames, but Chase seemed obsessed with tending the fire, constantly shifting the coals and poking them with a stick. She excused herself, suddenly stifled by the heat of the fire. Wandering into the deepening shadows, she drank in the fresh air and savored it. Stopping for a moment to take another deep breath, she looked up at the skies. Cloud cover was slowly breaking up, and a few stars were visible through the gaps.

Leaning her head back, she closed her eyes. She felt her mind expanding and perceived an almost audible click, as if a doorway in her mind suddenly opened. Her body felt intensely alive, every sensation magnified. With her arms wide, she stood, basking in the light breeze as it tousled her hair.

Chase yelled from the campsite, "Catrin, are you going to sleep out there?"

"It's such a pretty night," she said. "I think I'm going to take a walk. Would anyone care to join me?"

"Nah, we'll just stay here and eat all the food," he replied, laughing, but the boys roused themselves and joined her.

The night drew them on, pulling them into the ring of mighty trees. Beams of moonlight shone through the parting clouds, lighting Catrin's way. She let her body go where it wished, her path leading straight toward the center of the grove. The others followed in silence, as if entranced by her rhythmic movements.

Cold stone caressed her feet, soothing them as she strode upon it. Feeling as if she could ride the wind, Catrin whirled in a rhythmic dance. Around her pulsed the beat of life, and she danced to its lilting cadence. Life energy was everywhere, but it was more focused in the grove, almost tangible. Spinning on the wind, she closed her eyes and raised her hands to the heavens. Energy from above bathed her in its warmth, and she grabbed onto it with her mind, tasting its sweetness, smelling its fragrance, caressing its texture. Its beauty overwhelmed her.

She clung to the energy, letting it suspend and hold her. Overcome with joy, tears coursed down her cheeks. The boys' talking shook Catrin from her revelry. She opened her eyes to see the night sky and two bright sources of light. It took a moment for her eyes to focus; then she clearly saw the moon and another bright object. The second was like nothing she had ever seen. Elliptical, with a long trail of light in its wake, it sparkled with life and called to her. It was so beautiful, she could not look away.

"By the gods, do you see that?" Chase shouted, and Catrin returned to herself somewhat again.

Another, closer source of light stole the brightness from the doubly lit night sky. Lightning danced along her fingers in powerful arcs, and twin beams of liquid energy extended from the palms of her hands into the sky, twining themselves into a single thread of energy. Colors raced along it, constantly shifting and changing, each moment bringing something new.

Catrin heaved, her mind finally reconciling what her eyes reported. She yanked her hands down violently, feeling an awful tearing sensation as she pulled herself away from the massive energy flow. In that moment, she realized her feet were not touching anything, and she had no time to brace herself before they struck the black stone beneath her. Even in her confused state, she realized she must have been high above the ground, judging by her impact, which buckled her knees and tossed her onto her back.

She remained supine for a moment, staring at the sky, and she caught another brief glimpse of the comet before fast-moving clouds once again obscured it. The clouds, Catrin realized, were moving far too fast; a storm was upon them. Lightning ripped across the sky in a vast web of light, and the wind howled as bands of horizontal rain assaulted them.

"Run for cover!" Catrin shrieked above the wind, and they fled to the relative shelter of their campsite. Hail pelted them as they ran. The stones were small at first but steadily grew larger and more dangerous. The light of their windblown fire illuminated their belongings as they were scattered around the campsite, sent tumbling by the wind. After scrambling to collect their things, they huddled under their packs, watching helplessly as gale-force winds snuffed their fire.

The darkness was nearly complete, broken only by monstrous bolts of lightning as they set fire to the thunderheads. The wind howled and intensified, screaming at them, sucking their belongings into the night. Thunderous cracks and booms mixed with the wailing call of the wind and battered Catrin's senses, making her think she was about to go mad. Dirt and debris, carried by fierce gusts, stung her exposed skin.

Catrin screamed as lightning illuminated the plateau long enough for her to see a mass of branches and leaves hurtling toward them. It struck the ground in front of them with incredible force, driving the air from her lungs. Startled but uninjured, Catrin and her friends huddled under the massive limb, hoping nothing else would fly from the darkness.

* * *

From the deck of his flagship, *Rebellion's End*, General Dempsy stared at the skies in disbelief. It was not the storm that came as such a surprise; it was the comet. Archmaster Belegra had told him it would come, but he had not believed; instead he had chosen to deny the truth, to go into the greatest of peril unprepared because of his own blindness. It

69

took some time for him to accept this new reality, since it seemed everything in his world had suddenly changed.

Next came his anger. What did Archmaster Belegra expect him to do against the ultimate adversary? How could he ever be expected to achieve victory? His father had taught him that joining a battle where there is no chance for victory was to die a noble fool, but General Dempsy could see no honorable way out. No matter what his father had said, honor was a thing worth dying for, and he would not back away from his responsibilities because of fear.

In his mind, a plan began to form, and his face settled into a look of determination. Whether his plan would achieve victory or utter defeat, General Dempsy would use every trick he had ever learned. May the Herald beware.

Chapter 5

In our darkest moments, we come to know the true measure of our souls.
--Ain Giest, Sleepless One

* * *

As dawn illuminated the valley, turning it into a rippling palette of light and shadow, Catrin and her friends could see the full extent of the storm damage. The majestic grove that had drawn them was no more. Not even one of the greatoaks remained standing. They were strewn about the plateau as if felled by a mighty hand. Some were almost whole but had been torn from the soil and apparently flung about. Others had been twisted then sheared off, leaving fingers of wood sticking out from stumps like splinters of bone protruding from grisly wounds. It was the lightning-struck trees, though, that disturbed Catrin most. The bark was blasted off in many places, and the exposed wood was so warped, it resembled partially melted candle wax.

Catrin surveyed the damage, walking ahead of the dispirited group toward the place that had once been the center of the grove. Her heart was hurt at the sight of the ruination, but some morbid sense drew her on, forcing her to commit the images to memory. Since passage was hard to find among the fallen leviathans, their progress was slow, but no one spoke a word of protest. Catrin ran her hands along the fallen trunks as she passed them, bidding them a silent farewell.

It took her a moment to recognize the center of the grove when she reached it. Tears filled her eyes, and her body trembled as she gazed upon the black stone. None of it had escaped damage. That which was not crushed under the fallen giants had been blasted by lightning and pounded by massive hail. All that remained was a mass of rubble and gray powder that crunched under their boots. Grapefruit-sized hailstones still littered the area, serving as poignant reminders of nature's power. Catrin turned wordlessly back

71

to her friends, who remained downcast and silent; they had tears in their eyes, and she could see the fear in them.

"It was so beautiful," Osbourne said in a low whisper.

His words stung Catrin like a physical blow, and she moved away from the place quickly, trying to escape the oppressive weight settling on her shoulders. She wanted to believe the destruction of the grove was not her fault, but she found no comfort . . . only tremendous shame and grief. Her father had finally trusted her enough to share the knowledge of how to find his special place, and she had destroyed it. Her depression deepened when she realized it had not really been her father's place at all. Someone planted the greatoaks, by her guess, many generations ago. She had entered a sacred place and, by some unconscious action, had brought about its desecration. She felt as if she had betrayed her ancestors, and she could almost sense their accusing stares on her, denouncing her. Tears clouded her vision as she stumbled through the maze of debris.

When she reached what remained of the campsite, she began to gather what she could find of her gear. Chase reached her side but remained silent for a time.

"You can't blame yourself for the weather, Cat. This wasn't your fault. This was just like the storm we had three weeks ago. That funnel cloud did a lot of damage too, and you had nothing to do with it either," he said.

Catrin wanted to agree with him. She was no goddess or sorceress with influence on the weather. To believe she was would be silly. But she still needed a reasonable explanation for the strange occurrences that seemed to center on her. She supposed her dance above the stone could have been a hallucination, but such rationalizations did not ring of truth. When she considered the appearance of the comet, the odds against it all being coincidental were staggering. Perhaps, she thought, she had just been in the wrong places at the wrong times, but things were too similar for those events to have been purely accidental.

Once she and the others finished packing what they had left, Catrin shouldered her pack and looked at her companions. They looked away, and she understood their fear because she, too, was terrified. They probably believed she was somehow responsible for the devastation of the grove, and she feared they could be right.

"What happened last night, Cat?" Osbourne asked. "What happened to you?"

"I don't know," she said, her voice shaking. "I'm so sorry. Let's go home."

The others nodded and followed her wordlessly. They picked through the storm-tossed foliage but had to backtrack several times before finding clear passage. When they emerged in the eastern clearing, they found that it, too, was littered with debris and slowly melting hailstones. The forest trail was blocked in many places, and they had to shoulder through the brambles and thorns that abounded alongside the trail.

When the forest eventually thinned, they emerged into a bright and sunny afternoon. The valley ahead appeared largely untouched by the storm, and it seemed as if they were drifting out of a nightmare and back into a pleasant reality. Catrin relaxed when she saw a part of her world unblemished, but the images of the grove were still vivid.

Travel was easier when they were clear of the forest, and they soon approached the stairs. They descended carefully, aware that the slightest misstep could send them tumbling. Strom lost his footing once and slipped, frightening them, but he caught himself, and only loose chips of rock dropped over the edge. It took a few moments for them to calm themselves before continuing at a slower pace, and they were relieved when they finally reached the bottom.

The misty air surrounding the falls drove them onward. Once clear of the spray, they found themselves at the shady spot where they had eaten lunch the day before. They stopped and ate the last of their provisions in silence.

Familiar sights and smells brought Catrin some comfort, and as the group neared her home, she began to feel almost safe again, but the illusion was shattered when Benjin seemed to materialize from the shadows. He placed a finger to his lips, motioned for them to follow, and led them into a dense stand of pines. Catrin grew even more concerned when she spotted leather bags and packs stacked in an orderly pile, filled nearly to overflowing. The boys followed her gaze and seemed to come to the same cold realization: something else had gone very wrong.

"Don't have much time to talk, but I'm so glad you're here. Wendel and I guessed the storm might bring you home early. Couldn't be certain, but it saved me coming to find you," Benjin said just above a whisper. "Yesterday afternoon, y'see, there was a huge crowd at the Spring Challenges, even though it looked like bad weather. The games were over before the storm hit, but it was dark when everyone started to leave. Then a swift wind parted the clouds. Don't know who saw it first, but people shouted and cried when the comet appeared and didn't know what to do with themselves. They just stood and gawked and carried on about it until Nat Dersinger climbed up onto the reviewing stand.

"He started out rambling on that Istra had returned to the skies of Godsland, and Catrin's power meant she was the Herald of Istra. Yes, li'l miss, he called you by name. And now, this morning, over a dozen fishing boats came back early, each saying they had seen foreign ships. The details varied from ship to ship, but they agreed on one thing: a large host of ships is approaching the Godfist.

"When they heard this, people panicked and started shouting. A bunch of angry citizens went to the farm looking for you," he said, nodding at Catrin. "Your father and I had anticipated trouble, and I was already packed when they got there. I hid until they left. Your father knows how to deal with people, and he managed to convince them he'd sent you to the cold caves. He said you were retrieving supplies and would return on the morrow.

"He told 'em he'd let them know as soon as you came back, li'l miss. He need not have bothered with that, for I'm betting the townsfolk are now watching every road and trail that enters Harborton. I'm just glad they didn't post a sentry here at the mountain paths, or we'd have been hard pressed. Your father wanted to be here, but he knows he's being watched. He sends his love and will join us when he feels it's safe for him to escape."

"Where are we going?" Catrin asked, her voice wavering.

"High in the mountains, there's a spot Wendel and I found years ago. It's a good hiding place, and it has most of what we'll need to survive. Now we need to get going. We don't want to meet up with the townsfolk, and they could send sentries here at any time.

"Strom, Osbourne, come with us if you wish, but if you decide to stay, you must not tell where we are going. Chase, your father asked me to take you along, and I hope you want to come. He fears for your safety and thinks you'll be a help to us."

"I'll go with you," Chase said.

"Sounds like a long camping trip. I want to go," Osbourne added a moment later.

Strom seemed to struggle with some inner turmoil, and they watched as they saw him thinking. "I hate to leave Miss Mariss without a stable boy, and my mother will be without the extra income, but I'm a terrible liar, and I'd surely give you away if someone asked me. I think I should come too," he said.

With that settled, Benjin repacked the provisions and distributed the bags. Each of them was carrying a great deal when they set off, their burdens heavier than just the weight of the packs. Benjin led them through the trees, staying as far from the open trail as possible and keeping to the shadows, even though it slowed their pace.

They had covered very little distance when the fire bells began ringing. Even from a distance, the cacophony was startling and disconcerting. Benjin motioned for them to stop, dropped his pack and bag, and climbed a nearby tree. It took him a few moments to gain a clear view of the harbor. Once there, he scanned the horizon. Cursing, he scrambled back to the anxiously waiting group and tried to catch his breath.

"What did you see? What's happening?" Chase asked, fear in his voice.

"The warning fires are lit," Benjin said.

"Which fires? Is the one near the Watering Hole lit?" Strom asked anxiously.

"All of them are lit. The Godfist is under attack." His words seemed to linger in the air, and a feeling of impending

75

doom crept across the group. Benjin cocked his head to one side as if listening intently. "We need to go. Now."

"But my father . . ." Catrin protested.

"Your father can take care of himself, li'l miss. He'd wring my neck if I let you go back there after 'im. You know he would. You're in far more danger than he is. Now go!" he said firmly, his tone leaving no room for argument. He led them on a meandering trek from shadow to shadow. They moved as quietly as they could, but every noise seemed to echo across the valley. They heard no sounds of pursuit, but they would have had to struggle to hear anything over the pounding of their hearts and their labored breathing.

Rather than head for the falls, Benjin angled north and east, and when they reached the eastern ridgeline, he started up the incline. It was a difficult climb, but it would take them into the neighboring valley, Chinawpa. It was narrower than the fertile Pinook River Valley. Bramble and thorn bushes grew thick, and few ventured there.

After having been hidden by the shadows, Catrin felt as if the whole world could see her on the face of the mountain. They climbed in anxious silence, occasionally disturbing loose rocks, which bounced down the steep incline with what sounded like a terrible clatter. Benjin occasionally stopped to scan the valley for signs of pursuit, but he saw none.

Sweaty and tired, they crested the ridgeline and stared into the valley below. The descent into the Chinawpa Valley was not as steep as their climb had been. Benjin continued to lead, moving carefully down the ridgeline at an angle to make the descent more gradual. Daylight was failing them, and he cautioned them to beware of loose rock and scree. A few tenacious trees growing out of the rock face steadied them in treacherous places.

It was early twilight when they finally reached the valley floor, tired, sore, and in need of rest.

"I know you would all like to stop, but we have to get as far away as possible before we camp for the night," Benjin said, although it was unnecessary to tell them what they already knew.

Catrin trudged along behind him, not really paying attention to where she was going, just following the body in front of her and concentrating on staying upright. She was exhausted, her muscles cramped, and she clutched her side as she walked to try to ease the aching. Staying near the ridgeline, where the vegetation was sparse, Benjin seemed to be searching for something.

"Are we looking for something specific?" Catrin asked in an irritated tone. She knew she sounded childish and contrary even as the words left her lips.

"There's a place up ahead where your father and I once made camp; it provides some shelter, but it is primarily defensible should the need arise. I don't think we'll be found tonight, but it's better to be prepared for the improbable-- and sometimes the impossible. You'll have to trust me that it's the best place for us to stop," he said, continuing to walk.

Darkness settled over them and slowed their progress. The skies were overcast, and Catrin could barely make out the moon and comet behind the clouds. She could feel the energy enveloping her, but it was strange and frightening, and she closed herself to it. Still, it pulled at the edges of her mind, promising warmth, security, and power.

"Are you all right, li'l miss?" Benjin asked, concern clearly audible in his voice.

"I'm just tired and not feeling well," she replied, feeling guilty for telling only part of the truth, but she wasn't going to tell them about her strange yearnings for power. She wouldn't blame any of them for thinking she was a witch, and at this point, she was decidedly unsure of herself.

"We're just about there. We'll be resting soon, I promise. Just a little farther," Benjin said, and soon they approached a huge split in the rock face. An enormous slab of stone leaned against the valley wall, leaving a gap several paces wide. It was open on both ends, providing two routes of escape. They filed into the gap and dropped their packs. Chase began to set up a fire circle, but Benjin waved him from the task.

"No fire tonight, I'm afraid. It's just too risky."

The others knew he was right, but that did little to improve the atmosphere. They ate a cold meal in relative silence; then Benjin urged them to get some sleep, saying he would take the first watch. Deep breathing and occasional snores soon surrounded Catrin, but she could not sleep. Despite her weariness, she lay awake, wondering if she would ever feel safe again.

* * *

From high on a hill, Wendel watched the Zjhon come, frozen in morbid fascination as what looked like a wave of fire and destruction rolled through Harborton and the lowlands. He'd come here to survey the situation, to reassure himself that his friends, neighbors, and countrymen would be fine and that going after Catrin would jeopardize no one. Watching the horror unfold before him, he was faced with a new question: Would staying to defend his homeland make any difference?

His awareness was flooded with a vision of Catrin, hunted by the Zjhon, vulnerable and calling out for him. Never before had Wendel ever been so conflicted, he felt as if his spirit were being torn apart, ripped into pieces by a decision no one should ever have to make. He felt Elsa looking down on him, and he wept as he shamed her and shamed himself. His feet had taken him to the barn, where he had already, subconsciously and automatically, started saddling Charger. From beneath a pile of hay, he pulled his portion of the supplies he and Benjin had stashed away. From one of the bags protruded a painful reminder, a physical representation of his guilt and weakness. Elsa's sword reminded him of all the things he was not, of all his failings and shortcomings. It challenged him to save his countrymen *and* find Catrin--Elsa would have saved them all.

Wendel found himself in the saddle, ready to ride away from his farm, his friends--his entire life. Just as he gave Charger his heels, he caught movement from the corner of his vision. Turning his mount with his knees, he saw a mounted soldier closing on a single-horse cart. Driving the cart was Elianna Grisk, a woman of more than eighty summers. She was as sharp as a sword and took no guff from anyone, but she was more than overmatched. Her

78

horse was little more than a pony, and he was weary with age; he labored to pull her at little more than a walk, and the soldier's horse showed only the beginnings of a sweat.

Wendel cried out in dismay. His mind had been made up, his course set, but now he found himself swayed. Reaching back, he grabbed Elsa's sword and released a battle cry that had not been heard in many seasons. As he charged toward the approaching soldier, he saw the look of relief on Elianna's face; she believed he would save her. Life had given Wendel no other choice; there was only one way he could ever live with himself: he had to save them all.

* * *

In the darkness, all of Benjin's fears came to life and stalked him from every direction, waiting for him to let down his guard for even a moment. He was soft and slow with age, and he was unprepared for what lay ahead. Too long had he lived an easy life, forgetting the lessons his father and grandfather had taught him. He had always thought there would be time to prepare, time to train his children to face the coming storm, but now the storm had come early, and his work was not even begun.

Things most people thought of as legend were now here as flesh and blood, wood and iron, pain and fire. The Masters had always said it would only cause a panic if the truth was known to all, and thus they kept their knowledge hidden. The citizens of the Godfist would pay for the Masters' folly . . . and his.

Chapter 6

Men are fickle creatures, capable of kindness and compassion yet fascinated by the basest atrocities.
--Argus Kind, Zjhon executioner

* * *

When Catrin pulled herself from her bedroll, all but Benjin still slept. Their shelter blocked much of the morning light, and the air was still cool in the shadows. Benjin stood at the southern opening of the crevasse, his silhouette standing out in stark contrast to the bright landscape beyond. Catrin padded silently to his side and put her arms around him. He gave a start at her touch, and she knew he must have been in deep thought since he was usually impossible to sneak up on.

"Sorry," she said.

"It's all right, li'l miss. You just startled me."

"Not just that. I'm sorry about all of this. I never meant to cause so much trouble. I'm not even sure what I did, but now I've dragged all of you into my mess," she said, and she leaned her head against his shoulder for comfort.

He patted her on the head and guided her into the sunlight. "None of this is your doing, Catrin."

She looked up at him, surprised he would call her by name. She was so accustomed to "li'l miss" that her name sounded odd on his lips.

"We live in times of change, and all of us will be affected whether we wish it or not," he continued.

"But it seems, everywhere I go, trouble follows. It doesn't seem safe to be near me," she said, wanting to tell Benjin about the destruction of the grove, but she could not bring herself to speak of it.

"You can look at it that way if you wish, but I suggest you concentrate on what you can do to make the situation better. You cannot change what has already happened, but you can prepare yourself for the future. I can't say what this day will bring, but I vow to face it with my head high and my wits about me. I suggest you do the same. You can wallow in

80

self-pity if you like, but it'll only bring you misery. There's a greatness in you that you don't realize yet, Catrin, so you must not lose hope. We'll get through this together and be stronger for it."

"I know you're right. I'm sorry."

"And no more 'sorrys' from you," he said, shaking his finger at her. "I'll strike a bargain with you: If you promise not to intentionally hurt me, and I promise not to intentionally hurt you, then there will be no more need for another 'I'm sorry' between us. Do I have your word?"

"You have my word," she said with a small smile.

"And I give mine," he replied with a flourish and a bow. He smiled and touched her shoulder. "C'mon, let's go make the best of things."

Catrin felt a great deal of comfort from their talk. He'd forgiven whatever mistakes she might have made, and now maybe she could forgive herself. She made a conscious effort to tell herself she was forgiven and was surprised at how much it eased her guilt and anxiety.

She acknowledged that most people never intended to hurt her; her pain had been an unintentional by-product of their actions. A great weight seemed to lift from her soul, and she decided to focus on positive things. Taking a deep breath, she released her anger in a long sigh. A renewed Catrin strode back into the crevasse with confidence.

After they broke camp, Catrin helped the others stow their bedrolls and check their packs. Benjin led them by memory, and they often had to backtrack when the way was blocked. Numerous game trails crossed the valley floor, and he seemed to have trouble finding distinguishable landmarks. By noon, it seemed they had covered very little distance.

Chase, Strom, and Osbourne talked quietly among themselves. They were worried about their families and the other people they had left behind. They speculated about the invaders: who they might be and why they would attack.

Catrin listened in silence. She ached to know her father was safe, and she tried to have faith. Her mental image of him was one of strength and unbending integrity, and bringing that image to mind soothed her. She could not picture a man of such goodness and fortitude ever being in danger, and she clung to that illusion.

"I heard said some of the ships bore a symbol of a man and woman in an embrace. Sounds like the mark of a Zjhon warship to me. As much as I hate to speculate, I fear invaders have come from the Greatland," Benjin said.

"The Greatland!" Strom snorted. "I thought that existed only in fairy tales and legends. There's been no contact with other civilizations for thousands of years. Only the old texts mention the Greatland and the Firstland, so what reason do you have to believe they even exist?"

"I assure you the Greatland does indeed exist, and the danger presented by the Zjhon empire is all too real," Benjin stated flatly.

"You talk like you've been there," said Strom.

"That's because I have been there, but that's a story for another time. What's important now is that you know the Zjhon empire has not forgotten about us. They believe the Herald of Istra will be born on the Godfist and will be revealed through great acts of power. The Zjhon prophecies say the Herald will betray them and destroy their nation . . . or something like that. It's hard to tell just what they mean.

"I believe they'll go to great lengths to capture and kill anyone they believe could be the Herald. As much as I hate to admit it, I think Nat Dersinger was right: they've come to destroy us in a desperate attempt to save themselves. They will not find the Godfist an easy place to conquer, though; the Masters and a few select families have been making preparations for decades."

"You knew they were coming?" Osbourne asked, incredulous.

"In a sense we *knew*, but our information was thousands of years old, and it was nearly impossible to tell truth from fairy tale. Huge amounts of information were lost during the great wars and the Purge, and no one knew if the prophecies were anything more than legend, but we did know the Zjhon believed them to be sacred and quite real. We did our best to prepare for an invasion, and seeing their ships over the years kept us vigilant, but we thought we'd have much more time before it would happen. I guess our calculations were wrong," he said, stopping to untangle himself from a thorn bush.

"I don't understand," Chase interjected. "How could you *calculate* when they would attack?"

"It's a long story and rather complicated, but I'll try to explain. About twenty years ago, we heard the Zjhon Church had started quoting certain scriptures again, the ones that tell the Zjhon their duty is to fight in the name of Istra. The scriptures also say Istra's return will be the divine signal to embark on their holy war. We know they calculate the Vestran cycle to be about 3,017 years, but by our reckoning, it has only been 2,983 years since Istra departed."

"I *still* don't understand," Chase persisted. "I thought Istra was a goddess. What do you mean she has returned to the skies? All I've seen in the sky is a comet."

"A long time ago, people made up stories to explain things they couldn't understand. When a comet storm lasted over a hundred years and seemed to grant otherworldly powers, they glorified it and named it 'Istra, Goddess of the Night.' The comet we saw was most likely the first of many to come.

"It's said that during the Istran Noon, some seventy-five years into the storm, there can be as many as a thousand comets visible in the sky on any night. Some of the old tales refer to the first comet as the Herald of Istra, but others say it will be a person born here on the Godfist. I'm not really certain what I believe," Benjin added.

He called for a quick break, and while the young people rested, he walked a short distance in each direction. He was pushing his way into some heavy underbrush when he exclaimed, "Aha! I knew we were going in the right direction." He emerged from the underbrush with a gleam in his eyes.

"What did you find?" Catrin asked, and he beamed at her.

"When your father and I came this way, we left a few markings in case we ever wanted to find our way back. Beneath the underbrush and a thick layer of moss, I just found one of them. We carved it deep, and, luckily, it survived the passage of time. Our destination is due east, about a day's walk from here."

They were encouraged that they were on the right path and glad they would not have to carry their packs much farther. Benjin's excitement urged him to move on, this time leading them on a much straighter path. "Try to leave the forest undisturbed," he said. "Any sign we were here will help trackers."

Now there were fewer times they had to double back, and as they ascended a sloping hill, the forest became less dense, allowing them to move with greater speed. Just before nightfall, they crested a large rise. Tall trees provided cover, and there were a few open spaces for camping. They made no fire, for fear of being seen, but the mood was cheerier than it had been the night before. The evening air was cool and not uncomfortable. They snacked on their provisions and drank springwine, but Benjin cautioned them not to overindulge.

"Your packs may seem heavy now, but soon you may wish we could've carried more."

Chase and Strom both volunteered to take the first watch to let Benjin get some rest. "Thanks, boys. I'll fare better if I can get some sleep. Sentry duty is no pleasure, and it requires concentration. Your first duty is to remain awake. Sleep has claimed many sentries, and their groups have perished. I suggest you try to achieve a restful but alert state. Quiet your minds and concentrate on your breathing. The trick is to keep part of your mind focused on sight, hearing, and smell. It takes practice, but once you master it, you'll be able to achieve it at will.

"Don't shout or make any loud noises if you spot someone, as that might draw them to us. Wake the sleepers quietly, and sleepers should try to remember to wake quietly. Our sentry's stealth may go for naught if one of us wakes in a panic," he lectured. "I trust you will do your best to remain alert during your watch, but I think it'd be best if you double up for now. Chase and Catrin, take the first watch, Strom and Osbourne, the second, and I'll take the third.

"Periodically report to each other during your watch. Walk to where the other one is posted to check. Plan to alternate which sentry goes to the other. Changes will help keep you from getting sluggish."

The night was quiet, and Catrin dozed off during her watch. She flushed with shame when Chase woke her from a deep sleep, and she stood for the rest of her watch. When morning came, Strom and Osbourne admitted they had also fallen asleep, and they vowed to do better.

When they began their hike the next day, Benjin told them to be watchful for game trails, likely watering holes, and streams or ponds where the fishing might be good. "The land we're crossing now should be within our hunting range. There's a lot of game, but it's crafty because it's had to learn to avoid wolves and mountain cats. Animals are large out here, and they can be dangerous. Keep your wits about you."

* * *

Deep in the heart of the Masterhouse, within the mountain rock that held the most sacred halls, far from the stench of refugees, Master Edling paced. Here, fresh air vents allowed him to breathe freely for the first time since he awoke. Like so many vermin chased upward by floodwater, they had come to the Masterhouse, expecting to be fed and protected, and like the great soft-hearted fool he was, Headmaster Grodin let them in. It was suicide. With the emergency provisions stored deep in the mountain, those who dwelt in the Masterhouse could have easily lasted several winters, but with the boiling refugees, they would be lucky to last until spring. Even with strict rationing, they would most likely starve.

"We should send them to the cold caves with the Volkers," Master Beron said. "They've got plenty of food."

"Grodin would never allow it, the boiling fool. He doesn't deserve to be Headmaster. That position is reserved for someone with a strong enough will to make tough decisions when they need to be made," Master Edling said. "There must be another way. The problem we have right now is that the refugees are everywhere, like lice. Thank the gods that Grodin has at least the decency to maintain the sanctity of the sacred halls. If we could get him to agree to

85

isolate the refugees in the audience halls, we could collapse the entrances and be rid of them."

"And let them starve?" Master Beron asked, looking as if he might be sick.

"That's a big part of your problem, Beron; you've got no backbone. Would you prefer we offer them up to the Zjhon as slaves? Would you rather be a slave or die free?"

Master Beron sat for a moment before responding, but Master Edling's glare demanded he say something. "I suppose I'd rather die free," he said with uncertainty.

"You're boiling right you would. Now act like a man. These are terrible times, and if we're to survive, then terrible things must be done."

* * *

By midday, they reached an area where the vegetation thinned, giving way to mature trees that were widely spaced. Benjin scanned the valley walls, looking for another landmark.

"There was an ancient landslide--huge boulders in an enormous mound of rubble that was grown over with moss. It looked like a sleeping giant leaning against a cliff," he said as he searched, growing anxious as they traveled with no further sign of a landmark. "Wendel and I carried lighter packs, and maybe we were able to cover more ground. It was a long time ago, and my memory is not what it once was." They continued their hike for what seemed like ages, and still they found no signs of the sleeping giant. Benjin called a halt and looked for a place he could climb the valley wall.

"Maybe from a height I'll be able to see it," he said.

"I'll go with you," Chase said, following him. Catrin, Strom, and Osbourne settled into the shade to rest while they climbed.

"We've gone too far," Benjin announced when they returned. "Chase spotted some trees growing high and at odd angles, and I think they are growing out of the mound."

"Great job, you two. We must be getting close now. I trust your instincts," Catrin said.

After a short hike, Benjin smiled widely. "I think we're almost there!"

He walked closer to the cliff and found another set of marked stones, and they soon saw signs of the ancient rockslide.

"Chase and I will climb up first to locate the entrance. The rest of you stay here and remain alert. You'll want to back off a ways because we could loosen some stones," he warned. Using trees and bushes for support, they climbed the rocks, nearly slipping on places slick with moss.

In a loud whisper, Benjin said, "The entrance is blocked. We're going to have to clear it, and some debris may fall."

Chase and Benjin stacked the stones they removed to the side of the entrance, trying to keep them from falling, but a few still tumbled down the slope and crashed through the trees. The shadows were long by the time they cleared an opening large enough for Benjin to squeeze himself through to take a look.

"The place looks about the same as when I last saw it. Let's finish getting this opening cleared," he said. From inside the entrance, he was able to dislodge large sections of rock. They took two ropes and tied them to a remaining boulder and tied small stones to the other ends. Chase and Benjin tossed down the ropes, and although the stones helped to propel them through the foliage, only one reached the ground; the other caught high in the branches. Chase pulled it back up and tossed it again; this time the rope got low enough for Strom to reach it.

"Secure the packs, one at a time, and we'll haul 'em up," Benjin said. "Gather wood and kindling, preferably dry," Benjin called down after they began pulling the packs up. "Tie it off in bundles, and we'll haul them up."

Catrin and Osbourne scrambled to find wood in the failing light while Strom tied the bundles and guided them as they rose. Benjin's request for wood meant they would have a fire, which was reassuring because it meant he felt they were safely away from any pursuers. When darkness threatened to make scrounging impossible, they made the climb while they could still see, a relatively easy task when unencumbered.

No one spoke as they passed through the entrance and stared at the sight before them. The narrow opening emptied into a spacious hallway, which sloped downward at an angle. Perfectly rectangular, the hall was clearly not a natural formation, which was further evidenced by the worn scrollwork that decorated the lichen-covered walls. A short distance ahead, the hall gave way to a cavernous chamber. Its floor was littered with debris and the bones of small animals, and despite its relatively smooth appearance, it was pocked with small holes.

A narrow opening in the ceiling let in moonlight, which was reflected by the still waters of a subterranean lake. As they crossed the area that stood between them and the lake, the massive size of the cavern became apparent, and the scale of it dwarfed them. The vaulted ceiling was almost invisible in the growing darkness, and the dark waters of the lake seemed to stretch on forever in the distance.

"What *is* this place?" Catrin asked.

Benjin stood up from the bags he had been unpacking and joined the others. "Your father and I found this place by accident when looking for shelter from a storm. We couldn't figure out much about it other than the fact that this chamber had once been inhabited, possibly before the Purge. Other passages once led to this chamber, but they had all been blocked or the ceilings had collapsed. We investigated a bit, even built a small raft we used to explore. I bet it's still here." His eyes took on a faraway look as he remembered the time long past, but he pulled himself from his memories and returned to the present. "Let's get a fire started, shall we? I'm hungry and I'd really like some hot food. We can explore later."

Catrin got the tinderbox from her pack and started a fire. "Don't make the fire very large, li'l miss," Benjin warned. "We haven't put anything across the entrance yet, and the light could give us away. The cavern's big enough that it'll take up the smoke before it escapes through that hole up there, but we'll still need to be careful.

"The lake water should be safe to drink," he continued, "but I think it'd be best to boil it first. There's a kettle in one of the bags. After the water is boiled, you can put the kettle in a shallow part of the lake to cool it quickly. Let's fill our flasks too."

Catrin and Strom set about boiling water and getting ingredients together for a stew. She was glad to see Benjin pull recurve bows, strings, and several quivers of arrows from one of the long bags, along with a couple of short fishing poles.

Long before the stew was really done, they decided it had cooked long enough and fell to it. Full stomachs made them sleepy, and they were soon curling up in their bedding, letting Benjin take the first watch.

* * *

On trembling legs, Nat approached the ruins of the greatoak grove. Tears filled his eyes as he beheld what had once been a sacred and beautiful place. Now it looked more like a battlefield of epic scale, like a vision of what was yet to come.

Catrin.

This was where she and her friends had come to camp. They were here when the storm struck. She had to be connected to the destruction. This place had been undisturbed for thousands of years, and after only one night in her presence, it was destroyed. The evidence around him only served to strengthen his convictions. He had to do something, but he lacked the resources and connections. There was only one person who could do what needed to be done: Miss Mariss. Only she was powerful enough within the Vestrana to make such a decision.

As he crept back to town, sliding from shadow to shadow, his mind was consumed, trying to find the words to convince Miss Mariss that he was right. It would not be easy, but he had to succeed. To fail again would mean certain disaster.

Chapter 7

With dogma and aspiration, one can spin sand into gold.
--Icar the glassmaker

* * *

In the late morning, Catrin awoke and saw Benjin looking exhausted. As soon as she stood, he stumbled to his bedding.

"Don't leave the cavern," he mumbled then flopped down heavily and fell asleep.

Catrin used a stick to stir the remnants of the fire, and she added twigs to the glowing coals beneath the ash. She soon had a fire large enough to boil water. Kettle in hand, she approached the lake, and it shimmered in the light breeze, its surface rippling like the scales of a snake. Concentric rings added to the impression of a giant serpent curled around itself. She wondered at its beauty, amazed that something so massive and alluring could lie hidden inside a mountain for ages.

Was something beautiful if no one saw it? Her life had been that of a farm girl, and she hadn't entertained such philosophical thoughts that she could recall, but she had changed lately. Perhaps it was the bizarre events she had experienced recently, or maybe she was growing up; either way, she knew she would never be the same. It occurred to her that she and the rest of the group, with the exception of Benjin, would be growing up fast.

Curiosity gnawed at her, and she decided to wet her feet in the lake, if only to conquer her fear of something grabbing her and pulling her in. She let the water cover her ankles, finding it curious that little sand or mud covered the lake floor. The black stone was smooth and cool under her toes, almost too slick to stand upon. With the kettle filled, she pulled herself away from the mysterious serpent lake. The entire place intrigued her and sent her awareness into motion. So much of the cavern was obscured by darkness; her imagination bridged the gaps with grand images. Some of her mind's creations filled her with an almost irresistible desire to explore; others urged her back to the relative safety of camp.

Walking toward the fire, she looked up at the distant ceiling, which appeared to be a natural stone formation, in contrast to the man-made entrance hall. Stalactites reached inexorably toward the water below. When she looked ahead again, she saw Chase about to walk into her, his head craned upward. He, too, was caught up in the majesty of their hideaway, and a fair amount of water sloshed from her kettle onto his feet when Catrin stopped short to avoid the collision.

"Sorry," she said.

"No problem. I should've seen you coming. It's just that this place is so mystifying. It's not that it scares me or anything, but there's a strange feeling in the air--or something."

"I know what you're saying, and I feel like that too. I like it, and yet it frightens me a bit. Let's just sit by the fire while you dry out."

Strom and Osbourne came over to join them by the remains of the fire, bringing their mixture of nuts and dried fruit and hard, dark bread. As their eyes adjusted to the relative darkness of the cavern, they found they could see quite well despite the low light. Revitalized by the snack, Chase suggested they have a look around, and Osbourne agreed to stand guard.

As they skirted the lake, the walls began to close in, and the rock shoreline tapered to a narrow point, beyond which the water lapped directly against the nearly vertical walls of the dome. They couldn't quite make out the far side of the cavern, but they could make a fair guess at the distance. It was farther than any of them thought they could swim, not that they wanted to swim in that ominous-looking water.

The place had a powerful energy, and the black water brought to mind visions of giant serpents lurking just below the surface, lying in wait for unsuspecting swimmers. They had seen no indication of fish or any other creatures in the lake, but that seemed logical considering the lack of sunlight. They continued on along the shoreline, which was relatively smooth and free of debris.

Along the opposite shoreline, Catrin spotted an irregular shadow against the cavern wall. Moving in for a better look, they found the remains of the raft Benjin and Wendel had made years before. It looked as if they had pulled the raft to shore, stood it up, and propped it against the cavern wall. The logs were crumbling, and the rope had long since deteriorated, falling away when Chase gave it a tug. They left it where it was so Benjin could see it. Perhaps, Catrin thought, it might spark some good memories.

When they returned to camp, Benjin was pulling the kettle from the smoldering coals. He strode to the lake, kettle in hand, and it hissed as he placed it in the cold water. He dropped the handle and hastily pulled his hand away then waved to the returning group with a smile.

"Well, did you find anything exciting?" he asked.

"We found your raft," Chase announced with pleasure. "It definitely needs some new rope to hold it together, but I think it could still float."

"There really isn't much to see from what I recall, but if we find the time, we could lash it back together just for old time's sake," Benjin said then paused a moment before addressing them in a more serious tone. "We may need to stay here far longer than we are prepared for, and we need to get ready so we have food during the winter," he said as he walked over to where he had unpacked the bows and fishing rods.

"Catrin, you and Chase are both experienced hunters, and I'd like you to see if you can bring down any game. We can't afford to be picky. We're going to need as much meat as we can get. I believe there's a stream to the north and east of here. If you find it, look for a good fishing hole. I don't think there are any fish in this lake, but you never know. On a rainy day, we could try dropping a line." He handed Chase and Catrin each a bow, string, and a quiver of arrows.

"Try to retrieve any arrows you loose. My fletching skills are not what they used to be, and I was never very good to begin with," he said.

Catrin and Chase strung their bows, and Catrin was glad to have her familiar hunting tool in hand. After drawing her belt knife, she cut off a length of rope and coiled it around her belt. Chase seemed satisfied with Benjin's bow, and he got some dried beef strips from their provisions so they would have something to eat while they hunted.

"I want Strom and Osbourne to help me gather wood so we can build a small smoke room inside the cavern. We can also work on getting more water boiled, cooled, and into the flasks," he continued. With the responsibilities assigned, they got their gear and set off.

"Be back before dark," Benjin instructed. "Stay quiet and always remain alert. If you need help, howl like wolves."

Catrin and Chase made short work of their descent and headed east. They saw a few game trails, and Chase spotted a couple of buck rubs on the trunks of some nearby trees, but they found no other signs of wildlife.

"We need to find water. If we find water, we'll find game," Chase said.

They stood quietly, listening for the sound of moving water, but they heard only leaves rustling in the light breeze. Catrin checked the air for the scent of apples or berries, knowing that those, too, would attract animals, but she didn't detect anything. They turned toward the east since Benjin had mentioned a stream somewhere in that direction. Walking in stealthy silence, they were alert for any movements, large or small.

Chase stopped to wipe the sweat from his eyes. "It may be hot now, but there's a storm coming. I can smell it."

"I smell it too," Catrin said. "Let's hope it waits till after nightfall to rain. We better get moving."

A moment later, though, Chase stopped and stared, open mouthed, at a large eagle, which swooped in for a kill just a short distance ahead. Catrin watched in awe as the magnificent bird smashed into the ground and just as suddenly propelled itself back into the air with a huge black snake in its claws. The eagle had to work hard to gain the air, the weight of the snake holding it down, but it pumped its powerful wings and flew back into the treetops. They soon heard the screams of the eaglets demanding their turn to be fed.

Catrin and Chase pressed on, hugging the valley wall to keep from getting turned around in the cover of the trees.

93

Catrin froze when she heard a branch snap off to her right. She and Chase nocked their arrows and took up positions behind nearby trees, but nothing emerged from the woods. Catrin was about to give up when Chase tapped her on the shoulder and pointed.

A little farther north from where the noise had come, a medium-sized spike buck was following a pair of does into a narrow clearing. Catrin took aim at the buck, the largest of the three. Her arm trembled as she held the bowstring taut, waiting for a clean shot. The buck suddenly flicked both ears forward and snorted, and all three deer turned and fled, their fluffy white tails standing up straight.

Taking hasty aim, Catrin loosed her arrow. Her shot flew over the buck's head, but it didn't miss by much. The sound of the arrow frightened him, and he turned aside, giving Chase the broadside shot he'd been waiting for. Chase's arrow hit just behind the buck's shoulder, and he reached the deer almost before it hit the ground. Catrin held back a moment and allowed him time to grant the animal a quick death. She understood the need to hunt, but she didn't like to kill or see anything die. Chase would take care of that part, and she was grateful. She tossed him a length of rope with a sad smile, and he tied the buck's ankles.

"Nice shot," she said.

"Couldn't have done it without ya, Cat. If you hadn't panicked and taken the bad shot, I might never have gotten a good one. Your shot wasn't even close, you know," he said, grinning.

"It was close enough to make him hesitate and change his course, which gave you a sleeping bull for a target," she scolded and set off in the direction her arrow had gone. She pushed her way farther into the underbrush, and caught a sudden movement from the corner of her vision.

Stumbling backward, she found herself staring down at a large boar. She let out a yelp as she met the boar's eyes and knew immediately she had made a big mistake. The threatened boar interpreted her direct eye contact as a challenge and dropped its head as it charged. Catrin backpedaled as quickly as she could, and she could hear Chase scrambling behind her, trying to come to her aid. In a

94

split second, she realized she could not possibly outrun the boar and knew her best chance was to shoot it before it gored her.

She spun gracefully, pulling an arrow from her quiver as she turned. With practiced precision, she nocked the arrow and drew, but in mid-draw she realized that she was not going to be fast enough. The boar was going to reach her within an instant of her firing. She leaped into the air as she loosed her arrow, and she heard the air whistle as Chase's arrow whizzed by. Both arrows struck the beast in the chest, but the boar's momentum carried its enormous weight forward and sent it crashing into Catrin's legs while she was still in midair. She felt a tusk stab her in the shin as she was tossed higher into the air by the impact.

Face-first, she landed on the flailing hooves of the mortally wounded boar. Her landing knocked the wind out of her, and she was kicked in the face several times before she could get her breath and roll free. Fortunately, the boar was in its death throes, and the kicks had little force behind them. Chase quickly finished off the boar and turned to Catrin, who sat dazed and winded.

Her vision clouded as her eye started to swell shut, and blood poured freely from her nose and lips. The boar's tusk hadn't penetrated her leather pants, but her leg felt as if it were bruised to the bone. She sucked air through her teeth as she pulled her pant leg up to expose the wound. Her leg was swelling, and she soon had a large lump on her shin.

"I'll go back for help," Chase said just as a light rain began to fall.

"I can walk," she said, but she winced when she put weight on her wounded leg.

"Our kills weigh more than the two of us combined. I'm going for help," Chase said firmly. He turned and jogged back toward the cavern, occasionally howling like a wolf. He and the others returned more quickly than Catrin would have thought possible. She stood to greet them, and Benjin's face paled when he saw her. Her wounds were not as bad as they appeared, but she made a ghastly sight. The rain had streaked the dirt and blood on her face, and the swelling was getting worse.

"Cripes, Cat. You were supposed to shoot the game, not tackle it," Strom said. "It looks like he put up a pretty good fight."

Benjin gave her a thorough looking over and shook his head. "You got mighty lucky, li'l miss. Not many survive facing a boar that size. I'd say you fared pretty good by the looks of things. D'ya think you can walk?"

"Yes. It hurts a bit, but I don't think anything is broken," she said through gritted teeth. She put some weight on her leg and it held, but it throbbed painfully.

Benjin looked for a fallen branch but found none that suited him. He cut down a nearby sapling, stripped it of branches, and cut it to be as long as Catrin was tall. He handed her the makeshift walking stick. "We all need a little help sometimes. Lean on this."

Chase and Strom hacked at a couple of saplings with their belt knives and stripped them of branches. Benjin tied the animals' ankles then inspected the saplings. They slid the smaller sapling under the ropes that tied the buck's ankles and took the larger sapling to the boar.

Benjin helped them get the boar on the pole then stood and wiped his hands on his pants. "Strom and I will take the boar. Chase and Osbourne can carry the deer. Are you sure you want to walk, li'l miss? We could come back for you."

"I can make it," she said, wiping blood from her nose, but she leaned heavily on the walking stick. Benjin and Strom each put a shoulder under the sapling and struggled to get the boar off the ground.

"I know I said we couldn't afford to be picky, but in the future, let's stick to game smaller than a horse," he said between clenched teeth. With that, they began lurching back toward the cavern.

Chase and Osbourne moved in behind them, struggling a bit with the weight of the buck. Catrin limped along, lost in thought as she struggled to keep up.

They reached the base of the rock pile where the cavern was located, dropped the boar and buck to the ground, and flopped down beside them. They lay there, exhausted. Catrin leaned against a tree and tried to ignore the pain in her face and leg.

96

"With these kills, you and Chase should be able to sit back and relax. My stomach thanks you," Strom said with a smirk and a quick bow. Benjin had rigged a harness to lift the kills up to the cavern while Chase and Catrin had been out hunting. After they raised the deer and the boar, Benjin gave her his shoulder to lean on as she carefully put her injured leg into one side of the harness he had crafted. She leaned heavily on him as she gingerly lifted her other leg into the apparatus. "We'll take it real slow. Just let us know if you need help or if you feel you are in trouble," Benjin said.

As soon as her feet left the boulders, she started spinning, and she had to catch herself on a nearby branch. Chase did what he could to steady the rope from his perch in a tree above her, but his movements shook the tree, showering her with rainwater. He pushed the rope out away from a large branch, and she passed well clear of it. When she finally cleared the ledge, they looked at the boar then at the deer and finally at their small smoke room.

"We're going to need a bigger smokehouse," Osbourne said.

Benjin attended to Catrin's wounds while the others dressed the carcasses. She winced as he wiped the dried blood from her face and nose. Her eye was nearly shut, and her nose was sore, but those were barely noticeable compared with the throbbing pain in her shin. She pulled back with a sharp intake of breath when he lightly ran the damp cloth over it. He got his wax-sealed herbal kit and another flask of clean water and told Catrin to tilt her head back and open her mouth. She did so reluctantly, knowing what was coming. He sprinkled a fair amount of ground humrus root into her mouth and handed her the flask. She gulped, and water splashed down the sides of her face as she hurried to wash down the bitter-tasting herb. She took several more large gulps before she would let Benjin take the flask from her.

He put a bit more of the powder in his palm and poured a small amount of water on it. He mixed it into a paste and told Catrin to lie back and relax. She sprawled on her back but could not relax; her leg was still throbbing, and she tensed in anticipation of his touch on her swollen shin. He

97

did it as quickly and gently as he could, but she cried out in pain, and tears flowed down her cheeks.

"It'll take a little while for the humrus root to dull the pain, but it should help you sleep tonight," he said. Soon, mercifully, the potion began to take effect. Her pain was mostly dulled, and exhaustion overtook her. The herbs and the rhythmic sound of the falling rain soon lulled her into a deep sleep.

* * *

Though he had met with General Dempsy in the past, Kern felt an ache in his stomach and his knees trembled. This mission was different from all that had come before it, and the general's mood had been ranging from seething to bitter. The men had come to fear him more than ever as he lashed out in anger. His judgments over disputes became increasingly harsh, often punishing both the accused and the accuser. Most disputes were now handled between the individuals for fear of General Dempsy's decisions.

Biting his lip, Kern rapped on the general's cabin door.

"Come."

"Good afternoon, General Dempsy, sir."

"Overseer Kern. Report."

"We've covered the farmlands, sir. She's not there. I've sent men into the mountains, but I've received no reports yet. We'll find her, sir. You can depend on that."

"You'd better. Your men are supposed to be the best. I suggest you prove it, or your next medal could be posthumous."

"Yes, sir."

Chapter 8

* * *

The next few days passed more quickly than Catrin had thought they would. Her wounds were healing well, and she spent most of her time dressing, butchering, salting, and smoking the game Benjin and Chase brought back. Strom had had some luck with a fishing hole, and there were fish to be filleted then cooked, salted, or smoked. Racks made of fresh-hewn saplings now lined one of the cavern walls, and a few were already laden with cured venison, pork, and fish. Strom had been elected to find fruits and nuts, and he brought in apples, berries, and sacks of black walnuts.

As the provisions mounted, Benjin said, "I'm pleased with your work, but we still need at least three times what we have if we're to survive the winter."

"I'd rather not live here, but if I must, I don't want to go hungry." That was the mantra that kept the young people working. No one was happy with the prospect of a prolonged stay, but they tried not to dwell on it; their lives depended on the work they had to do, which meant less idle time to speculate about the future and the fates of their loved ones.

Despite Catrin's rapid recovery, Benjin continued to apply humrus paste to her shin, though he used it sparingly to conserve his supply of herbs. Catrin gladly retired her walking stick when she could put weight on her leg without any pain.

Benjin described a few herbs he thought might grow in the area and asked them to harvest only half of any plants they found, making sure to leave enough for repopulation. "If you only find one or two plants, just pick a few leaves. Some will be better than none," he said.

Within a few weeks, they had food to last until spring with strict rationing. They had to use the last of their salt supply, however, and their herb-gathering efforts had produced little. "There's no help for it, I suppose," Benjin said when he shook the last of the salt from the bag, too little even to cover a perch fillet. "We can't smoke too much meat without giving away our location. We'll need to eat as much fresh meat and fish as possible until we can no longer hunt. Any food that'll keep is off limits. We'll need it before spring arrives, no doubt. I want Strom and Catrin to gather more black walnuts, since they seem to be plentiful, and any other nuts or fruits you find.

"I know I've been pushing you all hard, but I've little choice in the matter. The storms can be intense this high in the mountains, and the snow doesn't melt till spring. Once the snows start, we could be trapped in here until spring. We need to gather more food so we can eat comfortably this winter, and we're going to need a much larger supply of firewood. I want you to spend half of each day hunting and foraging and the other half collecting wood. If you can do both at once, then you'll certainly impress me. I'm going to look for herbs. Our supply is far too small for my liking, and I know the places they like to hide," he said with a wink as he shouldered his pack.

When Benjin returned that evening, he was laden with plants and roots, and he entered the cavern with a big smile. "I feel a bit better now, I should have enough medicinal herbs to deal with most ailments, but try not to fall off any cliffs and watch out for snakes," he said. Along with the herbs, he produced turnips, asparagus, and even some wild garlic, which he used to make a delicious soup.

* * *

"I hope we don't have to eat all of these walnuts to survive," Strom said while he and Catrin were returning from one of their many nut-gathering outings, and she admitted that she was dreading the winter as much as he.

Tension grew as the weeks passed, and even Benjin began to show signs of worry. One night he sat them all down around the fire. "Wendel and I made an agreement. If he hadn't joined us within forty days, then I was to sneak back as close to Harborton as I could to see what's going on. I'm going to leave tomorrow before dawn, but I only plan to be gone for four or five days. You all know to remain quiet and stay hidden, keep the fires small, and try not to leave obvious signs of your passage when you're out hunting and gathering," he lectured.

"Maybe I should go with you," Chase offered.

"It'll be a very dangerous task, and I'm more experienced at this kind of thing. I want you all to stay here and continue on as you have been, but be extra careful; you must protect one another."

"What if you don't come back in five or six days?" Osbourne asked, concern written clearly on his face.

"The best thing you can do is keep yourselves safe and carry on as you have been. If you think you've been spotted, or if you need to escape, try to go east. About a half a day's walk from here, there's a large river. Follow the river north. When you reach the waterfall, climb to the top if you can and then follow the valley north by northeast," Benjin said, pausing a moment to look into the troubled faces in front of him to gauge their concern.

"I don't think you'll have any trouble; you're well hidden here. Just remember to stay inside as much as possible and keep quiet. You'll have enough provisions to last through the winter if you use good judgment. Strom, take the first watch and wake Chase for the second. I'm going to need my sleep tonight," he said before retiring to his bedroll.

Catrin and the others exchanged worried glances but didn't speak. They wanted to know what was going on outside their hideaway, but they feared for Benjin's safety. The tension in the cavern was palpable.

Catrin woke in the dead of night to find Benjin already gone. Chase sat near the fire and waved when he saw her sit up, and she joined him by the fire.

"How long ago did he leave?" she asked quietly.

"It's been quite a while. His idea of morning is more like the middle of the night," he replied. He declined her offer to take the rest of the watch, and instead they talked until dawn.

* * *

101

Though most of his wounds had healed, Peten Ross still walked with a limp, and not a moment passed that he did not feel pain. Yet no one showed him the slightest bit of favor or kindness--he was just another refugee, lumped in with commoners and men he wouldn't let shine his boots. The stench alone was enough to make him want to escape, but it was the chance to prove his bravery and worth to Roset and everyone else that was too alluring to resist.

She and the others had shunned him ever since the snake incident. Even knowing the snake was harmless, Peten recoiled from the thought of its touching him. He would prove Roset and the others wrong. While most chose to spend their time wallowing in self-pity, Peten had been looking for a way out. There were too many people confined in the Masterhouse, and he was convinced that Wendel Volker and those who followed him to the cold caves were getting fat on the Ross family's meat. For generations his family had been storing sides of beef in the cold caves, but only now did that practice seem a liability. It infuriated Peten that he should have to endure a strict ration when those who didn't deserve it dined on his food.

Things had seemed hopeless until Peten met a dirty little man whose name he did not remember nor care to know. All that was important was that this man was willing to reveal some of the Masterhouse's secrets for nothing more than a few silvers.

When everyone else was asleep, Peten walked on the tips of his toes over the still bodies that seemed to carpet the cold flagstones. One man cursed him when he stepped on a finger, but no one else seemed to notice or care.

At the entrance to the hall that led to the sacred chambers, those denied to the refugees, a bored-looking guard seemed to be having trouble keeping his eyes open. It seemed an eternity that Peten waited, but then the moment came: the guard let his eyes droop closed. After waiting for a few more anxious moments, Peten moved as quietly as he could past the guard, his limp making the act of being silent even more difficult. His right foot seemed to want to drag across the stone with every step, and he gritted his teeth against the pain.

Voices carried through the halls, and Peten flattened himself against the corridor wall, feeling exposed and vulnerable.

" . . . can smell the boiling vermin from here."

"Won't be much longer before that problem is . . ."

The voices faded and Peten hastily resumed his quest, suddenly panicking, worried he had forgotten what the man told him. Was it left at the fifth hall then right at the third? Or was it the other way around? Sweat dripped into his eyes as he concentrated. Part of him wanted to give up, to go back and hide with his family and friends, but another part seemed to have awakened. He could make a difference. His actions could save countless lives. In his mind he played through the drama and pageantry that he imagined would follow his great victory. His people needed a leader, a person who would take action in the face of death, and he was that leader. All he had to do was prove that to everyone.

With determination, he strode forward as fast as his limp would allow. Following his gut instinct, he turned left when he reached the fifth hall and right at the third. No more voices broke the silence, and finding the room the man had told him about sent Peten's confidence soaring. If only his confidence could defeat the smell, which was worse than the smell of the refugees. The thought of climbing through a sewer made Peten want to wretch, but it was the path to his salvation. Driven by his need for power and a deeper, almost unrecognizable, feeling of responsibility for those he cared about, he entered the sewer.

The journey was something he hoped he could erase from his memory for all time, but he doubted it. At least the man had been true to his word about leaving a torch. Obtaining flint from a fellow refugee had cost him another silver, but it was coin well spent. Without the torch, he would have been lost. When he rounded a corner and saw a splash of dim light illuminating the way ahead, though, he quickly tossed the torch into the fetid water.

When he reached the grate, he nearly wept. Grasping at the bars that blocked his way, he cursed the dirty little scoundrel who had sent him on a fool's quest. Anger boiled in his belly, and he growled in fury. It took every scrap of will he possessed to refrain from crying out, from venting his rage on the heavens. In his anger, his muscles contracted and he could feel the bars digging into his flesh, but then something amazing happened: One of the bars began to move. It was only the slightest movement, but it was enough. Increasing the pressure, Peten began to push and pull on the bar as hard as he could. Mortar fell away in large chunks, and with a suddenness that sent Peten stumbling backward, the bar gave way.

Again Peten had to refrain from crying out as he pushed his way past the remaining bars. Rock and metal bit into his skin and left him with a dozen minor cuts, but he gained the fresh air and his freedom.

The drainage ditch that ran from the mouth of the sewer ended at a small cove so fouled and stagnant that no one would stay near it for long, and Peten decided that it could be no worse than the sewers had been, and it was his best chance to slip into the water undetected.

Beyond the cove he bathed in the crashing waves, letting them blast the foulness from him, but the smell seemed to follow him no matter how hard he scrubbed. In the end, he gave up washing and concentrated on swimming and, at times, wading his way along the coast. The sun began to rise, as if Vestra wished to expose him to the Zjhon.

Peten cursed his luck and looked for a good place to leave the water and gain the shore. He had seen no shadows and heard no voices for quite some time, and he knew he needed to cover a lot of distance in a hurry. When he reached the shore, he climbed a pair of massive stones that cradled an ancient tree between them. Using a branch to pull himself up, he had no time to react and not the slightest chance of avoiding the boot heel that was hurtling toward his face. In an instant, the world went dark.

A broken twig and a plant that stood at an angle, its leaves crumpled and broken, were Benjin's first warning, and it was far too close to their hideaway for his comfort. There were more signs as he moved closer to the populated lands. Years of training became fresh in his mind once again, as the need for stealth became paramount. When he neared the farm, his fears grew. It seemed the Zjhon were everywhere at once. Their numbers were difficult to believe, and he considered abandoning his quest, but the need for information drew him on. It was all too clear to him now that they would not be able to remain in the cavern until spring, the Zjhon would tear down the forest and pick the mountains clean if that was what it took.

When he reached the tree line that bordered the farm, he crouched behind a tree and waited. Soldiers milled around the area, and he thought he might have to wait until after dark. In the distance, a bell rang, and many of the soldiers stopped what they were doing and headed back toward Harborton; a few remained. "Not perfect," Benjin said to himself, "but it's an improvement."

One man went to the well, and two others walked toward the cottages. No one else could be seen. Benjin made his move and charged up to the back of the barn. Looking through a knothole in the barn door, he checked for Zjhon but saw none. Doing his best to be quiet, he slid the door partly open and slipped in. First he went to the feed stall, and was pleased to find that the Zjhon had not taken everything. A salt block sat in the corner, and there were still some oats in one of the barrels. Being as quiet as possible, he broke up the salt block and put it into a couple of sacks that had been hanging from a wooden peg. He put some of the oats in a sack as well, but he did not take too much, knowing he could carry only so much and still maintain his stealth.

It took time to carry each sack into the loft, but he figured this was the safest place to hide them until he came back. The loft was also where he'd hidden his sword, and he pulled it from behind some bales of moldy hay. He had considered taking it with him when they first left for the mountains, but he hadn't been able to bear the thought of talking to Catrin about her mother. He could not lie to her, and if she saw the sword, she would surely have questions. Any answers he gave to those questions would certainly have led to questions about Elsa. The memories were still painful for him, and he could see no good that would come from revealing things to Catrin that would only confuse and hurt her. Now, though, his need outweighed his desire to spare Catrin the pain of knowing.

Even as the thought occurred to him, he heard the barn's front door open and the sound of horses walking into the barn. In the next moment, he heard something that chilled his bones and made him curse his own stupidity: "Why is the back door open?" someone asked in Zjhonlander. Benjin hadn't heard it spoken in many years, but he recognized the peril of his situation immediately. After making sure the sacks of salt and grain were well hidden, he climbed over the bales of straw that were stacked almost to the angled roofline. Squeezing himself through the cobwebs, he ducked under the rafters that gave him barely enough room to pass. When he finally reached the other side, he quietly slid down into the small open area between the straw pile and the back door of the loft.

From what he could hear, the soldiers below had not called out or raised the alarm, but he heard them climb to the loft. As quietly as he could, Benjin opened the loft door just enough to see if anyone was outside. When the way looked clear, he opened the door and climbed out onto the narrow ledge that ran along the top of the barn doors. With his back to the barn, Benjin closed the door and scooted himself sideways until he reached the makeshift ladder he'd built many years ago. It had taken a only few scraps of barn board cut into short strips and nailed to the side of the barn to create a nearly invisible ladder. As he climbed down it, he was thankful for his own ingenuity.

When he reached the bottom, he saw the soldiers coming back down from the loft, and he raced to the fence. Using his momentum and a hand on the top rail, he launched himself over the fence. In truth, he was lucky his grip did not miss the top rail since the entire fence was overgrown with honeysuckle and blackberry bushes. It was the growth that gave him cover while he fled. Running while crouched is not an easy thing to do, and his knees ached terribly when he finally reached the tree line. From there, he watched and rested.

The Zjhon seemed quite relaxed. They had taken Harborton and the highlands, and now those who remained to hold these seemed content to get fat on what had been left behind by the people of the Godfist. Anger and resentment burned in Benjin's belly, and when a sentry came too close, he moved without hesitation. Silently he approached the bored-looking soldier and caught him completely by surprise. Using his momentum and leverage to focus the power of his muscles, Benjin landed a devastating punch that dropped the soldier without a sound. After dragging the man back to the tree line, Benjin took his uniform and left him there.

Knowing it was only a matter of time before someone noticed the sentry was missing or found his body, Benjin hurried through the trees, looking for the game trail he used to hunt. When he found it, he took a moment to change into the soldier's uniform, and he stashed his clothes near the trail. He tucked his hair beneath the jacket collar and hoped his disguise would be sufficient, though he knew it was thin.

Getting to Harborton was as easy as following a series of trails through the woods that dominated the foothills, but when he reached the edge of town, his task became a great deal more difficult--the darkness his only boon. After sifting through a garbage heap on the outskirts, Benjin found some things that might help him get to the Watering Hole without having to answer any questions. He cut the top off an old leather flask and filled it with a noxious mixture of rotting vegetables and stale wine, and he hid the flask within his coat.

When the moon was high, Benjin walked the streets, doing his best to look as if he belonged there. Careful planning took him along a route that he guessed would have the least traffic. One street ran along a narrow canal whose smell kept most people at a distance, and another was little more than a dirty alley between two rows of buildings. The refuse that had accumulated there over many years made getting through difficult, but Benjin was grateful for it.

At the end of the alley, he could see his destination. The faded and chipped sign above the inn had always been a welcoming sight, but now Benjin knew better. The Zjhon religion declared churches and libraries sacred and decreed that they must not be destroyed during the conquest of a city, but it was the soldiers who declared inns sacred. It was a long-standing practice that those the Zjhon conquered were allowed to continue a limited and heavily taxed business, and it appeared this was still the case, for the sounds coming from the Watering Hole indicated the inn was still operating. Benjin could only hope that Miss Mariss was well and still running the inn.

Taking a deep breath, he prepared himself for what would likely be the most dangerous part of his journey. A patrol of soldiers walked the streets looking half asleep and utterly disinterested, and Benjin waited for them to pass. As soon as they were out of sight, he left the safety of the shadows and walked into the moonlight, hoping no one chose this moment to leave the inn. As he crossed the street, a loud outburst of laughter emanated from inside, and Benjin nearly leaped from his skin, but no one emerged.

With an ill-advised burst of speed, he covered the last bit of distance between himself and the shadows alongside the inn. Just as he rounded the corner, he encountered a soldier who'd been relieving himself in the bushes.

"Who's there?" the man asked in Zjhonlander, and Benjin nearly stumbled as he was taken by surprise. Quickly he turned and leaned over, making vomiting sounds and pouring some of his foul mixture on the ground. "If you can't hold your drink, you shouldn't indulge," the man said as he came closer. "What's your name, soldier? Whom do you serve under?"

Benjin felt a hand on his shoulder, and he prayed for good luck. As he turned toward the soldier, he never raised his head, and he made more retching noises, and then he poured the rest of his mixture on the man's boots. The soldier stepped back, and Benjin waited to see if his plan had worked or if it would be the end of him. The soldier must have gotten a whiff of the foul mixture and Benjin heard his stomach heave. Without another word, the man turned and left, probably hoping to keep the contents of his stomach where they were.

As soon as the man turned the corner, Benjin stumbled around the back of the inn and was pleasantly surprised the find the back door unguarded. Miss Mariss's kitchen looked much as it always had, save there were fewer people and a lot less food to be seen, and now there was an oppressive pall of desperation that hung in the air.

When the kitchen door suddenly swung inward, Benjin crouched down, but Miss Mariss saw him instantly. Her face registered no surprise or fear; she simply held a finger to her lips, grabbed half a loaf of bread, and walked back to the common room. Admiring her strength, Benjin moved to a darkened corner and waited. It took some time for Miss Mariss to convince her unwelcome guests that the inn was closing for the evening, but she eventually came back to find Benjin. Again she held a finger to her lips and led him to the cellar, which, like most cellars, was damp, cold, and had a smell like moldy soil.

"It's good to see you, Benjin," she said after leading him to a place between the stacks of crates and barrels, most of which appeared to be empty. "There's been much worry over the safety of you and those in your care."

"We've worried about you as well."

"I've got it good compared to most. I have to put up with the scoundrels in my inn, but I have most of my freedom. As for the rest, things could be a great deal better."

Benjin nodded his agreement, and they settled down to discuss their plans.

* * *

When five days had passed and Catrin and the others still had seen no sign of Benjin, they were worried, but they tried to be optimistic.

"I'm sure he's just being extra careful, and all the rain we've been having is probably slowing him down as well," Chase said.

"Knowing Benjin, he's probably so overloaded with salt and cheese that he'll barely make it back before the first snow." Strom laughed.

After ten days, the group was anxious and restless. Catrin had so much pent-up energy, she thought she could probably sprint all the way to the ocean. She was fretful and paced constantly.

"I'm going fishing," Strom announced, clearly wishing to escape the oppressive atmosphere, even if it was only to sit in the rain. Chase seemed to share his desire.

"I think I'll go hunting in the high reaches today," he said nonchalantly.

"The high reaches?" Catrin asked. "What kind of game do you expect to find up there? Goat?"

"Perhaps no game at all. I want to find a high place with a good view of the valley. I have a bad feeling about Benjin."

No one disagreed, and Strom offered to go with him, but they jointly decided one person stood less of a chance of being spotted than two. They were going against Benjin's orders, but they all felt compelled to do something--anything. Catrin and Osbourne felt helpless, left without much to do.

"I think we should keep watch while they're gone," Osbourne said, looking pale and shaken. "I'll take first watch."

"I'm going to look again for another exit from the cavern in case we need it," Catrin said.

She retrieved a coil of rope and a couple of torches that Benjin had fashioned and made her way back to the old raft. She lowered the logs to the ground and lashed them together. It was a hot job, and her eyes burned with sweat by the time she finished, but the raft looked strong. She grunted with effort as she pushed off into the dark water. The raft seemed to float well, and she hoped it would be stable. She pulled it back to shore.

Searching through the woodpile, she found a branch she could use to push herself across the water. It still had leaves on one end, and she hoped it would work like an oar if the water got too deep for poling. When she returned to the fire to light one of her torches, Osbourne looked concerned.

"I don't think it's a good idea for you to go off on that raft. It's not safe."

"Nothing we do these days is safe. But don't worry; I'll be fine."

Catrin put her spare torch on the raft along with the rope and her makeshift oar and climbed tentatively aboard the awkward craft, holding her lit torch aloft. Her weight caused the raft to sink lower into the water, and at times it was almost completely submerged; only her quick reactions kept the second torch from getting saturated. The sudden movements threatened to overturn the raft. It was precarious, but she was determined.

Poling and holding the torch up at the same time was hard, but she managed to move along the shoreline, still staying close to the cavern wall. There was no real shoreline this far out, but she did occasionally come across what appeared to have been other passageways leading into the cavern. They were all blocked with fallen rock and debris, and none appeared passable.

As she became more adept at poling, she moved more quickly toward the far end of the cavern. The water grew deeper, and she had to put her entire arm in the water to reach the bottom with her pole. Eventually the water was too deep to reach the bottom, and she pushed off the cavern walls when she could. Occasionally she pushed herself out too far and had to paddle back. Her branch made a poor paddle, and at times she made more progress by setting the branch on the raft and paddling with her free hand.

When she reached the back of the cavern, she came on a collapsed corridor that was larger than all the others. Fallen stone blocked this one too, but the size of the arch intrigued her. As she began to wonder if someone hadn't blocked the tunnels intentionally, a small breeze caressed her cheek. She sniffed the air--a bit dank but not foul.

After pushing the raft closer to the doorway, she latched onto some of the rocks that blocked it. She wedged her torch into a nearby crevice and pulled herself onto the top of a protruding rock, hoping the raft would not drift off. There wasn't much room for her on the small shelf of rock, but she managed to balance as she reached out to the raft. She had to stretch to grasp her rope, which she used to secure the raft to one of the jagged rocks at the bottom of the doorway.

Cooler air continued to seep through the rocks, and Catrin loosened some of the top pieces. It was slow work, but she cleared a hole about the size of her head. She poked her torch into it to see what lay beyond. She could see very little, but it did appear that the corridor was mostly clear beyond the initial blockage. When she pulled her torch back, she noticed a narrow rectangular slit in the stone above the doorway and shivered as she recalled the lessons that spoke of old castles having arrow slits above the entrances, often referred to as death holes. The sight of it was unsettling.

She needed a much larger opening to crawl through, but several large stones were wedged tightly just below the hole she had created. She finally got one of the large rocks to wiggle and rocked it back and forth, moving it a little more with every sweep. She gave it a hard yank and nearly fell from her perch when it jerked free, the stone hitting the water with a loud splash. Catrin leaned back against the rocks and took a couple of deep breaths.

"Are you all right?" Osbourne shouted across the water, and his words echoed loudly in the cavern.

"I'm fine. I've found another passage, and I'm going to see where it goes."

"Don't be gone too long, Cat," he said in a quieter voice. "I don't want to be here alone."

"I'll be back as soon as I can."

The hollow left by the large stone gave her more room to work and made the removal of the next one a bit easier. She soon had a hole she thought she could squeeze through. With her torch held through the hole, she saw the rubble pile sloping down and away on the other side. Dropping the torch onto the rocks on the other side--carefully so as not to extinguish it--she wriggled her way through the hole, getting slightly stuck when her belt knife caught on the stones. After freeing the knife, she slid farther through the hole. A rock broke away and moved out from under her hand, and she began to slide. She landed noisily, her face just inches from the burning torch she had tossed into the space. She wasn't bleeding, but she was a sore in several places.

After gathering her gear, she moved past the rest of the debris. The ceiling and walls were unbroken, and Catrin was convinced these halls had been sealed intentionally. It also occurred to her that whoever had done it had most likely done it in a hurry. Otherwise, the barrier would have been much more substantial. She recalled the arrow slits above the doorway and thought perhaps they had not needed much more of an obstruction.

When she moved her torch closer, she could see how cleanly the stone had been cut. There were no visible seams in the smooth walls, which seemed to be one continuous surface. The floor was also smooth, though covered with a thick layer of dust and dirt.

Walking slowly down the corridor, Catrin felt like an intruder in a place long lost to the living. Ahead she saw a doorway, but there were no tracks in the dust on the floor, so she didn't think she would encounter any wildlife. Still, she crept ahead slowly, half expecting a specter to jump out at her. Instead, she found a short hall with several doorways on either side. She looked into one of the rooms and saw some crumbled pieces of pottery and rotted wood that may have once been a bed frame. In the other rooms, she found similar hints that these had once been sleeping chambers, but the rooms were rather small. She doubted they had been rooms for the wealthy, and she wondered if they had been servants' quarters.

In another she found a washbowl behind the ruins of another bed frame. The bowl was almost perfectly preserved, with the exception of one sizable chip out of the rim. It was unlike anything she had ever seen before. She bent down and wiped her finger across the surface to find under the dust that the bowl was shiny with elaborate designs below the glaze.

As she bent down to inspect it more closely, a clump of reddish clay caught her attention. It was wedged inside one of the bed frame's wooden joints, as if it had been hidden there when the bed was still whole. Drawn to the clump by some mysterious desire, she pried it away from the disintegrating wood, and a small shape revealed itself.

In the dwindling light of her torch, it appeared to be a carving of a fish, made from some kind of milky crystal, its surface porous and rough. She placed the little carving in her pocket and in that moment saw her torch was not far from burning out. She had been gone a while, and she figured Osbourne was probably worried. She turned back, eager to tell him what she had found.

Though she hoped not to use it, her spare torch was tucked into her belt. When the first torch sputtered out, she had to quickly decide if she wanted to light the spare while the first was still hot enough to ignite it. She decided to save it since she was not far from the opening, and her vision would eventually adjust to the darkness.

Shuffling along the smooth wall, she worked her way back to the pile of stone and poked her head through the hole. The raft waited below, and she was grateful it had not gotten loose. Looking across the water, she saw Osbourne's silhouette leaning against the wall near the cavern entrance. Sliding forward carefully, she was in a very awkward position when shuffling noises and deep voices shouting words she did not understand suddenly echoed in the cavern.

Twisting her neck and body so she could see across the water again, she saw three shadowy forms outlined against the light of the no-longer-shaded entrance. Helplessly, she watched as two large men tackled Osbourne and tied his hands and ankles behind his back. Two more forms entered the cavern, and she knew she needed to escape. Jerking herself back through the hole, she retreated into the dark corridor.

For a brief moment, she stopped to think; there was nothing she could do to help Osbourne, but horrifying visions of Osbourne as a captive tormented her. She was no match for two grown men, let alone four, especially not men as large as those, and she had no idea what her next move would be.

With four redfish in his sack, Strom stood and stretched
his legs. A light rain fell, thoroughly soaking him, but at least
he was outside. He had never been afraid of confined spaces,
but the cavern made him feel like the world was closing in
on him. Breathing in the fresh air, he started back toward the
cold and dark of the cavern.

His fears returned as he got closer, and he wondered
what would happen to Catrin next. It was as if the gods were
toying with her. Thoughts of the gods had always seemed
distant to him, but now he was overwhelmed by nagging
questions. The rules of his world had suddenly changed, and
he was no longer certain what was real.

It was almost too much for him to absorb, and he
turned his mind to the task of getting back safely. Not far
from the cavern entrance, he encountered Chase.

"Did you see anything?" he asked.

"There's an army coming from the north, and I thought
I saw movements in the trees, so I came back to check on
everyone."

"Did you hear that?" Strom asked. "That sounded like it
came from the cavern."

Chase didn't bother to respond; instead, he took off at a
run, Strom close on his heels.

* * *

When Benjin reached the farm, he sneaked back into
the hayloft to retrieve the things he'd hidden there. Under
the cover of darkness, he carried the sacks down from the
loft and used a piece of rope to tie them together before he
slung them over his shoulder. Then, knowing every moment
he stayed only increased the danger, he made his way along
the fence.

Morning would arrive soon, and Benjin knew the
chances of his escaping were rapidly dwindling. Surely
someone would find the man he'd stolen the uniform from,
and it was obvious that men were searching the mountains

for Catrin. Quickening his pace, he tried to cover as much ground as possible before sunrise.

When he reached the place where he'd first seen signs of soldiers in the mountains, he froze. Nearby the snap of a branch warned of imminent danger, but he couldn't pinpoint from what direction it had come. Not wanting to lead anyone to Catrin and the others, he began moving in the opposite direction. The sound of moving leather was all the warning Benjin received before a sword whistled by his ear. Reeling from his evasive maneuver, Benjin let go of the string that held the sacks over his shoulder and rolled away from them.

The soldier who stepped out from behind a nearby tree was a giant of a man with muscles like cords of thick rope. His face showed no fear or battle frenzy; instead what Benjin saw was the cautious confidence of a seasoned warrior. Benjin managed only a single swing of his sword. The ill-timed and out-of-practice attack proved to be a critical mistake. Even as he swung, Benjin saw the man raise his thick sword to meet his strike. On the bottom of the soldier's blade, just before the crosspiece, was a large notch. With the precision of a practiced movement, like a dancer spinning in time with the music, the soldier lodged Benjin's blade into that notch and used his strength, leverage, and a quick snap of his wrist to shatter Benjin's sword.

Left with only the handle and crosspiece of his sword, Benjin could only hope that a technique he'd learned long ago would allow him to use his opponent's size and strength against him.

Chapter 9

Mistakes are a necessary part of life, but they should never be repeated.
--Wendel Volker, horse farmer

* * *

Shrouded in darkness, Catrin continued along the wall. Her hand glided over the smooth stone, and she slid her boots across the floor, testing each step as she went. Her fingers found another doorway. She peered inside but could see nothing in the darkness. There were side passages and doorways at irregular intervals but nothing to indicate a way out. Each junction tested her will. Could it lead to daylight? Her gut told her to continue straight and let any pursuers explore the rest of the place.

In the darkness, tactile imagery gave her a sense of her surroundings, but she felt lost without her sight. In her fear, she moved with exaggerated caution, anticipating unseen obstacles. When she heard muffled shouts, though, she became desperate to move with greater speed, and she stumbled several times in her rush to put distance between herself and those behind her. Her instincts screamed for her to run as fast as she could, but she made herself take it slowly for the sake of safe passage, knowing that even a minor injury could lead to her death in these circumstances.

No more shouts broke the silence, but that did little to ease her anxiety. Only when she was far into the depths of the mountain, by her reckoning, did she begin to let down her guard. Beyond a steep incline, the hall grew level. A few steps beyond the plateau, her fingers encountered what felt like cloth that had been attached permanently to the stone, and it crumbled under her touch. Her imagination conjured up the image of an ancient tapestry, depicting heroic lords as they performed mighty deeds. Unwilling to damage whatever it might be, she used only the toe of her boot as a guide; beauty, even imagined, should not be destroyed.

Occasionally she tested the wall with a finger, but the tapestry stretched on for what seemed an impossible distance. Her mind could not conceive a work of art so massive, and she began to wonder if she were fooling herself. When her finger once again met bare stone, she was almost surprised. The stone felt cool under her hand, and she let her fingers glide along, feeling her way into the unknown.

Her thumb encountered a deep swirl carved in the wall, and that was all the warning she had before she walked into a stone column. The pain and shock left her shaken for a moment, but then she explored the column with her fingers: The top was tapered gracefully, and the bottom was broad. At the base, she found elaborate carvings, which felt like oddly shaped faces. Hopeful, she stepped to the center of the corridor and through an arched doorway, beyond which she discovered a cavernous hall. Towering pillars, so massive their scale was difficult to fathom, were illuminated in the pale light.

The distance separating her from the light source further revealed the enormity of the hall, and she almost doubted what she was seeing--this hall dwarfed any man-made structure she had ever heard of. Even the floor was a marvel, covered with an uncountable quantity of tiny tiles. Large sections of the design were missing, and the loose tiles made for lousy footing.

Distant rumblings of thunder warned of a storm, and in the stillness, Catrin thought she heard rain. Straining her eyes in the darkness, she headed in the direction of the diminishing light but was soon plunged back into near blackness, and she feared she would fall if she tried to go much farther.

Exhaustion drove her to the nearest column, and she settled near its base, her knees pulled to her chest. Anxiety burned in her belly, and fear iced her spine. She worried about Osbourne's safety and that of everyone else she knew and loved. Unable to sleep, she tried in vain to find her meditative state of awareness. Occasional flashes of lightning illuminated the great hall only long enough to produce quick and frightening glimpses, and the thunder and the rush of rain left distorted echoes lingering in the air. Images of demons and phantoms, lurking in the darkness, tormented her.

She didn't remember falling asleep, but when she woke, she saw the far end of the cavern bathed in a soft, pale glow. A jagged chasm, high in the wall, was the source of that blessed light. Her muscles protested when she stood, but she rolled her neck, stretched her legs, and started toward the light.

What appeared to be a throne of rough-hewn rock seemed to grow out of the far wall beneath a colossal bas-relief. The throne was grossly oversized--large enough to hold ten men--and was flanked by a pair of statues in the shape of men. Similar figures lined the walls, and they made Catrin's flesh crawl. She soon realized they were not statues, but suits of heavy armor, the likes of which had not been seen in recent history. Under her breath, she muttered, "Strange. Empty armor guarding an abandoned throne."

The magnificence of the hall left her awestruck, and she wondered what kind of person would sit on such a throne. How could anyone not have felt tiny and insignificant in this enormous display? She pictured herself in that high seat, and seeing herself sitting there in her leathers and homespun made her smile. Thoughts of Osbourne and the others, though, soon banished all humor.

The chasm bisected the wall above the relief like a gaping wound, and Catrin desperately wanted to reach it. She tried to gauge the distance from the ledge that ran along the top of the relief to the bottom of the gap. It was at least three times her height, and she knew she would never be able to jump that far. There didn't seem to be any other way out, so Catrin decided to inspect the wall above the great mantle.

Climbing onto the throne, she hoped the ghosts of whatever kings may have occupied it would not be offended by her trespassing. The relief was easy to climb, its worn image providing an easy grip. She hated to climb on that ancient beauty, but it was unavoidable. The wall above the ledge was rough hewn, like that of the throne, and it bore many scars and cracks. Running her fingers over it, searching for any notches she could use during her climb, she was disappointed to find no suitable handholds within her reach. She needed something to stand on.

The suit of armor on the far side of the throne was in fairly good condition, and she approached it apprehensively, halfway fearing it would come to life and attack her. It remained still, and she ran her hand along the breastplate; it was pocked and corroded, but it still had much of its tensile strength and mass.

Weight was a problem. She would be able to carry only so much while climbing. Knocking on the side of the helmet, she found it was quite solid and pulled it free from the rest of the armor, marveling at the craftsmanship. Even covered in dust and grime, she could see it was beautifully done, and she hated that she was going to use it as a stool.

Climbing the relief with one hand was out of the question. She considered tossing the helm onto the ledge but feared the noise. Finally, she decided to wear the helmet. After cleaning out the inside with her shirt, she gingerly pulled it over her ears. It was too big for her and flopped from side to side whenever she moved her head. Her vision was partially blocked, and the smell was most unpleasant, but she endured the discomfort and made her way to the top of the relief. She set the helmet in the most stable position possible, and after a deep breath, stepped onto it with one foot. Slowly, carefully, she put her weight on it and brought her other foot up to rest on the best toehold she could find.

The toehold was not so good, but it took some of her weight off of the helmet and allowed her to extend herself. At the top of her greatest reach, she felt a knob of rock. Hopeful, she climbed down and slid the helmet perilously close to the end of the ledge. When she stepped back up on it, the helmet shifted and nearly upset her balance, but she caught herself in time.

The protrusion above was wide but not well enough defined to provide a firm grip. Frustrated, she used her belt knife to chisel around the top. The tip of the knife snapped off, and she cursed her luck, promising herself that her next belt knife would be more like a pickaxe.

Using what was now the blunt point of her knife, she fell to work on the stone. What remained of the blade was not as sharp, but it was thicker and stronger, so it had become a better tool for the task. She worked in a precarious position, perched on the helmet and overextended, but she landed several solid blows on the rock. Chips of stone and sparks flew before her determined stabbing.

With her handhold more defined, she began the perilous climb in earnest. She had to expand a few chinks while she clung to the wall, and her energy was nearly spent by the time she reached the large crack, but getting to it gave her a burst of energy. Grappling her way to the base of the opening, she found it difficult to enter. The bottom was too narrow for her to fit through, and her feet scraped against the rock below, unable to find purchase.

With an effort born of desperation, she used her arms to heave herself into the crevice. Dangling in what was an extremely uncomfortable position, she rested her quivering arms. Breathing heavily, she remained there for a few moments before pulling herself the rest of the way in. Catrin knew how close she had come to falling, but her curiosity won out over fear and physical exhaustion, and she moved on.

The crevice continued for a short distance before it opened into fresh air. Catrin made her way to the opening, and she felt moist, chilly air on her face. The sight below terrified her: a sheer drop of several hundred feet was all that stood between her and the valley floor. She realized she was now on the opposite side of the mountain. Edging herself out of the opening, she craned her neck to see how far she was from the crest.

It looked as though she might be able to climb it, and she knew she could not descend the cliff face safely. Gathering her strength, she climbed to the top of the crevice. There were large foot- and handholds, and the opposite wall of the cleft gave her leverage. The ledge above the crevice provided a commanding view of the Pinook Valley, and Catrin saw the sun for the first time in many days.

121

Columns of smoke, far to the north, rose into the sky. It did not look like a forest fire, and the recent rains reduced that possibility even further. A cold feeling crept into her stomach as it occurred to her that she was seeing the smoke from hundreds of campfires. Her gut told her that an army approached from the north.

She felt naked and exposed on the side of the mountain, especially knowing the men who captured Osbourne might have been army scouts and they could still be looking for his companions. Though she didn't think Osbourne would tell them anything, the supplies and bedrolls in the cavern clearly indicated he had not been alone. She simply had to trust her luck and hope she would not be seen, but she was not optimistic.

From atop the crevice, she had a better view of her climb to the peak. It didn't look easy, but it was certain to be a great deal easier than her escape from the throne room. Having no desire to remain in the open, she began to climb. The incline was fairly gradual, and she walked much of the way. Occasionally she had to get on her hands and knees to make it through a tough spot, and in several places, she had to climb over large rock formations that stuck out of the mountain. From her higher vantage point, the rock face below resembled the edge of a huge crater, as if some god had taken a bite out of the mountainside.

When she gained the crest, she flattened herself down against the rock and crept along to look into the Chinawpa Valley. Trying to take advantage of the excellent view, she searched for the cavern entrance, but she had lost her bearings and was unsure how it would look from above. A small ridge sloped gently down the mountain face, and she decided to follow it to the base. About to stand, she caught movement in her periphery. Flattening herself further, she turned to look.

Nothing stirred, but she remained as still as stone. Fear paralyzed her when two figures emerged from behind a rock outcropping. They were south of her but near the top of the ridgeline, concealed by the shadows, and they seemed to be trying to stay in the darkness. Catrin froze and tried to become invisible. When the forms stopped and turned in her direction, tears came to her eyes and her lip began to quiver. She saw one motion to the other then point in her direction. Escape was unlikely, and she decided she would rather throw herself from the cliff face than be captured.

Standing quickly, she turned to make her desperate retreat. She had taken only three steps when some instinct made her look behind to see if she was being pursued, and she nearly shouted out for joy.

Benjin and Chase emerged from the shadows, waving their arms at her.

Stopping in midstride, she nearly fell. Rushing to meet them halfway, she hugged each of them and asked, her voice trembling, "Osbourne?" She was shocked to see both of them smile.

"He's fine," Chase blurted, unable to control his excitement. "Strom and I saw the soldiers approaching the cavern, and we sneaked in behind them. They were busy tying up Osbourne, and we caught 'em by surprise. We used the rocks we had by the entrance to kill one and knocked the other one out," he said matter-of-factly. "Benjin got back late last night," he added.

"We'll talk about this later," Benjin said. "Right now there's an army approaching, and they have two scouts who haven't returned. They look to have been a few days ahead of the army, but they'll soon be missed. Let's get back to the cavern."

Catrin swayed on her feet when she realized the second set of shadowy forms she had seen had not been soldiers at all; it had been Strom and Chase. Had she stayed a moment longer, she would have seen them rescue Osbourne. All the fear and pain she experienced in the past day had been for nothing. She began to cry as she realized she could have just climbed back onto the raft and poled herself safely back to camp.

"Are you all right, li'l miss?" Benjin asked, looking her over for any signs of injury.

"I'm fine," she replied, but the tears of mixed joy and frustration kept flowing.

Chapter 10

Security is the blindfold worn by those who cannot accept the uncertainty of the future.
--Mundin Barr, speculator

* * *

One of the soldiers lay supine near the fire, still unconscious, and Benjin seemed to think there was little chance he would ever wake. They hoped he would regain consciousness soon so they could squeeze some information out of him. For the moment, though, he would give no more information than his deceased companion. Catrin did not want to know what they had done with the body of the other man, so she didn't ask. The thought of Chase killing someone, even to defend himself or a friend, seemed so out of character with his gentle nature that she blocked any image of that from her mind.

Not far from the lake lay a new raft made of many saplings that had been hastily bound together with rope and vines. When Strom saw her looking at it, he walked to her side. "I was coming to look for you," he said. Catrin felt tears filling her eyes, and in a rare moment, Strom put his hand on her shoulder. "Come on. Let's get something to eat."

Seeing their provisions, still intact, brought a wave of relief; she had feared it all lost to the attackers. It was odd that she had gone a relatively short time without food, yet she felt as if she had not eaten in weeks. It was as if the time she'd spent thinking about starvation had had a physical effect on her. Though she was able to eat only half of what she took, she kept the rest nearby for when her appetite returned; its very presence brought her comfort.

Benjin filled her in about his journey. "Let me first say that I believe your father is well and is adequately defended in the cold caves. Miss Mariss is also faring well, given the circumstances. I was unable to get information regarding Osbourne's family, and the only information I got about Chase's father was that he was last seen with Wendel. I'm guessing he's in the cold caves as well.

"Miss Mariss said Wendel led many people to the cold caves, and once inside, they blocked the entrances with rocks and hastily laid mortar. As far as she knew, they are continuing to build up the blockade even as the Zjhon remove it, but that process is slowly forcing them farther back into the caves. Others fled to the protection of the Masterhouse--far too many to be comfortably housed there. Riots broke out when the Masters began strictly rationing food and water since their supplies were not plentiful enough to support such numbers," he said and stopped to consider his next words.

"There is a bit of good news and more bad news. First the bad news: Peten Ross was captured and forced to talk. Peten told them he thought Catrin was the Herald and about the day Osbourne was attacked. He also described each of us, as well as a few others, in great detail. He told them that Strom, Chase, and I had mysteriously disappeared, and he thought we had run to hide in the mountains with Catrin," he continued.

"The good news is also bad news. I guess I failed to mention that. The Zjhon know who you are, what you look like, and that you are most likely not in the Masterhouse or the cold caves. Because of this, they have changed their strategy. Now they only wish to contain the people who are trapped and use their numbers to scour the rest of the Godfist looking for you. This'll take much of the pressure off of those who are under siege, and there should be less loss of life. The bad part, of course, is that they'll be combing the mountains looking for us."

Catrin shivered and pulled her knees to her chest as the weight of his words settled into her consciousness. The Zjhon wanted only her. Maybe if she gave herself up to them, they would leave the people of the Godfist alone.

"There is another part of this story I've not told you yet," Benjin said. "I must stress how very important this is. You are being entrusted with sacred information that you must never reveal. Can you all promise me that you will never reveal any of what I tell you to another living soul?"

They all nodded solemnly.

125

"Miss Mariss told me things she was strictly forbidden to tell anyone not of the Vestrana." He paused and looked at each of them solemnly. Catrin tried to remember where she had heard the word *Vestrana* before, but all she could recall was some talk about a secret society that was shrouded in mystery.

"In order for me to tell you these secrets, you have to swear the Vestrana oath, but first I must explain some things so you'll know what you're swearing to. You don't have to swear the oath, but if you don't, I'll not be able to tell you some things, and neither will anyone who has sworn." The young people looked at each other, wondering if any would refuse to swear.

"At the end of the last Istran phase, the Varics were nearly destroyed, and they went into hiding to survive. They knew their knowledge and beliefs were important and needed to be passed on, so they formed a secret society known as the Vestrana, and my family has been a part since its inception. My grandfather swore me in when I was still a boy," he confided.

"The Vestrana opposed the Zjhon and their practice of conquering lands and then forcing the conquered peoples to convert to their religion. The penalty for refusal was death. Our secret exile has gone on for thousands of years, and we have replenished our numbers. We'll not dictate religious beliefs to others, as we wish every person to choose his or her beliefs freely and not be persecuted for them. We strictly oppose any religion that mandates killing people simply because their beliefs are different. Do you all understand?" he asked.

"I'm no good at lying," Strom admitted for the second time. "Every time I try to lie to Miss Mariss, she calls me on it--on the spot. I'm just not good at keeping secrets, so I don't know if I should take the oath."

"The choice is yours; I'll not force you to take an oath you feel you cannot keep. I will tell you, however, that you won't have to lie. You just cannot say certain things. You can be completely honest with someone without revealing any of the things you must keep safe," Benjin said.

126

"I *can* be quiet, and if I don't have to lie, well, then, I think I can do it," he said, looking a bit more confident. Benjin gave him a moment to reconsider before he continued.

"Before I can tell you any more, I'll tell you the oath, and if you feel it is right, you should swear it.

"Here it is: 'I swear to uphold the values of the Vestrana. I will not divulge any information considered within confidence of the Vestrana. I will seek to free the oppressed and vanquish the oppressor. I will give my life before I will betray myself or the Vestrana,'" he intoned.

It was simple enough, but Benjin made them explain it back to him in their own words to be sure they understood its meaning. "I must ask you to understand that people generally prepare for several seasons before they are allowed to take the oath. There are many things you do not know, so you must not say anything at all about *any* of this to *anyone* for *any* reason. Ever! Is that clearly understood?"

They all nodded soberly.

Once he was satisfied they understood the gravity of the situation, he asked if any of them wished to swear the oath. All of them wanted to, and each recited it individually. Benjin made them repeat it until they could speak it from memory, and he formally welcomed each of them to the Vestrana and kissed them on their foreheads.

"I've never sworn anyone in before," he admitted and seemed much more relaxed when he spoke again. "Many innkeepers across the world are members of the Vestrana and serve as part of a huge information network. Miss Mariss is one of those innkeepers, and she has access to information few else on the Godfist are privy to. The Vestrana have many allies, some of whom may make a living in shady dealings, but they honor the Vestrana. Miss Mariss suggested we seek out one particular ally. In doing so, she had to reveal one of her most trusted secrets to me.

"There is a harbor on the east coast of the Godfist; it's along a rough section of coast that offers very little safe anchorage because of the many surrounding islands and reefs that'll sink an unwary ship. The only ships known to

127

safely dock there are pirate ships, and even those are somewhat rare events.

"The Godfist is pretty far outside established trade routes, and pirate ships only dock here to avoid pursuit, though sometimes they trade goods and information with the Vestrana. There are now two ships docked at the cove, as far as we know. They sought refuge from the Zjhon fleet, fearing the ships had been sent after them. The last Miss Mariss had heard, they were still there. She's going to try to get word to them and arrange passage for us. Though they are not here with us, agents of the Vestrana are doing all they can to help. I know the Zjhon are going to scour the Godfist in search of Catrin, so I propose we travel to the cove and leave the Godfist with the pirates. Even if Miss Mariss is not able to contact them, we may be able to work something out, and to be completely honest, I don't have any better ideas."

His words were met with utter silence, and Catrin struggled to make sense of all of it. She could not imagine leaving the Godfist, her home, and had never thought about going any other place. The others seemed to be having similar problems assimilating the information. Chase was the first to find his voice.

"Where would we go?" he asked.

"We should go to the last place they would expect us to go, to the Greatland--into the heart of their empire."

"Do you really think that's the best thing to do?" Catrin asked, incredulous.

"The Greatland is the largest and most heavily populated landmass on Godsland. We can disguise ourselves and hide much more easily among so many people, not to mention the huge area they would have to search to look for us. It may also be that getting you to the Greatland is the best way to help fulfill the prophecy."

"You really believe I'm the Herald?" Catrin asked, fearing his answer.

"I'm not sure what I believe," he said, "but I know you have important tasks ahead of you, and no matter what you or I believe, you have already done some important work. There's no going back, I'm afraid. From now on, you'll be the one who was declared the Herald, whether you are or not. Truth can be a difficult thing to find."

Catrin had never heard Benjin speak so profoundly, and she wondered what else she didn't know about the man she had worked beside for so many years.

"I'm sorry I don't have all of the answers. I wish I did," he said, shaking his head. "In many ways, I'm just as confused as you are. To follow our hearts and hope we make the right decisions is the best we can do. Do we agree we should make for the cove?"

He knew their answer and told them what to pack and what to leave behind. During this activity, he pulled Catrin aside but seemed to have trouble choosing his words.

"I've sworn the Vestrana oath," he began. "A message given into my trust must be delivered, unopened, to the intended recipient unless it cannot be done. There is a strict protocol on this, and I must honor it, even when I don't want to. I considered breaking my oath when Miss Mariss gave me this message. I thought about reading it before I gave it to you. I even considered destroying it without reading it. I'm ashamed to admit I was tempted, but I will keep my oath. This unopened message is for you. You don't have to tell me what it says. I'm just the messenger," he said as he handed her a tightly rolled parchment closed with wax. The seal impressed in the wax belonged to Nat Dersinger.

After moving off to a quiet place by the fire, Catrin stared at the parchment. She did not want to open it, afraid of what it might say. Nat was a pariah, his outlandish ranting about the coming of Istra and the dawning of a new age too disturbing for most people to give any credence to. Some said he was mad; others claimed he was afflicted with some disease, but most agreed his public sermons were the ravings of a deranged mind. Catrin had to wonder, now that many of his prophecies were actually coming true, whether Nat was mad or everyone else was.

An uneasy feeling gnawed at the pit of her stomach as her beliefs began to crumble beneath her. Fear crept in where her fallen truths no longer held sway, and yet she felt liberated to pursue limitless possibilities that would open to her. She tore the wax seal away and unrolled the parchment.

My dearest Catrin,

My fondest wish is that you will walk in peace and light and that your mind will always remain free.

Some say I'm deranged, but I leave that for you to judge. What I am sure of is that you must embrace your role as the Herald. I implore you to use the divine gift you have been given and that you do not squander it.

I have studied all scriptures and holy books available to me, and I want to help you learn to use the power of Istra's light. You have experienced its improper use, even though you did not intend to exploit it, so you are aware of its power.

If you choose to pursue the divine gifts you have been given, I beg you to seek knowledge. I hope to bring knowledge of these to you, but if I cannot make my way to you in time, seek out the Cathuran monks; they may be able to help you.

Before your journey takes you beyond the Godfist, you will be besieged.

Remember these words when you fear you have made the wrong choices:

Vestra's light warms Godsland.

Water ascends upon the wings of his warmth, and the skies disperse it at will.

Rain shapes the land and gives life to the fishes, and the fishes sparkle in Istra's light.

May Istra and Vestra guide and bless you,

Nat

Catrin sat back, confounded by what she had read. Nat was right about the disastrous results of her tapping the strange energies, but his words of warning were unclear to her. That he would make this effort to get a message to her only to leave her with a riddle seemed ludicrous. Frustrated, she tucked the parchment into her pocket, hoping to make sense of it at some later time.

When she rejoined the others, Benjin's eyes met hers. When she had no comment, he simply nodded and finished checking his pack. He then stood and pulled several pieces of rolled parchment from his pack.

130

Addressing all of them, he said, "You've been sworn, and this information is in the Vestrana confidence. You must not divulge it to anyone, and you must destroy this if you believe it could fall into anyone else's hands," he said, handing a copy to each of them. "The journey we're about to undertake will be perilous. I wish I could offer you the chance to walk away, but our situation is too dire; you are in peril if you stay or if you go. I think we should stick together, but I want each of you to have a map in case we get separated.

"This is a highly unusual practice. It's dangerous in the extreme to have so many copies of anything in the Vestrana confidence, but this is a highly unusual case, and I've made an exception. Be certain no one else gets these maps," he reiterated firmly. "We leave before dawn, and I want a double watch tonight."

* * *

The snap of a branch in the distance behind Nat increased his level of panic. For weeks, he'd been hiding in the hills. Miss Mariss had urged him to find Catrin, but he had no idea how to do that. Only his visions and dreams provided any guidance, but those proved difficult to interpret and decipher. The only things he knew for certain were that Catrin must survive and that she was in terrible danger. In the end, he was left to wander in the wilderness, battling his own despair as he searched for someone who did not want to be found. He could have passed her and her companions a dozen times and he would never know. He was a fisherman, not a tracker.

Finding Catrin was now the least of his problems, though. The Zjhon were searching for her as well, and they were close behind him. If they found him . . . He tried not to think about the horrors he might face. Even with his staff, he was no match for a trained swordsman. Instead he concentrated on moving into the thickest and most forbidding undergrowth he could find. When he could no longer make forward progress, he curled into a ball beneath a veil of thorn and briar, hoping those who pursued him would simply pass by.

Eventually the light began to fade, and the beat of Nat's heart slowed. Weariness more complete than any he'd ever known began to wash over him, coaxing him to sleep, luring him into the land of dreams.

Somewhere between sleep and wakefulness, the scene before him changed, no longer did he see a canopy of twisted vines and curved thorns bathed in moonlight; instead he watched as Catrin was surrounded by the shadows of death. Moving like the wind, the darkness closed in on her, blocking out the light and her life. Just as he thought her flame would be extinguished, Catrin fought back. To Nat's horror, she did not attack the darkness directly; instead she tore the land asunder and hurled it at her foes. Her every step rent the land, leaving cavernous gouges and craters wherever she trod, and still the darkness came, unthwarted and undaunted.

Clawing his way through the darkness, Nat clenched his jaws as the thorns bit deep. He could not stop, though, no matter how great the pain--he had to find her.

Chapter 11

One man's offal is another man's harvest.
--Icari Jundin, mushroom farmer

* * *

Benjin woke them early. When he checked on the health of the unconscious soldier, he seemed almost relieved the man had died in the night. He and Chase dragged the dead man from the cavern and hid the body with the other.

When they returned, Benjin examined the pile of armor and weapons the soldiers had carried. He took a short sword, belt sheath, and bracers for himself. The sword had a black leather handle and a decent edge--not a fine blade but good to have. He motioned the others over and began to distribute the dead soldiers' belongings to the rest of them. He gave Chase the other short sword, belt sheath, and bracers. The boots went to Strom and Osbourne to replace their lighter shoes.

Catrin asked for one of the belt knives left in the pile, and Benjin handed her one still in the sheath. She was hesitant to discard her old knife and decided to wear both, not wanting to abandon the old one with the broken tip.

Osbourne pulled the other soldier's knife from its sheath; Catrin expected some sort of noise when he unsheathed it, but it slid free without a sound. The wicked-looking blade curved slightly before the tip. Its upper edge was serrated, and it had a straight edge on the bottom. He pronounced it perfect for him.

"The plan is simple," Benjin said. "We travel north and go straight at the approaching army, but we stay high in the mountains. Once we sneak past them, we will turn east, toward the desert. Perhaps we'll get lucky and have foul weather to hide us, perhaps not; either way, we'll need to be ready to take cover at all times. Keep your eyes open for places to hide as you may only get a moment's notice. We could go due east from here, but I fear those passes are heavily guarded. As outrageous as it may sound, sneaking past the army is probably our safest choice.

"I doubt the patrols will be this far out by first light. We need to get to the next plateau soon if we are to avoid them," Benjin said, and he set out at a breakneck pace.

When they crested a rise, Benjin paused and strained to see into the distance. "We should be able to see the falls from here, but I can't make them out," he said. Catrin and the others squinted in the predawn light, but visibility was low.

"I think they are still a long way off," Chase said.

Benjin nodded. "Let's go. We've no time to waste," he said, heading off at a brisk walk.

As they drew closer, Catrin saw the falls. They did not seem as grand as Benjin had described them, barely visible in the distance. Perhaps they had been larger when Benjin last saw them, but she wondered how that could be possible when this was the rainiest spring any of them had ever seen.

They froze when Benjin hunched down and signaled them to do the same. "I thought I saw something moving in the trees," he said after a few moments. "I think it's clear, so let's move."

As they neared the base of the falls, the banks of the river came into view. "Above the falls there is no eastern shore. The river runs along the rock face. We'll need to stay on the west side for now," Benjin said.

As they came closer to the river, they were surprised by what they saw: the water level was extremely low, the flow muddy and sluggish. The water was well below the normal watermarks, and they estimated it was less than half what it should be.

By the time they reached the base of the falls, the sun was high in the sky, and Benjin said he planned to use the sun for cover. They would climb the jagged cliff wall while the sun was high, which would make it harder for soldiers to spot them with the sunlight in their eyes. He found a place far enough away from the falls for them to remain dry, and there were many irregularities in the rock face, which would make for an easier climb.

Their ascent was slow and tenuous, irregular rocks providing some handholds and footholds, but in many places they were widely spaced. In some instances they had

134

to scale the nearly sheer face with little, if anything, to grab onto. When they finally reached the plateau, they did not find the river they had been expecting and instead saw a muddy lake that covered almost the entire plateau. Chase spotted the cause of the flooding near the top of the falls. The recent storms had downed a large number of trees. At least a dozen had been swept away by the river and were creating a dam just before the falls, where the river narrowed. Only a fraction of the water flowed past the debris; the rest continued to flood the plateau.

A narrow ribbon of land separated the newly formed lake from the cliff, but it was clearly saturated. The valley beyond the plateau was completely swamped by the backed-up river, effectively cutting off their escape.

"Cripes," Benjin said, "we're going to need to find a way around this. Stay alert." An enormous rock finger jutted into the air above the valley. Skirting the lake, they plodded through the mud, which threatened to remove their boots with every step. At times they walked through ankle-deep water. Around the rock finger, the soil border was less than a pace wide. The promontory was slender and appeared fragile, warped and twisted by eons of windborne sand.

"Stay back. I'm going out for a look," Benjin said.

"You aren't really thinking of walking out on that rock, are you?" Strom asked, incredulous. "That thing looks like it could fall at any moment, even without your weight on it."

"It's been here for thousands of years, and I'm betting it'll be here for thousands more; its frailty is only an illusion."

Benjin crept onto the rock; the winds whipped around him, and he was nearly blown off. He caught himself, but the movement sent rocks bouncing into the valley below.

"I think we've been spotted," he said. "There are soldiers below, and they are climbing toward us. We need to retreat as fast as we can; we must go back the way we came. I don't think we'll be able to get through the flooded valley without ruining our food supply or drowning."

Catrin sat to one side, absorbed in her thoughts, and with every moment her anger grew. The Zjhon threatened everything she held dear. Struggling to think of a way to stop

135

the approaching army, or at least hamper its progress, she stewed, biting her lip. Benjin interrupted her thoughts.

"C'mon, li'l miss, we need to get out of here."

Catrin wondered if she was making a mistake; then she recalled the words Nat had written: "Embrace your role as the Herald. I implore you to use the divine gift you have been given." She considered those words, and they urged her to act.

"No," she said in a firm voice. "I will not run from this challenge, and I will no longer tolerate these invaders of my homeland."

"What would you have us do, Catrin? I am yours to command," Benjin said, shocking everyone. He knelt in the sodden soil and bowed to her. Chase, Strom, and Osbourne stood silently.

Catrin considered her next words carefully, not knowing what she was going to say or do. She looked around her, and the muddy water brought back a part of Nat's message, one line in particular, and she said, "The water shapes the land."

"I want you to dig. From here," she said, pointing to the soil around the base of the finger of rock, "to here. We need a trough from the dry to the wet, and it should be as deep as possible."

"What are you talking about, Cat? We don't have time for this; we need to get out of here," Chase said.

"We cannot run anymore, Chase; there is nowhere safe to hide. I choose to fight," she said, and she began to dig with her bare hands as Benjin loosened the soil with his sword. All but Chase began to dig, but he soon crouched down along with the rest. The trench grew quickly, the sodden soil making their work easier.

"Stay on the north side of the trench," Catrin warned.

"But we need to go south to escape," Chase argued, looking at a massive fist of rock that blocked their path and would not budge.

"Just dig around it," Catrin said, following Chase's gaze. "The trench need not be straight." As they dug their way closer to the water, the ditch began to flood, and they continued to dig from higher ground. As water began pouring over the cliff's edge, Catrin and Benjin looked over to see what was happening below.

A few soldiers watched from the valley floor, but most were scaling the cliff face in an effort to reach them. Catrin and the others watched the water move through the ditch, eroding the soil around it. Deeper and wider the trough grew, gradually sending larger amounts of water into the valley, but it was not enough; it was happening far too slowly to make any difference. It mocked their meager effort, and helplessness washed over Catrin.

She watched the flow intently, seeing tremendous potential energy latent in the calm water, and she knew there must be a way to unleash it. Without realizing it, she opened her mind to Istra's energy and attempted to ply it with her will. She started by trying to push the water over the edge, hoping to make it go faster, but the water repelled her.

Any force she exerted on the water became fragmented, scattered in a hundred directions, and her efforts had no visible effect. Her frustration flared into anger, and she turned to the rest of the group. "Go north. I'll catch up with you soon."

"But, Cat--" Chase began, but she cut him short.

"If you value your lives, go north. Now!" she said in a commanding voice, despite her fear. Her legs trembled; her face flushed and nostrils flared; her heart pounded in her ears. Chase and the others headed north, frequently looking over their shoulders. A strange feeling came over her as she watched Chase walk away. So many times she had followed him on his adventures, but now she knew she must stand alone. As she embraced the energy around her, she prayed she would not unwittingly create another disaster. The lives of her friends now rested in her hands, and she was determined to save them.

With confidence born of every lesson her father and Benjin and Chase had ever taught her, Catrin moved to the finger of rock. Its base had been exposed by the modest flow of water that rushed by, but she strode to the end of the finger, seemingly oblivious to the winds tearing at her. Doing her best to keep from trembling, she spoke in a voice that carried across the Pinook Valley.

"Armies of the Zjhon! You are not welcome here," she began. In the next moment, though, she panicked. No more words would come; her throat was closing. She was no hero; she felt like just a little girl. Old fears constricted her heart, and she nearly fled, but then, in her mind, she saw the faces of Benjin and Chase and her friends. With a fire burning in her belly, she renewed her commitment and tried to find words befitting a great hero. "I am the keeper of this land, and I forbid you passage. Retreat now, or feel the weight of my wrath!" she said, and her statement carried on the air to the soldiers below.

They laughed at such threats coming from a girl, and Catrin turned without another word. She strode back to the edge of the widening trough, gazing at it a moment more before moving north. Some fifty paces away, she stopped, hoping Chase wasn't right. Maybe she had lost her senses, but it was far too late to turn back. She would have to endure the consequences of her decisions and actions.

Facing the cliff, she felt the heat of her anger toward the invaders, and it purged her fears. Her body quivered with energy as she gathered it and pulled it to her, reveling in its glory. She could smell its fragrance and taste its sweetness, but a searing pain in her left thigh distracted her for a moment, feeling as if her limb were on fire. She ignored it and drew in a deep breath, letting the soldiers' laughter feed her rage.

"You bear witness to the Call of the Herald," she announced. "I have warned you, and you have mocked me, and you will suffer for that." She clasped her hands high above her head, energy swirling through her fingers and dancing over her palms. It pulsed around her. She brought her hands down in a powerful arc as she shouted, "You will not pass!"

When her fists struck the soil, a huge shockwave sent ripples of power through the plateau with a massive, echoing boom, and the land pulsed as if it were liquid. Waves of energy rolled away from her. The floodwaters transferred the energy as waves crashed against the irregularity of the far cliffs and returned to punish the saturated shoreline. Unable to withstand the power of the water, large sections of rock and soil were dislodged and pushed into the Pinook Valley.

As tremors shook the ground beneath her feet, Catrin ran toward her companions. The massive chain reaction gained momentum, and the thunderous roar became nearly unbearable, but even in her retreat, Catrin was compelled to witness what she had wrought. Water crashed around the finger of rock, carrying gobbets of dirt and rock away with it, and with an ear-shattering crack, the rock slumped forward and leaned into the valley. Water rushed in eagerly to fill the gap, and a tremendous roar reverberated through the valley; Catrin watched in disbelief as the finger of rock tumbled away in the deluge.

In a massive release of potential energy, water assailed rock and soil, and the cliffs parted. Gravity pulled the water into the valley, and the din of a massive rockslide accompanied the rush of the fall.

Rock and debris clogged the valley, and a towering wall of water rushed to greet the main body of the advancing army. Cries of man and horse rose above the din, but Catrin had no time to consider what her senses told her as more of the plateau began to collapse. She fled the devastation and tried to catch up to the rest of the group, already moving swiftly north. The Upper Chinawpa Valley, which lay ahead, drained quickly, and muddy shores rose from the depths; there Catrin's friends stopped to wait for her.

Unsure of what to say, she approached them tentatively, half expecting them to tell her she was crazy or leave her behind, but they welcomed her silently.

Chase grabbed her in a bear hug. "I'm sorry I doubted you," he whispered.

Benjin held up his hand to speak. "You have followed me, but I can no longer lead you," he said. "I've heard the Call of the Herald, and I will go wherever she leads me, I will do what she asks of me, and I will lay down my life to save hers," he finished, bowing to Catrin.

The others made similar vows, and Catrin was left to stand in wonder. She'd had no preparation for this, and she did not know what was expected of her. She knew that she was leaving one reality and stepping into a new existence, and she was unsure of the consequences of this new power.

Finally, Strom broke the uncomfortable silence. "I'm just glad Catrin's on our side."

* * *

Sweat dripped into Nat's eyes as he scrambled down a craggy face. He climbed with a mixture of haste and care. His experience urged him to exercise caution, but his instincts told him he must flee. The Zjhon were close--closer than ever before. Already he had been near enough to see their eyes. Using his staff to steady himself, he climbed past an awkward outcropping.

When he reached the narrow band of greenery that stood between the base of the mountain and the sand, Nat cursed. He was starving and exhausted. After giving up on finding Catrin, all he had wanted was to get back to town, to find some way to get to Miss Mariss and food. The need for food and water was sapping his strength and his sanity. Several times he had found himself wandering without any idea of where he was going or where he had been; all he could remember was that he needed to keep moving.

Suddenly stopping, he realized he'd done it again. Ankle deep in sand, he turned and only the mountains behind him gave him a sense of where he was. What he saw when he lowered his gaze made his location seem irrelevant: half a dozen mounted men were heading straight for him, and there was little Nat could do but wait for them to arrive. Maybe they would give him food, he thought, but what was left of his reason suggested it was unlikely. Turning away from the Zjhon, back the way his subconscious had been leading him, he walked. When he raised his eyes again, certain the Zjhon would overtake him at any moment, he was confused to find that he must have gotten turned around again, for before him came riders in a cloud of dust.

Chapter 12

If you wish to find yourself, you must first admit you are lost.
--anonymous philosopher

* * *

Catrin left the crumbling plateau behind, her body throbbing with energy, her senses heightened. As the breeze caressed her skin, the hairs on her arms and neck stood up. The roar of the mudslide pounded against her overly sensitive hearing, and she retreated from the din. Followed by Benjin and the others, she headed toward the northern end of the valley. There the mountains turned east and the valley grew wider. With little dry ground, they had to slog through a foul morass. Clinging mud made loud sucking noises as it hung on to their boots, weighing them down.

As the valley widened farther on, small sections of dry land appeared more often, like giant turtles in a sea of murky water. The valley floor was made up of rolling hills, and when they found dry spots at the tops of hills, it was only before they descended into valleys of muck. Puddles harbored fish stranded by the rapidly receding water.

Catrin wanted to take the fish back to the river, but she knew it would require too much time to do it right. She and Benjin had spent hours once catching fish in buckets after they were stranded by the Pinook River, which had overflowed its banks. Because the fish would die if they were quickly moved from warm water and put into frigid river water, they put the buckets into the river at the shallows until the water temperature gradually dropped. Then they tipped the buckets over so the fish could swim out. She had enjoyed seeing the fish disappear into the river, safe, and wished she could save these fish too, but there was no time.

The mountains threw long shadows as the waning sun set fire to the skies; bold strokes of crimson and ocher made for a breathtaking display. Patches of dry land gradually became larger, and some were almost suitable campsites. "I think that hill up ahead looks like a good place to camp," Catrin announced.

"There's not much cover there. I think we should try to find a better hiding place," Benjin advised.

"No," she said quietly, determined to embrace her new role, despite her insecurities. "I'm not going to hide anymore. I have to show the Zjhon I don't fear them. Instead, I will strike fear into them. Let them find us in the open, sitting by our fire, and let them see we are not hiding. Let us invite them to take us if they will. They will feel my wrath if they do."

No one but Benjin seemed to know what to make of the change in Catrin. He had accepted her as the Herald and let her be in complete control of their destinies. The others had known Catrin most of her life--and theirs--and seemed to have a difficult time accepting her now as the figure of legend from the prophecies. But they had seen too much of her power to deny it, and slowly they came to believe.

"As you wish," Benjin said with a short bow. He walked ahead to look for dry wood; Chase matched his stride. Strom and Osbourne remained alongside Catrin as she headed toward the campsite.

"Is there anything you need us to do, Miss Catrin?" Osbourne asked, looking uncertain.

Catrin sighed. "Please don't call me 'Miss Catrin' . . . not you or Strom or Chase. You're my friends, and I need you. I'm sorry I bossed everyone around and was so mean," she said, sounding much more like herself.

"Oh, that's all right, *Miss Catrin*," Strom said with an impish grin. "We know you have the whole 'Herald of Istra' thing to contend with. We could probably forgive you for being weird."

"I want you to dig," Osbourne said in a high-pitched voice, "from here"--he posed and pointed--"to here," he finished with a flourish.

"You best be careful, Osbo. You don't want risk the wrath of Miss Catrin. Fear the wrath, boy. Fear the wrath," Strom said as he ducked away from Catrin's playful jab.

While she was relieved to know she had not lost her friends, Benjin's behavior concerned her. His sudden change in personality was as bizarre as her own, and she needed to talk to him soon, but she feared she would insult him. She had looked up to him for so many years, and he had always been the first one to help her with her unusual ideas. She would never hurt him on purpose, but she did need to understand some things about him.

When they reached the top of the hill, Chase and Benjin were setting up a fire circle beside a small supply of firewood already stacked to one side.

"You're absolutely certain about the campsite and the fire, Catrin?" Benjin asked.

His use of her name annoyed her for reasons unknown, and she suppressed her irritation. "Yes, this will be fine. Strom, Osbourne, you asked if there was anything you could do, and now there is. Would you gather fish from the puddles please?"

Strom and Osbourne both nodded, and they left seeking fish.

Catrin turned to Chase. "Can we talk for a moment, please? I really need to know your opinion on something."

Chase raised an eyebrow and nodded before following her. A nearby tree grew around a large bolder, cradling it in its massive trunk, like a great claw clutching a mystical orb. Catrin climbed atop the bolder and sat cross-legged.

"Do you believe I'm truly the Herald of Istra?" she asked. Chase had always been her closest confidant, and they trusted one another. Before their tragic deaths, their mothers had been quite close, and Chase and Catrin had spent most of their childhoods together. Chase had the same pain she had, and she knew he would be honest with her.

"I think . . ." He paused a moment, thoughtful. "I think I do, Cat. I mean, all the signs are there, and you have shown your power." He pondered for a moment then returned the question. "Do *you* believe you are truly the Herald of Istra?"

"Yes, I do," she replied. "I didn't want to believe at first. I tried to tell myself it was all coincidence, but things just kept happening, no matter what I believed."

"What is the Herald supposed to do?"

"I have no idea," she admitted. "I wish I did know; it would certainly make things easier. I guess I'm supposed to destroy the Zjhon, but I'll be boiled if I know how or why."

They sat quietly for a while. Strom and Osbourne returned with an abundance of fish, and Catrin watched them while her thoughts drifted.

"What did you do on the plateau today? I mean, how did you hit the ground so hard? I've never seen anything like that."

"It's hard to explain," she began. "It's like trying to describe an eagle's call to someone born deaf or a sunset to someone born blind. I guess in this sense, *I* was born blind, but something opened my eyes. I'm still uncertain about a great many things, but I'll give you my best guess. I think the comet flooded our world with energy, and somehow I can gather that energy, focus it, and release it. I'm not exactly sure how I do it; that's just how it feels when it happens."

"I think I understand. What opened your eyes?"

"It could have been a number of things, I suppose, but I think it was Peten's staff." She paused. "Something inside me snapped. I can't tell you exactly what happened, but I'll tell you what I remember. When I saw my reflection in the wood of his staff, I knew I saw my own death approaching. I think my conscious mind accepted my fate and waited for the killing blow. Perhaps it was my unconscious mind that reacted instinctively." She realized how strange her words sounded, but they were the closest thing she had to an explanation.

"Well, Cat, this is how I see things: You're the Herald and you have great power, but you don't know how to control it. Your instincts seem to tell you things the rest of us cannot hear. I don't think you're any different from the rest of us, except that you've had some experiences that expanded your mind. The prophecies say you'll destroy the Zjhon nation, so I guess we should concentrate on doing that first."

Catrin saw thousands of complexities, and Chase had reduced them to a few simple statements. She shook her head and laughed. "I'll get right on that nation-destroying thing."

The pain in her left thigh got her attention as she got down from the boulder. Most of her body was sore, but her thigh felt different; it felt as if she had a small spot of sunburn. Then she recalled having pain in her thigh while she was engulfed in power. She reached for the tiny carved fish still in her pocket, precisely over where she felt the sting.

The carving looked worse than she remembered, now dull and chalky. It retained its shape, and even in its current state, it was oddly beautiful, and she was surprised it hadn't been broken or crushed during her misadventures. She guessed it must have bruised her leg during the climb, and when she could find no other reasonable explanation, she accepted that.

"What've you got there?" Chase asked.

"I found this while I was exploring the passage beyond the cavern; I had completely forgotten about it. It looks like a carving of a fish, don't you think?"

"It's pretty crude, but yes, I'd say it resembles a fish. I don't think you want to keep it in your pocket if you want it to stay whole. Here, I have something for you." He reached into his shirt and pulled out a plain and simply made silver locket, its worn surface dented and scratched. Catrin had seen the locket many times but had never seen what was in it. It hung from a necklace made of thin leather strips braided together and tied in a knot.

He deftly separated the strips and removed one. He retied the two remaining strips and slipped his necklace back on. "You never know when these thongs will come in handy," he said with a wink. She watched him form a tiny noose from the leather thong. He extended his open palm, and she placed the small carving in his hand. He looped the little noose around the tail of the fish, and created a necklace that firmly secured her carving.

"May you wear it in good health," he said, placing it in her hand. She admired his handiwork, holding it up and studying it for a moment before slipping it around her neck. She let it hang outside her shirt, so it could be seen.

"It's beautiful in its own way. Don't you agree?"

"It's a lot like you, Cat. If you look hard enough, it's kinda pretty," he said with a smirk. "Perhaps you're both jewels in the rough."

He ran ahead of her back to the campfire, drawn by the smell of cooking fish. Benjin and the others were eating fish and drinking the last bottle of springwine. More fish roasted over the fire, with a plate of fillets waiting to be roasted.

"I give thanks to the mighty fishermen who have provided so well for us. My compliments to your skills," Catrin said with a smile.

The day had left them tired and hungry, and the fish were satisfying. The springwine disappeared, and they wished that bottle were not the last. Despite their exhaustion, restlessness set in. Benjin kept a watchful eye on the surrounding land, alert for any movements, but the night remained peaceful and still.

Catrin longed for something sweet and, thinking she smelled apples, stood and said she was going to look around. Clear skies and a full moon illuminated the night, and she searched the sky for the comet. It was smaller and farther across the sky, but when she spotted it, her thoughts focused on it, and she was drawn to it. It mesmerized her and drew her closer, but she became frightened and turned aside when arcs of power leaped between her fingertips. Shaken, she walked on, following a trail defined by smell alone. She was nearly at the base of the hill when she spotted the trees, mere paces above the mud line.

They were few and stunted, but they were heavily laden with fruit. Catrin scanned the branches for ripe apples and picked those within her reach, but she wanted a few more. As she stood on the tips of her toes and stretched toward an apple, hands grabbed her waist. She gasped when they lifted her into the air but was reassured when she heard Benjin chuckle. She snatched four beauties from the highest branches, and Benjin lowered her gently.

"It looked like you needed a lift."

"Except for the fact that you frightened me out of my wits for a moment, I thank you. I'm glad you're here too. I need to talk to you." He nodded, and she went on. "Do you believe I'm the Herald of Istra?"

"Yes, I do believe you are," he replied slowly and deliberately. "I believed it the instant you said you were. I was undecided until that moment. When I returned from Harborton and found out you were gone, I was worried beyond reason. Chase and the others were just as distraught, and we reviewed everything we knew. They told me about the night in the greatoak grove. I'm truly sorry about that, Catrin."

"Why do you keep calling me that? You've called me 'li'l miss' for as long as I can remember. Why don't you still call me that?"

"I'm sorry, Cat--uh, li'l miss," he fumbled. "You've changed in the last year . . . and for the better; you're becoming a strong young woman. It's not the changes in you that caused me to use your name, though," he said, and Catrin glanced up in surprise. "I've been remiss, you see. I have failed to properly perform the duties of a position passed to me by my grandfather.

"When I was a boy, he said he had a very important job for me. He said we were Guardians of the Vestrana, though I knew very little of what that meant at the time. I had already been sworn to secrecy, and he knew I could keep a secret. I guess he was right about that, at least, because you are only the third person I've ever told.

"He said our job was difficult but had a single aim: we were to protect the Herald and their line and swear our lives to them. Since I didn't understand at first, he explained it. 'A time will come when the Herald will need protection, and our family will answer the call; that is our destiny and our duty,' he said to me. He told me to train myself both as weapon and shield, and so I became a soldier." Fascinated, Catrin nodded for him to continue.

"That's why I started calling you by name; it is my duty to show you proper respect." Catrin needed time to absorb what she had heard. Her perceptions of events and people kept shifting.

Benjin had always lived at the farm with her and her father and had been a part of her world. She'd never before wondered why he lived there and had no wife or children of his own, and she began to see him in a new light.

"Well, the Herald is telling you to stop it," she said, smiling and waving her finger in his face. "You can call me by name if you like but not solely because I'm the Herald."

Benjin smiled. "Li'l miss, consider it done."

"What do we do from here?" she asked.

"I think we should do what you think is best. I'll give you my best advice if you want it, and I'm sure Chase and the others will as well, but my first duty is to protect you. I hope you consider our advice, compare it to your senses and your gut, and then make your decisions based on those things. I'll do my best to help--no matter what you decide."

She felt inadequate and small, yet it was up to her to decide what actions to take, what course to follow. The responsibility was a little frightening. What if she made the wrong choices?

"I don't want you to stay with me because your family was sworn to protect the Herald. I want you to stay because you want to stay," she managed through tears she hadn't realized she was crying.

Benjin pulled her into his arms, hugging her close. "There, there, li'l miss. Don't you cry. I'm here because I want to be here, and no one could tear me away. My duty to the Herald is just a fortunate coincidence that tells me to do what I would have done anyway."

Catrin cried and hugged him back; then she wiped her eyes and gathered the apples, while he picked several that were not yet ripe, saying they would make a nice treat in a few days. When Catrin stood, he noticed her carved fish.

"I like your necklace."

"Thank you. So do I. I found it while I was exploring the cavern, and I just remembered it when I was talking to Chase. He made the necklace for me," she said.

"He did a nice job; it compliments you."

* * *

Premon Dalls shuffled along the halls with the rest of the refugees as they were moved to their new homes within the audience halls. As the seemingly endless line of humanity poured into the halls, pushing, shoving, and vying for any scrap of space they could claim as their own, Premon faked a coughing fit. Standing in the arched entranceway, flanked by the strange carvings that adorned the archway and pretending to catch his breath, he examined the mechanism Master Edling had told him about.

The entranceways were narrow, yet long, and they served more than one purpose. Though the ceiling was decorated and appeared to be of solid rock, it was a ruse. The designers of the Masterhouse had foreseen the possibility of a siege, and they had built defense mechanisms into their fortress. Above these corridors lay a mountain of rubble and rock supported by joists that could hold its weight but little more. Above that stood a massive shaft, and at the top, an enormous weight was suspended by a chain. All Premon had to do was retrieve the special rod that Master Edling had told him how to find, insert it into the mouth of either carving, twist, and yank. That was all there was to it, at least that was what Master Edling had said. How Premon was supposed to trigger all three collapses before anyone emerged was something of a mystery, but Premon didn't care. He had nothing to lose.

The thought of killing all those people, sentencing them to starvation, would have made most men sick, but Premon considered himself a practical man. The loss of the refugees would mean many more months before those in the Masterhouse would either starve or be forced to surrender themselves into slavery. When he had revealed to Peten Ross that he could escape through the sewers, Premon had known he was sending the boy to his death, but he had also known that it would mean one less mouth to feed. Now he would achieve the same result, only on a much larger scale.

Chapter 13

Even the greatest catastrophes bring new opportunities for life.
--Brother Ramirez, Cathuran monk

* * *

Eager to put the plateau behind them, Catrin set a brisk pace. The sodden valley reeked of rotted vegetation and dead fish. "This valley runs all the way to the coastline, but the mountains on our right turn south and open into this area, the Arghast Desert," she said aloud while glancing at her map. She remembered the Arghast Desert from school: a vast wasteland. Nomadic tribes were said to wander the area, but no one had reported seeing them in generations.

The ragged northern coastline bordered the desert and was lined with mountains, which dwindled in the east. The southern coast was flat and lined with long stretches of sandy beach. It would be a long hike south, but Catrin thought it might be easier going than the mountains. She thought of how nice it would be to walk along the ocean with the sounds of crashing waves to soothe them. "Do you think we should go north or south when we reach the desert?"

"North," Benjin replied immediately. "The southern coast would be a more pleasant journey, but there's no cover there, and those lands can easily be patrolled by ships. We'd be inviting the entire Zjhon fleet to intercept us. The northern coast is much less accessible to enemies. There is very little safe anchorage, and most of the shoreline is made up of steep cliffs and mountains. If we stay close to the mountains, we should only have to skirt around the edges of the desert, which is not only uncomfortable, but often deadly. However, it is our best route."

"How many days would it take us to walk straight across the desert?"

"It's hard to say," he said after a moment. "I'd say six days at the least and as long as ten in the event of sandstorms. The days are hot and the nights cold, and there's almost no water. Venomous snakes, lizards, and scorpions are almost impossible to avoid." Before Benjin could continue, Catrin cut him short.

"I agree we should avoid the desert, and I agree the southern coast is too dangerous, so let's discuss the northern coast. What kind of difficulties do you expect on that route?"

"There are venomous snakes in that area as well--but fewer. We must be watchful for glass vipers. They're deadly, and because of their ability to take on the color of their immediate surroundings, they can be almost impossible to see. Beyond that, there are predator cats, roaming packs of wolves, and possibly bears, but they should not pose too great a threat. We'll just need to be cautious. The foothills are partially forested, which should provide additional cover should we need it."

"How many days will it take us to go north around the desert? Do we have enough provisions?"

"I'd say fourteen days until we reach the east coast, and then another two south to the cove. We have enough food to last ten days comfortably, the full fourteen if we stretch it. Of course, we may find game along the way, but I wouldn't count on it. We've got enough water for three or four days, and we'll need to replenish our supply as we travel."

Catrin nodded, scanning her map for indications of water features, but they were few. "Are there other sources of water to the east? I don't see many marked on the map."

"We'll need to be watchful. I'm sure there are streams and creeks that aren't on the map, but we'll have to find them. Once we reach the desert and turn north, we'll be entering territory I've never traveled, and I'll know little more than what the map shows us."

The sun rose higher, and so did the temperature. As they were trying to get some relief from the heat, Benjin snapped his head to the left, squinting in the bright light. Chase saw it too.

"I saw something moving in those trees."

"I did too," Benjin said, "but I didn't get a good look." They all watched the trees for a long while, but nothing moved; if someone lurked there, he remained hidden.

"Probably just a deer," Chase said.

Anxieties ran high, and they often looked over their shoulders for signs of pursuit. The tension and uncertainty gnawed at Catrin like an itch she could not scratch. Distant noises and glimpses of movement were the only indications of pursuit, but each occurrence renewed their apprehension. Catrin tried to convince herself it was her vivid imagination that each distorted echo was an approaching battle cry and that within every shadow lurked men intent on killing them. Though she had vowed to show the Zjhon no fear, she hadn't promised not to feel any.

As the valley widened into a broad plain, trees became more numerous and thickets more dense, and they had to use game trails or clear paths of their own. The shade provided respite from the glaring sun, but the underbrush slowed their journey. On a steep slope covered with thorny bushes, brambles, and vines, they found a patch of berry bushes, but the fruit lay beyond a thick screen of the plants. Working with great care, they cleared a narrow pathway to the berries. Benjin knew which ones had poisonous berries and others whose fruit was edible. Soon they had ample raspberries, blackberries, and even huckles. In a brief moment of levity, they filled themselves with the fruit.

Once beyond the wall of thorns, the land became more hospitable; underbrush gave way to tall grasses, and trees were sparse. Ahead lay marshy lowland, and already dark clouds of gnats buzzed around them. Emerald biting-flies darted around their heads, and walnut-sized mosquitoes attacked in legions.

"When I last passed this way, a strip of dry land bordered this marsh on either side. Now it appears we'll have to wade through it," Benjin said, scowling with squinting eyes over the saturated lowland, which now stretched across the entire valley. Narrow islands appeared throughout the marsh, creating a disjointed maze of land almost entirely immersed in stagnant water, and the search for a dry path became paramount.

As they moved deeper into the marsh, the stretches of water separating the islands became longer and deeper. Osbourne was the first to notice the leeches, which had attached themselves to his legs. He yanked his pant legs up and pulled the leeches off, throwing them. The rest discovered the same effect, and Benjin suggested they tuck their pants into their boots.

Slogging through the mucky quagmire was difficult and unpleasant, and Catrin was relieved when the marsh began to give way to some patches of high ground. Then a nearby scream and a series of splashes broke the silence.

"I saw something flailing around behind those weeds, but I'm not sure what it was," Chase said. "Shouldn't we go back to check?"

"I think we should take a look," said Benjin. "That sounded like a man shouting, and it sounded like he was hurt. If someone is following us, I want to know for certain. Let's go, Chase."

When they returned, Benjin said grimly, "A soldier was tracking us. We don't know if he was alone, but he'll follow us no more; he was bitten by a poisonous snake, and he took his own life before we arrived. We didn't go very close, since the snake was coiled in our path, but I could tell the man was no ordinary foot soldier. He was a member of an elite unit; at least that's what I gather from his attire. Unlike the other soldiers, he was equipped to move quickly; his armor was light and his weapons advanced. We'll have to remain more alert. I suspect more soldiers are tracking us."

"Let's move on, then," Catrin said. "I'd like to put as much ground between us and this marsh as possible. I don't want to camp anywhere near here."

* * *

By the light of one of the precious few candles that remained, Wendel Volker packed his gear. Elsa's sword lay across the blanket-covered crates he'd been using as a bed. He took no food, and in no way, other than burning the candle, depleted the provisions that would be needed by all those who remained in the cold caves. A twinge of guilt made Wendel pause and reconsider; these people needed him, or at least so they thought. An equally painful guilt hovered over him for abandoning Catrin, and his duty as a father had finally won out over his duty to his people. Those

153

he had gathered in the cold caves were now as safe as they were going to be; there was nothing more he could do to ensure their well-being. In a moment of self-justification, he asserted that by leaving, he would consume less of the rations; therefore, he was doing everyone who remained a favor.

Like all others, that moment passed, and he was left to deal with guilt over leaving Jensen behind. He and his brother simply saw things differently. Jensen had as much anxiety over Chase's fate as Wendel did over Catrin's, but he steadfastly refused to go after them, and he had done everything within his power to persuade Wendel to do the same. When he was honest with himself, Wendel realized that Jensen was the only reason he had stayed as long as he had. With a deep breath, he firmed his resolve and shouldered his pack. The journey ahead would be difficult and fraught with danger, but the hardest part was behind him; as he stepped out of the chamber that had been his temporary home, the journey was begun. He would find Catrin.

His candle was not overly bright, but he shielded it as best he could while allowing enough light to guide his way. To those who were immersed in darkness, even the dimmest light can shine like a beacon, and Wendel had no desire to alert anyone of his departure. Fortunately, most avoided the deepest tunnels, where the air was the coldest and the feeling of the land pressing down the greatest. Wendel had grown accustomed to the feeling long ago, and he walked without fear, though not without anxiety. He should have left a note for Jensen, something to explain his motives and reasoning, but he could not turn back now, and there was no time to waste. Jensen would wake soon, and another day would be lost, and Catrin would be another day farther from him. In the back of his mind, a voice warned that she was already too far away, that he would never reach her in time. Ignoring that voice, Wendel moved as quickly and quietly as he could.

Deep within the network of tunnels and caves, the scent of fresh air drifted. Only in a few places did shafts penetrate the rock and allow air and, in some cases, light into the caves, but Wendel now stood below one of these shafts. He had never found one of the shafts from above, mostly due to the fact that this part of the cold caves lay directly below a series of steep and formidable peaks. Not knowing what he would face when he emerged gave him pause, and he took a moment to plan this critical part of his escape.

First he tied a length of rope around his waist and secured the other end to his pack. The knife on his belt was all that he would carry, and all that he could use to defend himself should the outlet of the shaft be guarded. Though he thought it unlikely, Wendel made himself consider the possibility. Chastising himself for allowing fear to stall him, he moved to the crates of cheese that were stacked nearby, and he placed them on top of one another beneath the air shaft, giving himself just enough of a boost to gain his first handhold. Once inside the shaft, the climbing would be easier since he could use both sides of the shaft to support himself. The fear of getting stuck in a section where the shaft was too narrow nearly made him abandon this course, but his decision was made.

"Only cowards and thieves sneak away beneath a shroud of darkness," came Jensen's voice from below. "I never believed you to be either of those things, yet here we are."

Nearly howling in frustration, Wendel cursed himself for whatever carelessness allowed Jensen to find him here.

"I could see it in your eyes, and I could hear it in your voice when we discussed the plans today. I knew from the way you held yourself that you had no intention of being here when those plans were put in place. You cannot hide things from me--never could. Thought you would know that by now. So . . . if you are determined to leave, at least come down here and face me like a man."

With a final glance toward the sky--though he saw little in the darkness--Wendel lowered himself back to the crates, wondering if he would ever see Catrin, Chase, or Benjin again. The thoughts were nearly as painful as seeing the disappointment in his brother's eyes.

155

* * *

As the trees grew thicker, the group moved slowly along a narrow game trail. The air vibrated with the percussive cadence of hammer-locusts, and Catrin could feel their call thrumming through her. A mass of downed trees suddenly loomed before them, deteriorating beneath a bed of moss and lichen. Thorn bushes around the rotting mass created a formidable barrier.

"These trees are crumbling, so you'd better watch your footing," Benjin said. Catrin made the climb easily, stepping lightly across the slick limbs. Just as she gained solid ground, she saw the trunk beneath Osbourne's boot collapse, and his leg was immersed in a writhing, humming, black mass. Playing harmony to the hammer-locusts, a growing cloud of angry hornets defended their nest.

Engulfed by the storm, Osbourne let out a cry and ran past Catrin, who sprinted after him. Burning stings on her neck and head spurred her to reckless speed, and she pumped her legs as fast as they would go. Each new pain drove her forward; unable to distinguish hornet stings from the bites of thorns, she fled. Dark shapes darted around her, striking without mercy. Her head throbbed in time with the pounding of her pulse, and her vision deteriorated as her eyebrow swelled.

A loud splash was the only warning she received before she hurtled through open air. Her brief flight ended as she struck water, which was deep enough to break her fall. She plunged under for an instant, but then her feet found bottom, and she propelled herself back up.

When she broke the surface, coughing and gasping, she was thankful no hornets awaited her. Her left eye was nearly closed, and the swelling in her neck made it difficult to turn her head. Osbourne was thrashing on the far shore in obvious agony, his entire head swelling. A moment later, Benjin and the others plunged into the water.

Catrin ran to Osbourne, who had gone still. His eyes were mere slits trapped between exaggerated folds of puffy flesh, and the flushed skin of his lips curled outward to

156

contain it. His skin deepened from mottled red to purple, and his body occasionally twitched.

"Cut his shirt away from his throat," Benjin barked, approaching with his herbal kit. "Pull his lips open and depress his tongue." Catrin pried open Osbourne's slack jaws and pressed his tongue down firmly with her fingers. Benjin pinched a generous portion of Celia's root, which he blew into Osbourne's open mouth; then he puffed the fine powder into Osbourne's lungs, using his hands to seal the opening of their mouths. A fine cloud of powder escaped when Benjin pressed on Osbourne's chest with his hands, causing Osbourne to exhale. Then Benjin blew into Osbourne's mouth again.

When Osbourne went into spasm and coughed, Catrin let out her breath, only then realizing she had been holding it. The boy was wracked with violent fits of coughing, which left him gasping, and each new breath tickled his throat, causing him to cough harder. Only wheezing and vomiting separated his fits, but he was breathing.

Chase had stings on his neck and arms, but the swelling was minor. Strom had been behind them and was untouched by the angry mass of hornets that had pursued the others. With Osbourne out of immediate danger, Benjin mixed a large batch of sting remedy from several of his powders and some clean water. When he looked up from his work, Catrin saw that his bottom lip had been stung several times and was twice its normal size. She realized then how painful it must have been for him to blow into Osbourne's mouth, and she marveled at his strength.

Osbourne's breathing gradually eased, but his eyes remained shut. Benjin told him to take shallow breaths until the tickle left his throat and leaned him against a tree. In time, the herbs took effect. His body relaxed, and though the swelling was not gone, it no longer seemed to be getting worse.

Benjin prepared another mixture, which he said would help with the swelling, but they would have to swallow it. It was bitter and left a vile aftertaste. Osbourne drank the mixture diluted with water, but he choked on it and suffered another coughing fit.

Benjin's lip grew huge, but he kept working despite his obvious discomfort. When he checked their packs, he sighed. The others watched as he removed the smoked and salted goods that had gotten wet, and the pile of food he discarded was distressing to see after the work they had put into preparing it. They sat for a while and watched Osbourne recover. He seemed to be having less trouble breathing, but his eyes were still shut. Catrin wanted to make for higher ground before they camped for the night, and she was trying to decide what to do when Benjin drew her aside.

"I don't think Osbourne should walk any farther today. I should go ahead and scout out a suitable campsite while the rest of you wait here. You all can rig a litter and attend to Osbourne's needs while I'm gone. Agreed?" She nodded. "Good." He got his bow and a quiver of arrows, set off at a rapid pace, and was soon lost from sight.

Chase and Strom found saplings, while Catrin unpacked her leather ground cloth and made a hole near each corner and several more along each side. She took a length of rope and unbraided it so she would have the six smaller lines she needed. She then lashed the ground cloth to the saplings to form a litter for Osbourne.

"Sorry I took so long," Benjin said when he returned. "I found a decent campsite and a fairly clear path there." After lifting Osbourne gently onto the litter, trying not to aggravate any of his injuries, they set off at a steady pace. Benjin and Catrin pushed bushes and saplings aside in narrow places, allowing room for the stretcher Chase and Strom were carrying.

The land finally began to slope upward, and Benjin led them to the top of a hill shaded by an enormous tree. Under the tree waited a pile of firewood, pears, and a brace of rabbits, which explained why Benjin had been so long in returning.

Catrin removed her ground cloth from the makeshift litter while Strom lit a fire and Benjin dressed the rabbits. They made soup for Osbourne because he was quite ill and might not tolerate solid food. The campsite was a good choice: the area shaded by the tree was soft and covered with spongy moss, making it far more comfortable than rough ground.

Strom, the only one unscathed by the attack of hornets, looked around the fire and shook his head. Benjin had a very fat lip, Catrin's eye was swollen nearly shut, Chase had large lumps on the back of his neck, and Osbourne was puffed up as if he were filled with water.

"You're a sorry-looking group, I have to tell ya," he said, grinning, but within moments he began to shift where he sat. He grumbled as he stood and vigorously scratched the seat of his pants, apparently wishing he'd been more careful selecting leaves after relieving himself. Benjin shook his head and retrieved his ever-diminishing supply of herbs. He made a suitable mixture, poured it into Strom's hand, and gave him a water flask.

"You'll have to apply that yourself, m'friend," he said, casting him a sidelong glance. "You're on your own."

* * *

Master Jarvis hurried along the inner corridors, his mouth and nose still covered with a scented kerchief to mask the smell. No one was immune to the effects of the siege, though he no longer even considered this a siege; it was more like containment. The Zjhon were not trying to get in anymore, they just didn't want anyone to get out. Master Jarvis could not decide which was worse.

The thought of Catrin in the hands of the Zjhon nearly made him sick; he'd taught her since she was a little girl, and she'd always been one of his favored students. The only thing that sickened him more was the thought of what Master Edling was trying to achieve. Some would say that Jarvis was seeing things that were not there, but he knew better; he'd known Edling for too long. Master Grodin had been swayed into moving the refugees into the audience halls based on the premise that the people would feel more secure surrounded by their peers than if kept apart. It was a ruse, and Jarvis knew it. Though some people had expressed feelings of loneliness and a sense of being disconnected, he doubted any of them would consider being crammed into the audience halls an improvement. The fact that one of the special release bars used to trigger the cave-in mechanism was missing only solidified the reality in Master Jarvis's mind.

When he finally reached Master Grodin's quarters, he was pleased to see the old man awake and alone. "May I trouble you?"

"Who's there? Is that you, young Jarvis?" Master Grodin asked. "There are some candied cherries in the dish there. Help yourself. I know how you like them. Then run along and be a good boy."

"Thank you, sir," Master Jarvis said, knowing that sometimes Master Grodin seemed to drift into the past, remembering a time when Jarvis was but a student of his. "The refugees have been moved into the audience halls."

"Yes, I know. They can all be together with their family and friends now. I wish I could do more for them. Maybe you could take them some candied cherries?"

"Perhaps I will," Master Jarvis said. "I'm concerned about Master Edling's motivation. I suspect he had another reason for wanting the people moved."

"You and Edling must end this rivalry between you," Master Grodin said as he wagged his finger. "Wasn't it just last week I caught the two of you fighting in the store room?"

In truth, that had been nearly thirty years ago, but Jarvis knew better than to tell Master Grodin he was mistaken; instead he tried to nudge his aging mentor back into the present. "I'd feel more comfortable with the refugees in the audience halls if all of the cave-in release keys were accounted for. One is missing."

Master Grodin turned sharply and chewed on his beard a moment before he responded. "I suppose that leaves me only one course of action," he said, his eyes clearer than Jarvis had seen them in some time. "Since Edling feels compelled to represent the refugees, then that is how it shall be. Let it be known that he and his must remain in the audience halls at all times, so that he can personally ensure the safety and well-being of his charges."

Jarvis left with a smile on his face, wondering how much of Master Grodin's condition was an act, and how much was the guise of a clever old man.

Chapter 14

The bitter taste of betrayal can be purged only by fire.
--Imeteri, slave

* * *

The next few days were long and miserable while they waited at the campsite to heal, taking time when they could to gather supplies. They were not in very good shape for hunting, so they settled for gathering fruits and nuts.

The weather was clear and warm, and light breezes carried the many scents of summer. The comet was no longer visible in the night sky, and no new comets showed themselves. Catrin wondered if it had all been just a cosmic joke, the first comet really being the only comet. She could still feel a charge in the air, but she wondered if it was just a lingering effect from the first comet.

"Do you think there'll be more comets?" she asked Benjin.

"Can't be certain, but I assume so. Legends say thousands of them crowd the night skies during the Istran Noon, which should occur some seventy-five years from now. I'm guessing we'll see a gradual increase over time."

They had seen no further signs of soldiers, for which they were grateful, but the fact seemed to disturb Benjin. He was nervous, edgy, and constantly looking for signs of the Zjhon.

"I know there're more soldiers following us. I'm almost certain the man who died in the marsh wasn't alone, but I can't understand why they don't attack. They're more heavily armed than we are, and they have to know that. They know where we are, and they've had time to bring a larger force here," he said.

"They may be heavily armed, but I bet none of them has ever changed the course of a river or knocked down the side of a mountain like I saw Catrin do," Strom said. His words sounded strange to Catrin--like something from a fireside story.

"But they knew they were coming here to face the Herald," Benjin replied. "They must have known she would have great power. I don't think they're totally reacting out of fear, although I do agree they have good reason to be cautious. I still think they must have some other reason for following us but not attacking."

"Perhaps they are bringing more troops here to confront us," Chase said. "Maybe the terrain has just delayed them. We should remain watchful."

"Maybe they don't need to attack us now because they already know where we're going," Osbourne observed. "They're probably just waiting for us to walk into an ambush."

Benjin nodded and hesitated before he said, "You may be right, but I'm not sure. They may have other plans for us. Still, we'll need to be alert for signs of either ambush or pursuit."

* * *

Catrin spent a long day looking for fruits, nuts, and the herbs and spices they needed to replenish Benjin's medicinal supplies. When she returned to camp, her companions seemed to be better, a great relief after days of misery. There was a strange look in their eyes as she approached.

Strom stared at her so intently that she finally couldn't stand it any longer. "What are you looking at?" she asked Strom more sharply than she'd intended.

"I'm looking at your necklace, Cat. It didn't look like that when you first showed it to us. It was all milky and dull, and now it's . . ."

Chase finished the sentence for him. "It's just beautiful."

Catrin lifted the leather thong over her head and examined the carving, amazed by what she saw. The carved fish was now clear and almost lustrous. It caught the light and sent small prisms dancing around her. She ran her finger across it and found the surface smooth where it had seemed rough and porous before. Trying to find a reasonable explanation for the transformation of the small carving, she wondered if it had just been dirty and in need of cleaning.

She tried to remember exactly how it had looked when she had first found it. It had seemed almost as if it were dried out rather than dirty.

"Maybe your swim cleaned it off," Chase said, which made better sense than anything else she had come up with, but Catrin wasn't so sure. She tried to put it from her mind, but in its place came anxious thoughts of Istra.

Somehow, the light of a comet, or a goddess--depending on how she chose to perceive it--gave Catrin access to powers of which she had no knowledge or aptitude. Through some unknown process, she knew she could gather the comet's energy and release it in devastating ways, but she didn't know how to control it. Only when her life was in danger did she even seem to have full access to it; most of the time it was a distant dream, tickling her senses then receding too fast to pursue.

She needed to know how to use the energy without hurting anyone. If she did not learn to control her outbursts, it might kill her and everyone around her. It was an uncomfortable feeling, and it put Catrin on edge. Her mind whirled with questions and only a handful of answers, and those answers only spawned more questions.

Trying to her calm herself, she sat down and closed her eyes. Fears and anxieties cluttered her mind and prevented coherent thought.

"Are you all right, li'l miss?" Benjin asked.

"I have too many thoughts in my head to concentrate on anything because other thoughts keep pushing themselves into my mind. It's frustrating, and I don't like it at all."

"I understand," he said with a slight nod of his head. "Let me try to help. There are many techniques you can use to quiet your mind and get a clearer view. Would you like me to teach you some of what I know?"

"Yes, please. Would you?"

Benjin told them to all sit in a circle around the fire, directing Catrin to sit directly across from him. Sitting with his legs crossed and his arms relaxed, he put his hands on his knees, palms facing up. The others followed his example.

"Close your eyes and concentrate on slow, steady breaths to the count of seven. Breathe in through your nose and out through your mouth. Keep your eyes closed, and relax your muscles," he said, watching them. "You need to relax a bit more, li'l miss; you're as rigid as stone. On every exhale, concentrate on your muscles becoming looser."

Catrin tried to calm herself, but the harder she tried, the more tense she became, and she grew angry with herself for not being able even to relax properly. How could she ever hope to control her power if she could not even control her own state of mind? Realizing her fists were tightly clenched, she opened her eyes with a frustrated sigh. The others still had their eyes closed and looked relaxed. Benjin's eyes met hers.

"Perhaps we should try another technique that can be useful when your mind refuses to be quiet. When our heads are full of thoughts, it can be nearly impossible to suppress them. It's often better to deal with each thought individually as they come to you. Not all of them are pleasant, but we have to learn to accept them; they are a part of us. We should deal with them and try to understand them, but at the very least, we should accept them.

"I want to teach you an ancient exercise. First, close your eyes and begin your breathing again. When a thought comes to you, grab on to it and accept it. Recognize it as your own, and try to understand why you are thinking it. Picture it as a small ball of energy; hold your hands out and cup that energy in your palms. Examine the energy and analyze it until you come to know it. When you are comfortable thinking about it, take a deep breath, and when you exhale, release that energy into the universe.

"Your thoughts are your own, but your pain and suffering can be eased when you let the universe help, and your joy and happiness can be shared with the whole of existence. Your hope can go to every part of creation. By sending out your thoughts, you will feel less alone with your feelings. You can help others find their happiness, and you will receive help dealing with your troubles."

Catrin was surprised by his philosophical words; she had never heard him speak that way, even in his previous lessons about meditation. She tried to concentrate on taking his advice rather than analyzing it, but concentrating was a challenge. Breathing deeply, searching for calm within the violent storm of her thoughts and emotions, she became detached from the world, transported to a place of her own making that was comforting yet unfamiliar. Letting the thoughts swirl around her for a moment, she tried to find her center and braced herself for the onslaught.

A feeling of anger and betrayal flashed into her consciousness: it was hot and painful, and further images of anguish and pain came to the fore. She remembered the townies' abuse of her and her friends; visions of the attack on Osbourne played through her mind. Then her dreamlike vision moved on to another scene: the townspeople challenging her father and accusing her of being a witch. Images of the invading army hammered her until she almost lost her focus.

After a deep breath, she accepted the anger that was part of her. Releasing the thought as she exhaled, she blew it away from her.

While floating between thoughts for a moment, she was surprised by the lull in the maelstrom of her consciousness. She felt a great release from the thoughts she had accepted; she chose to persist, believing she was ready for her next thought. It did not take long before it drifted in from somewhere in the back of her mind. This was a warm, comforting image, however, and it felt secure and safe. She realized that thought was Benjin.

She envisioned him with his salt-and-pepper beard, his long black hair with streaks of gray pulled back with a leather thong. She saw his strong features and muscular build. Pouring herself into the meditation, she concentrated on that thought, building it up for a huge release. She felt great gratitude to Benjin for protecting her, for being her friend and mentor, and for caring so much for her. She let the thought expand to include all those around her then to all those she had left behind. To all who had ever been kind to her, she sent out this thought as a gift of thanks. With her next exhale, she let it pour from her.

Catrin floated blissfully above her consciousness, having experienced a massive, gratifying, and unexplainably beautiful release of tension.

"Your minds have become very quiet now," Benjin said in a low and rhythmic voice, hardly more than a whisper. "Focus your consciousness. I want you to picture a strawberry. Focus on the details rather than the whole. Envision the colors and textures; picture the seeds and leaves until every detail is complete."

Catrin heard his words somewhere in her mind, and she tried to comply. She began to visualize the strawberry, and soon she tasted the sweetness of the freshly picked fruit, strawberry jam, and strawberry-rhubarb pie. All her memories of strawberries permeated the thought, but she was brought out of her meditation by the sound of Chase laughing and talking excitedly.

"That was great, I'm telling ya. I could actually taste strawberries."

"And strawberry jam," Osbourne added.

"I tasted pie," Strom said with a grin.

"Hey, Cat. Do you remember the time you tried to shove strawberries up my nose?" Chase asked, and Catrin laughed; she'd been thinking about the same thing.

"Did any of you experience anything else?" Benjin asked.

"When we first started, I felt angry," Osbourne said. "I remembered the way I was attacked and the way Catrin was treated."

"I felt a lot like that too," Chase said, "but then I got to thinking about how Benjin has protected us and kept us safe. And then I felt like I was a protector too."

"Me too," Strom added, and Osbourne nodded.

Catrin sat back, wondering if it was all coincidence. Could they all have been thinking the exact same things? Benjin met her eyes.

"I didn't want to say anything without some confirmation, but Catrin's powers are beginning to manifest in different ways," he said. "During your meditation, I could actually see the energy above Catrin's palms. It's difficult to describe. It shifted and moved, but I got a general sense of what she was thinking. It seems she was able to influence our thoughts."

"She can control people's minds?" Osbourne asked, his face pale.

"I don't think she has any control over our thoughts or any way to read them. It does seem, however, that she can project her emotions to those around her," Benjin said.

"I didn't try to make you think those things," Catrin objected. "Those were the things I was thinking about, but I just concentrated real hard on them; that's all. I wasn't trying to influence your thoughts. Honest." Her voice was practically pleading now. "And I'd never try to read your minds. Sometimes I can sense people's emotions, but I don't even do that intentionally."

"We know you wouldn't do anything like that on purpose," Chase said. "You should guard your thoughts more closely from now on, though. Try not to concentrate that hard on anything you want kept secret."

"Well said," Benjin said.

"I need to see this for myself," Catrin said. "I'm going to try to do it again."

Benjin did not discourage her, and the others looked as if they wanted to see it, so she took a deep breath and centered herself. The excitement made the meditation as difficult as her previous frustration had, but she closed her eyes and concentrated.

This was important. This was an opportunity to learn something about her powers, a chance to take control of her life. Hope, excitement, and curiosity were predominant in her thoughts, and she focused on them.

"Look now," Chase whispered.

It nearly cost Catrin her concentration, and she kept her eyes closed until she regained her focus. Slowly she opened them. The light was almost blinding, but soon she could see a ball of energy floating above her cupped palms. Like a shimmering jewel with countless facets, it was exquisite. It spun and danced in her hands, constantly changing.

The more excited and fascinated she became, the larger and brighter it grew. When she could no longer contain it, she tossed it into the night sky, where it burst into a cloud of twinkling lights no larger than grains of sand. They dimmed and disappeared before reaching the ground, but the air was charged with excitement.

"That was amazing," Chase said.

"I'd have to agree," Benjin added.

Catrin's mind raced with possibilities and questions. What else could she do with her powers? What other abilities might she stumble on? The thoughts were as terrifying as they were exhilarating. Even after she retired to her bedroll, she lay staring up at the stars, hoping whatever power she found next would not destroy anything or kill anyone.

Chapter 15

Bonds of blood are sacred and immutable.
--King Venes of the Elsics

* * *

Catrin woke during the night and decided to relieve Benjin from his watch. She figured it would be best if he were the one rested for the next part of their journey. Pulling her coverlet around her shoulders, she wandered past the glowing coals of the fire. She found Chase in Benjin's stead. He smiled at her.

"Couldn't sleep?"

"I slept great, actually. I just woke up for some reason . . . not sure why. How long ago did you relieve Benjin?"

"Not long ago. I'm awake and alert. I'll take the rest of the watch. Get some more sleep; you'll probably need it," he said. Catrin was glad to take him up on this advice. Her sleeping spot had gone cold and she shivered, but soon she slept again.

Chase woke them during the false dawn. Catrin felt she had closed her eyes only moments before, and they were still clouded with sleep. Their routine well practiced, they broke camp in record time, and Catrin slowly recovered from her disorientation.

Wanting to cover as much ground as possible while the air was still cool, they set off without delay. Catrin set a moderate pace for Osbourne's sake since he was still experiencing headaches and shortness of breath. His condition troubled her, but they had to keep moving. Benjin did what he could to ease Osbourne's afflictions using the few medicinal herbs he still had left, and Catrin hoped it would be enough.

The broad valley morphed into rolling hills, and as they crested a steep rise, Catrin caught sight of what lay ahead. The rising sun cast a myriad of colors across the sky and the desert below. The horizon was a lush canvas of texture and color, pastels and blush highlighted with hues of violet. Waves of sand appeared almost fluid, lapping against a meandering shoreline. The relative flatness stretched into the distance, the horizon broken only by distant, shadowy mountains. The sheer size and deceptive beauty of the desert cast an intimidating pall on those who viewed it.

Catrin had never been away from the mountains before. Realizing the feeling of security they had always given her, she was glad they would follow the mountains for much of their journey.

"Do not let its beauty fool you," Benjin said. "The desert is deadly. We'll be skirting it for some time, and though the mountains will give us some cover and possible storm shelter, we won't be immune to its dangers. Keep watch on the horizons and be alert for storms or large clouds of dust."

At the mouth of the valley, they turned north, following the narrow band of lightly forested grasslands that huddled between stone and sand like an emerald river. The air above the desert shimmered in the heat of the morning sun, and they moved along in relative silence to conserve their energy. They drank sparingly from their flasks, knowing they could run out before they escaped this arid landscape.

Catrin let Benjin lead and found herself walking in a trance, part of her mind watching where she was going, but another part deep in thought. She tried the technique of clearing her mind that Benjin taught her, but she could not focus, and she wandered from thought to thought, seemingly at random. The deluge of thoughts flowed past her consciousness, and she let them skirt her awareness, creating an odd, transitional state of mind. She became aware of a curious hum, like background noise in her head, a buzzing that seemed to be just behind her ears. She tried to focus on it, but it stayed at the edge of her senses, elusive and indefinable.

Taking a different approach, she tried to specifically not think about it and concentrate on something else. No matter how hard she tried to ignore it, though, the humming crept along the edges of her senses, tickling her awareness. She tried to evoke powerful memories and the emotions they brought, hoping to overpower the distraction. She called up the vivid memory of her first kiss, and the buzzing pounded into her thoughts. Grasping it with her mind, she latched on to it with all the focus she could muster.

Her body thrummed in the powerful chorus, a lilting melody that ebbed to a mere whisper only to resound again insistently. Concentrating on hearing alone seemed insufficient to perceive the energy, and she split her focus to include the vibrations she felt. At this point, she began to experience it in a completely new way. The energy took shape and form, though its form continuously shifted like the surface of a lake. Fragrances overlaid her other senses, and even the taste of the air colored her mental imagery.

After tripping on a gnarled tree root, Catrin caught herself on the trunk. Her palms slammed into the bark, and she was overwhelmed by her impression of the tree: Vitality and strength flowed through the physical bond like a torrent of life. The tree exuded ancient wisdom and lack of cares. It existed simply and simply existed. It did no right or wrong, made no mistakes, had no opinions. It was beyond reproach and indifferent to criticism. Catrin was comforted by its energy and felt a gentle calm wash over her. Chase stumbled into her back, jarring her from her mental state.

"Sorry, Cat. I didn't realize you stopped."

"My fault. I wasn't watching where I was going," she explained, not wanting to discuss her experience until she understood it better.

After her shocking contact with the tree, Catrin had a better idea of what to expect and how to interpret what she felt, and she began to sort through her perceptions of the various energies around her. Everything she saw had its own pattern, its own unique energy: her companions, the trees, grass, mountains, and especially the desert. She was surprised to find so much life energy within the desolation of the desert. Her senses skated along the sands. She didn't know what all the energies were, but she knew they existed.

The auras surrounding her companions were storms of emotional energy, which gave her a strong sense of their moods. She had always been sensitive to people's feelings and tried always to ascertain people's mental states in order to understand them. Posture, stance, and movements were all indicators, but none had ever given her such clear insight as she had now. Oddly, her new sense felt completely natural, as if it had always been a part of her, latent, waiting to be recognized and used. But it was also a burden. It made the fear and anxiety surrounding her companions almost palpable and impossible to ignore. Devoid of any means to assuage their fears, she simply accepted them and let them be.

A vibrant burst of energy off to her right caught her attention. It burned with life. She used her eyes to identify the source and saw an emerald hummingbird visiting the flowers of a trumpet vine. As if sensing her scrutiny, it flew in front of her face and hovered there. After a brief moment, it chirped, backed up, and darted into the azure sky. Catrin's impression of the hummingbird--vibrant and alive--stayed with her, its bold curiosity refreshing.

The more she used her new life sense, the easier and more natural it became. She found that, after a while, she could sense it without focusing on it, though it was most intense when she concentrated, just as she could hear without consciously listening.

New sensations invigorated her, as if feeling a cool breeze on her face for the first time, and she was exuberant. Another small life force moved nearby, and she was surprised to see a honeybee. It did not seem angry or aggressive, as she had always perceived stinging insects; it was just going about the business of being a honeybee.

There was an abundance of life in the soil itself, including things too small to be seen. Catrin saw the ways death served to feed life. Deciduous trees shed leaves, which fell to the ground and decomposed. Organisms that used the decaying leaves as food aided the decomposition. Their waste and the decayed matter become soil, which, in turn, nourished the trees and plants. Catrin had never recognized the chain of life as a varying cycle of composition and decomposition before, and such realizations were rapidly changing her perception of the world around her.

Nature, in all its majesty and glory, was beginning to be revealed to Catrin through senses she had not been aware of before. For the first time, she saw the ecosystem as a unit and saw how each part of the system contributed to the whole; without any one component, life could fail. Predators could not exist without prey, and herbivores would die without plants, and plants would shrivel without materials provided by the death and defecation of animals. When she considered how many factors had to be in place for life to endure, she was amazed it existed at all, and yet it flourished, even in the harshest of environments--simply astounding.

Involved in her thoughts, Catrin was surprised when Benjin selected a place to camp. Most of the day's hike was a blur to her, and she had to reorient herself with the landscape. The mountains cast long shadows over the grassland as the sun set; the air cooled quickly, and it was almost chilly by twilight. The campsite Benjin selected backed up against the rock face. Although a few trees dotted the area, they were weathered and twisted. It was not much cover, but it was certainly better than the open desert.

"I've been thinking about what Osbourne said about an ambush," Benjin said as they ate. "If there's a trap, I think it would be best to spring it without Catrin with us," he continued. "There shouldn't be many places for the Zjhon to hide near the cove, and if I make it that far without seeing anyone--"

Catrin cut in. "So your plan is to go into an ambush . . . alone? Without me?"

"Now, Catrin, please understand, it's to protect you," he began, but Catrin silenced him with a look. He clamped his mouth shut, his eyes down, and waited silently. Catrin knew she was being unreasonable, but the thought of him walking into an ambush was horrifying. Some other option must exist, one without Benjin as bait. No one spoke until Benjin drew a breath, but Catrin cut him short again.

"You'll think of another plan," she said with a sharp nod. "Our only recourse cannot be a suicide mission for any of us. I will not accept that."

"Why, yes, of course. There must be a better way," Benjin replied without looking at her.

Catrin looked out into the night, terrified by the thought of being without Benjin. He made her feel safe. Without looking at the others, she went to her bedroll. She knew her anger was driven by fear, and that was the only way she could hide it.

* * *

"Now what do we do?" Chase asked once it appeared Catrin was truly asleep.

"For now we just have to keep moving toward the cove," Benjin said. "We have few other options."

"Maybe you and I should leave now and scout the way," Chase said.

"I don't like that idea at all," Strom said.

"There has to be something we can do," Chase insisted, his own desperation driven by fear. Survival almost seemed too much to hope for given the circumstances.

"When we get closer," Benjin said, "we can sneak away to spring the trap. We'll speak of it no more until then. Catrin won't like it, but it's what's best for her."

"And what then?" Strom asked, anger clear in his voice. "You go off and spring the trap and die, and what happens then? Catrin, Osbourne, and I go off and fight the world? Cat's right; you're both being idiots. Should we run through the desert to see if it's hot? No." He paused a moment to return the stares currently aimed at him. "When we get close, we watch and we wait. If we're clever enough, we'll see some sign of activity before they see us. I'm not sure what we do from there, but that's a far cry better than running in there and jumping around like a couple of idiots with torches and getting yourselves skewered."

There was a long moment of silence when Strom finished speaking. He crossed his arms and dared anyone to challenge him.

"Nobody said we were going to go running in there," Chase said, slightly downcast. Strom glared at him.

"Especially not jumping around with torches," Benjin added.

Chapter 16

This life is but a brief tenure, one of many perspectives a spirit must experience in the quest for eternity.
--Sadi Ja, philosopher

* * *

The clear skies and cool air would have been perfect for hiking, but they were accompanied by gusting winds. Funneled closer to the sands by the narrowing grassland, Catrin and her companions were relentlessly pelted with stinging sand. They held pieces of clothing over their faces, but their eyes still suffered.

"Be watchful for water. We need to replenish our supply as often as we can," Benjin said. They saw troughs left by a previous deluge but no water. Catrin mentally explored the landscape as they traveled, hoping to find a spring, but the only water she sensed was deep beneath the sand.

"Do you see that dark column of rock? Is that a waterfall?" Strom asked.

"If it is, it's awfully small," Chase said.

Catrin cast her senses toward where Strom indicated, hoping she would detect water. She tried not to be upset when she found nothing, but she realized she had truly expected to be successful. Determined to make a thorough examination, she tried running her senses across the distant soil from another angle. Her spirit soared when she felt the slightest pressure of resistance.

Focusing on that place, she sensed a very small amount of water, but water it was. "You are both correct. It is a small waterfall," Catrin said, and despite some sideways glances, they began walking toward the waterfall. As they approached, the land rose at odd angles and was difficult to traverse; loose rock and scree made matters worse.

A small flow of water trickled down the rock face, a shallow pool at its base. The water was cool and clean, and they refilled their empty flasks. They tried to wash themselves in the small basin, but their results were only cursory. The murmuring water gave an air of tranquility; a tall tree provided shade, and moss grew thick over the rocks surrounding the basin. It would have been idyllic to stay there, but they knew they had to move on. Despite efforts to find anything edible, they had not found a morsel since leaving the valley. They were running out, thanks to the dunking most of their food had taken, and needed to find something soon.

As they departed, the wind died down, making the rest of the day's hike bearable. The northern coast loomed in the distance like the edge of the world. Trees and vegetation became sparse, and gouts of dust rose from their boots with each step. They continued on, well after sunset, despite their weariness. The nearly full moon in a clear sky provided ample light, and the air became cooler, almost comfortable. Catrin was still wary of seeing more comets. She yearned for the exhilaration of their energy yet feared the consequences.

An abrupt turn in the mountains and the rush of the pounding surf signaled their destination, and the exhausted group made camp in a stupor. In the morning they would turn east, marking another milestone in Catrin's mind. Another step completed and another step closer to safety--at least that was their goal. They ate a little that night, trying to conserve what they had.

The next few days were long and uncomfortable. They found no game and no water, though Benjin did find some edible roots and a couple of rare herbs.

"Beware the cactuses," he warned as the plants became so numerous, they were nearly unavoidable. "Those with fine, hairlike spines can be worse than those that look more intimidating. Stay alert and avoid them if possible."

The next day they picked their way along the coastline, and the mountains dwindled to hills. In a few places, as the terrain allowed, deep blue waters could be seen in the distance. Those waters were surrounded by a barrier reef and were said to be littered with rock outcroppings and extensions of the reef just beneath the surface.

Strom stopped abruptly, startling the rest of the group. "I saw a bright flash of light--over there," he said, pointing into the distance behind them. They watched for a few moments but saw no more flashes or signs of movement.

177

"You most likely saw one of two things: a soldier's gear reflecting light, or a mirror being used to send a message," Benjin said.

"Do you see that cloud of dust?" Chase asked, pointing into the desert. It appeared out of place. It did not look like a funnel cloud and seemed too narrow and isolated to be caused by wind.

Benjin shaded his eyes and gazed into the distance. "Take cover! Now!" he ordered.

"There is no cover," Strom observed darkly, but his voice shook with panic. All that dotted the landscape were small bushes and a few straggly trees, and a mass of riders was thundering straight for them, leaving little doubt they had already been seen.

"Boil them!" Benjin swore. "Draw your weapons and guard each other's backs. If we must die this day, then let's go down with a fight."

Belt knives and short swords seemed like a pitiful defense, but Catrin committed herself. She considered stringing her bow, but she knew it would do her little good in close quarters. Her hands shook and her heart pounded. She had never been so terrified. The roiling dust cloud grew closer, and she imagined hundreds of soldiers bearing down on them, intent on her destruction.

"Let them come," Strom said through gritted teeth. "I'm tired of running and hiding. Let this be done now."

They stood grimly, determined to face this enemy. Catrin's instincts shouted that they should find some hole to hide in, but she knew they would be found.

The shimmering air obscured the riders even as they came into full view, and they slowed gradually as they approached. They used no reins, which was foreign to Catrin. She saw, though, it was so each rider could carry spears, crossbows, and slings.

The horsemen were at ease in the desert environment. They expressed no hostile action, but neither did they appear overtly friendly. They just moved forward with the confidence of those who know their land and their horses. Lean and muscular, their mounts' coats were lustrous, and their manes thick. Even their fetlocks bore long, thick hair that draped over their hooves.

"The tribes of Arghast approach," Benjin said. "Sheathe your weapons and hold your ground. Don't do or say anything unless I tell you. It's said they'll generally only attack if you insist upon crossing the desert." The riders slowed their horses some fifty paces away.

Catrin estimated more than a hundred horsemen spread before her, and she studied them, needing to understand this new adversary. There were several distinct variations in their clothing and saddles. The differences were subtle, almost imperceptible. One group had thin, dark sashes across their chests. Another group was distinguished by the braided manes and tails of their horses and yet another by tattoos branded on their horses' withers.

Only the occasional rattle of a harness broke the silence, and the riders made no attempt to communicate, seeming content to wait. Catrin glanced at Benjin, who stood patiently. She could see no sign of emotion on his face, but she could feel the anxiety of his energy and marveled that he could hide his emotions so well.

Seven horsemen broke free of the line and walked their horses forward at a measured and deliberate pace. Six of them wore the same styles she had noticed, but the seventh rider was different. He rode clumsily and bore only a tall, iron-shod staff. His horse was tethered to the horse of the leading rider, and he appeared to be struggling to remove his headgear. They were close when he finally got the headgear off, exposing his frayed hair and wide, blinking eyes. Catrin drew a sharp breath when she saw Nat. He smiled sadly and waved as he approached.

When the horsemen stopped, they dismounted gracefully, except for Nat, who nearly fell out of the strange saddle. The Arghast gave a signal, and their horses backed away. An equally subtle command sent the horses to their knees.

"What do we do?" Catrin whispered to Benjin.

"You and I will approach them. The rest of you, stay here," he said.

Catrin felt her face flush, and her anxiety rose to a new level, but she would show no fear. She and Benjin approached the Arghast but remained silent. The still-hooded man next to Nat stepped forward and spoke in halting words.

"We leaders of Arghast tribes. I, Vertook of Viper tribe, speak for all tribes. This man say you Herald of Istra," he said, nodding toward Nat, who looked terrified. "True?"

Benjin nodded his head slightly.

"Yes, it is true," Catrin answered. Nat seemed relieved but said nothing. The tribesmen considered her answer and spoke harshly among themselves.

As Catrin turned her head to check on the others, her eyes swept along the horizon, and she saw a light flashing in what appeared to be a pattern.

"The Zjhon," she whispered to Benjin, and he nodded again. She turned her attention back to the tribal leaders. Their conversation had grown more animated, and hushed tones gave way to angry shouts.

Knowing the Zjhon's arrival could lead to a bloodbath, Benjin stepped forward. "Gracious tribal leaders, I beg your pardon, but I fear dire happenings."

"Who you?" Vertook asked.

"Benjin, Guardian of the Herald."

"Speak," Vertook said after a moment.

"Enemy soldiers follow us. They are signaling each other. We will all be attacked if we stay here," Benjin said with a slight bow.

Vertook turned to the others, and his words led to more shouting. He turned back to Benjin. "Soldiers follow this one too," he said, nodding to Nat, "but we take care of them. We no fear soldiers but will take you to safe place." He placed two fingers in his mouth and whistled a long, high-pitched note. Several horsemen broke away from the line and brought five riderless horses forward. Vertook pointed to Chase and the others and waved for them to come forward.

The approaching horsemen dismounted and presented headgear to each of them. A major difference between these headgears and the ones worn by the tribesmen were that they bore no eye slits, and they would not be able to see where they were led. Each of her party was paired with a tribal leader, their horses tethered to those of their custodians. The tribesmen waited for the others to put on their headgears then helped them onto the horses.

The headgear was suffocating, and being unable to see left Catrin disoriented and queasy. A sudden cry broke the air, and the horses whipped around, moving off at a fast trot. Holding on to the horse's mane, she tried to synchronize her movements with his, but it was difficult without her sight and what seemed an erratic path, but she let her other senses guide her. Through their physical bond, she made contact with the horse. She felt an overwhelming sense of power and endurance but mostly loyalty. When she dug deeper, though, she could not help but sense the overwhelming sadness. This horse would carry her to the end of the world if he was asked, but the one to whom his loyalty belonged was gone. A feeling of separation and loss washed over Catrin, as her mount projected his mourning. Tears soaked her cheeks and the inside of her headgear; her nose became congested and breathing became even more difficult.

By the time they finally stopped, Catrin was exhausted mentally, physically, and emotionally. A muffled voice told them to remove their headgears, and she wrestled it from her head. Her sweat-soaked hair clung to her scalp, and even the warm breeze felt cool on her face. She gulped air as if she had been suffocating. Leaning against her mount, she felt as if he were leaning equally on her, as if bearing her here had brought some purpose to his life. It shocked her to sense his gratitude, and she was trying to let the noble animal know she felt the same when she noticed Vertook watching her. He approached, pulled his flask from his belt, and handed it to Catrin. She nodded her thanks and drank. The liquid had a tingling sweetness that was warm going down even though the liquid was relatively cool. She wondered for a brief moment how he kept it so cool then handed the flask back to him.

"You feel better now," he said roughly.

She thanked him and realized her eyes had adjusted to the fading light. She was surprised to find herself in the mountains, but these were not like the mountains of her home. They looked more like enormous piles of clay that soared high into the sky, taller than any she had seen before. They formed an almost complete ring around the small valley, and it was cool in their shade.

The tribesmen attended their horses, removing saddles and scraping sweat. They used large leather bags to water the horses. It took Catrin a moment to locate Benjin and the others, and she was relieved to see them unharmed. When she found Nat, he was limping toward her, leaning heavily on his staff. The ride had been rough on him as well.

As Catrin strode forward to meet him, no one moved to stop her. She walked past many tribesmen, who paid her little mind, seeming to be utterly consumed with tending to their mounts. The leaders, though, were gathered in a tight circle, obviously involved in another heated argument. When she reached Nat, he spoke out of the side of his mouth.

"We have much to discuss, but I can't speak freely," he said just above a whisper, and at the same moment, the tribal leaders separated. Vertook glared at Nat, and he moved away quickly.

"Calm and confident, li'l miss," Benjin whispered as the leaders approached. Catrin tried to appear composed, despite her anxiety.

Vertook swaggered up to them. "You, Catrin Volker, claim to be Herald of Istra, yes?"

"Yes," Catrin replied, wondering why they would ask her again.

"Prove it," he said simply.

Chapter 17

That which is not broken can be made better.
--Ivan Jharveski, inventor

* * *

Frozen in place, Catrin was terrified that trying to prove her powers and failing would mean their deaths. Even success would be fraught with danger.

"Do your thought-isolation meditation, *now*," Benjin said to her even as Vertook's glare demanded his silence.

She wasn't certain she could do it, but she had no better ideas. She sat on the ground, cupped her hands, and closed her eyes. Her mind was hammered with intense thoughts too fleeting to grab on to. She focused on her frustration, squeezed her eyes shut, and ignored everything else.

The gasp from a tribesman distracted her, and she channeled it into annoyance, letting it feed her anger. She forced her mind to be consumed by a raging tirade that included a litany of irritants and annoyances. Each grievance was slammed into that thought. While some part of her cautioned against such anger in a meditative state, she slammed that thought inside too and let it feed the rest. She had no choice but to give this effort all she had.

When her energy reached its apex, Catrin could find only an angry haze of emotions. She raised her cupped hands slightly and threw them out wide. Concentrating on a second, more positive thought, she slammed her hands together, smashing the accumulated mass of negative energy with the positive charge. A blast of hot air rolled away from her, and booming echoes resounded.

Catrin opened her eyes to see what she had wrought. Benjin had sat down heavily, looking as if he had been assaulted. The others looked as if they had been struck by an enormous hand, so dumbstruck were their expressions.

The leaders once again convened in a circle, and the meeting almost instantly transformed into a brawl. Men quickly separated those who fought, and soon they were back to their heated argument. Several more scuffles erupted, and Catrin waited in silence for the madness to play itself out. No one said anything, lest the enraged group turn on them.

The fighting reached a crescendo, and it seemed all of the tribal leaders were involved. An elderly man advanced toward the writhing mass, shouting, waving his arms, and pointing at the men. Catrin did not know what he said, but his words seemed to demand order.

The brawlers removed their headgears and began to treat their wounds. Vertook's nose was bloodied, and he began to stuff small bits of cloth up his nose to stanch the bleeding. The old man lectured the leaders while they dressed their wounds, and it was plain that he shamed them. When the meeting reconvened, it did so in a much more subdued fashion. After what seemed an interminable time, they appeared to come to some conclusion, and they turned to face Catrin. Vertook stepped forward.

"We not believe you. Proof not enough," he said, having difficulty speaking with his nose plugged. Catrin heard his words and felt a cold, sinking feeling in her stomach. This was not going well at all, she thought, and Nat's stricken look confirmed her fear.

"One more chance; you show *big* power"--he waved his arms out wide--"or all die for trying to fool Arghast," Vertook said.

Catrin moved in front of each tribal leader and looked each one in the eyes. She measured them individually, and many became offended and enraged. One man had to be restrained by his tribesmen, but Catrin did not flinch. These men were threatening to kill her and her companions, and she had nothing to lose. She strode slowly back to the center of the group and addressed everyone in the valley.

"The tribes of Arghast have assaulted the Herald of Istra and her Guardians. They have asked for proof of the Herald's power, and they have found her demonstration insufficient. Now I will show the tribes of Arghast the true power of the Herald at their own peril. Power is a dangerous thing, and to see it is to be threatened by it. Once unleashed, fate will choose its targets. I have tried to spare you, but you leave me no choice; I must put us all at risk. You have made your decision. So be it."

Her words echoed and hung ominously over the valley. Not waiting for a response, she strode straight to Nat and looked him in the eye. His fear was showing.

"May I have your staff?"

"I can deny you nothing, Lady Catrin," he said loudly and bowed, presenting his staff. She accepted it, and it felt good in her hands, lighter than it appeared. The iron-shod tip somehow balanced the strange staff, and she could feel its strength, as if it had power of its own. The wood was smooth and highly polished but was not slippery or oily. She hefted it with a determined smile and turned to her companions.

"Guardians of the Herald, I call you to duty. Please assist me while I satisfy the curiosity of the mighty Arghast tribes."

Benjin winced as a few men reacted to her comment. He and her friends stood before her, awaiting her command. She was not surprised that Nat joined the group, but when Vertook stepped up, it gave her heart.

While the tribes had been fighting, Catrin had been scanning her surroundings for energy. The mountains revealed nothing to aid her--except a small clue: water. She guessed heavy rains fell there occasionally, and when they did, the runoff would have to go somewhere.

She looked at the sand, sensing the surface then delving beneath it. The sand was not very deep in the valley, and in some places it was only a couple of feet deep. Under the loose sand, a layer of compressed sand formed brittle sandstone. Not far beneath the sandstone, she sensed a layer of bedrock. When she cast her senses deeper, through the bedrock, she found water.

Her father had taught her about artesian basins, and she remembered her lessons well. This valley had all the criteria. Rainwater drained from the mountains and into the basin, where it fed an underground aquifer. Layers of rock that rose higher into the mountains also collected and held runoff. Water was trapped below an impermeable layer of bedrock and, subsequently, was under intense pressure.

Trusting her instincts, she scanned the bedrock for thin spots and found her target at the back of the valley, a short walk from where she stood. Asking her Guardians to follow her, she strode confidently toward that spot.

The valley floor sloped downward, and the sand was a shade darker in the area Catrin selected. She stood atop the spot, closed her eyes, and reached into the sand with her senses, trying to be fully focused. Her mind pierced the bedrock and felt the intense repulsion of the water. Moments passed while she considered her options. The lives of many depended on her decision, and she did not want to make it in haste.

"What do you want us to do, Catrin?" Chase asked. "I think they're losing patience."

"I want you to dig."

"Oh for the love of everything good and right in this world, not the digging thing again," Strom said, and Chase smacked him on the back of the head.

"We'll do what you say, Catrin," Chase said. "Just tell us."

"Dig a hole here, please. Make it as deep as you can," she replied, leaning on Nat's staff while the others dug. She needed to conserve her energy for the task ahead, although she was not certain she could do anything. The energy the comet had spilled into her world was fading like a scent on a breeze, and it was becoming increasingly difficult to detect its energy, let alone harness it.

Her senses seem to have dulled in the time since the comet was last seen in the sky, and she wondered if she could get those sensations back, but she put the thought from her mind and concentrated on what she must do. Her Guardians made good progress, and the hole was already quite deep. Chase stood in the hole, and only his head and shoulders were above ground level.

The initial dig had been relatively easy, allowing them to use their hands as shovels, but when they reached the layer of sandstone, they had trouble going deeper. They used everything they had to break up the brittle sandstone, and they removed it in large chunks. Catrin desperately hoped the tribesmen would have enough patience to let them finish, and as the last of the sandstone layer was cleared from a small area, she saw the bedrock.

Running her senses over it, looking for the thinnest point, she found a likely spot, but it was close to the edge of their hole. "Clear that area, please," she said, and they quickly removed the sandstone. "I need to finish this," she said. Benjin helped her into the hole and handed Nat's staff to her.

With a deep breath, she gathered all the energy she could pull from the night air. The moon was bright above the mountains, but she felt little energy from it. She mustered what she could and drove the staff into the bedrock with all her strength. The staff struck stone and rang a sharp discord through the valley. Sparks flew and a few small chips broke away, but her blow had done little damage. Her next blow struck with such force she felt the staff flex in her grasp, and she feared it might snap in two. She paused to catch her breath and looked up at the concern in her Guardians' faces.

The crushing weight of responsibility threatened to smother her, and she could almost feel the walls of the hole closing in around her. Struggling to stay calm, she reached into the rock, looking for any imperfection, any flaw she could exploit. Close to the surface, she found an almost imperceptible hairline crack, and her hopes soared.

She concentrated on the crack and focused on her target point. She hefted the staff and struck the bedrock hard, large chunks of stone shattering among the sparks. There was a long way to go, but she had made some progress.

"You'd best hurry, Catrin. The tribes are growing hostile," Benjin said.

As she leaned down to look closely at the rock, her fish carving fell from her shirt and hung just below her face. She pulled the leather thong over her head and held the carved fish in one of her palms, wondering if she could draw energy from it. She remembered how the carving had grown hot enough to burn her leg when she slammed the ground with power, and she wondered if she hadn't been drawing from it then. The carving had appeared to recharge itself when kept

187

in the light, and her gut said she had just stumbled onto its secret.

Grasping the staff in both hands, she held it aloft, the carving wedged between the staff and her palm. She centered herself as the carving grew warm, and she felt energy begin to flow into her. Her senses heightened as the power coursed through her veins, and as it entered her, she sensed it leaving the carving. Knowing she had no time to waste, she used all her strength and all her emotion to drive the staff into the bedrock, striking it with such force that the blow sent shockwaves echoing through the valley.

The bedrock gave way as she reached the bottom of her massive swing, and she fell forward for an instant as a large section collapsed downward. Almost instantly, the force of the trapped water sent the broken rock soaring into the air. Catrin fell back as the staff was ripped from her grasp by a huge column of water, which shot high into the night sky.

Catrin scrambled backward out of the hole, the powerful spray buffeting her as she clawed her way to safety. She retreated from the water's fury, and the Arghast backed away before her in fear and reverence. Vertook stared at the fountain, dumbstruck.

Chaos ensued as the enormous shockwave sent loose rocks and stone tumbling down into the valley. Several people were struck, the horses panicked, and men scrambled to reach them to prevent the frightened animals from injuring themselves.

They all stared at the towering fountain with amazement and disbelief. When the height of the fountain did not dwindle, they slowly began to believe that they were in the presence of the Herald.

Catrin watched as the water fell from the sky and seeped into the sand. The sand became saturated, and soon water would fill this end of the valley.

Benjin, Chase, Osbourne, and Strom moved to her side, overjoyed. They speculated on how long the fountain would last. Catrin was physically drained, mentally exhausted, and wanted nothing more than sleep. The carved fish still in the palm of her hand looked terrible; it was chalky to the touch, and its surface was again dull.

She leaned over and placed it back around her neck. When she looked up, she found herself surrounded by kneeling tribal leaders and tribesmen; even her Guardians knelt. Vertook was in the front and center of the mass, and she realized that he alone belonged to all three groups.

Nat retrieved his staff from the sand. Then he stood before Catrin, facing those assembled. "Behold the Herald of Istra! She calls you to your duty. Will the tribes of Arghast answer her call?"

Catrin was startled by the ululating cry that rose from the throats of the Arghast and was overwhelmed when she saw that the horses, too, had gone to their knees. And her mentor and strength, Benjin, was prostrate on the ground.

Her power and accomplishment would have exhilarated her at any other time, but the day's events had been exhausting and she was lightheaded. Her vision fading, she grew dizzy and fell to the sand.

* * *

Standing before the fountain, where before had been nothing more than sand and rock, Vertook was in awe. No power could have been more moving to him than to bring water to the desert, no feat more seemingly unachievable. All his life he had waited for this moment, waited for some event to prove his life had meaning. Now that he had witnessed that event, he realized his entire life had been wasted, wandering from one dried up hole to another. For him, nothing would ever be the same. The things that had meant the most to him in life, besides his wife and his horse, suddenly were meaningless. All that mattered now was to serve Catrin, to protect her so that she might bring water to all the world.

He made in a moment a decision that should have been agonizing, yet it was surprisingly simple. "Harat!" he said without taking his gaze from the water. Only a moment later, he felt Harat by his side, sensed the calm determination and sense of honor that had always marked him as a leader. Without saying a word, Vertook untied the sash that looped over his left shoulder--passing directly over his heart. He'd taken reassurance from it many times, knowing that the sash of the leader would protect his valiant yet frail heart. Now he no longer needed it, but even more, he could no longer uphold the responsibilities that came along with the sash. Remaining silent, he handed the sash to Harat, who hesitated to take it. Vertook thrust the sash into Harat's hand, his final command as tribal leader. Harat took a step back, placed his hand over his heart, and when he bowed down, tears fell from his eyes.

As Harat walked away, Vertook pulled his gaze from the fountain long enough to watch the man who would now protect and guide those he loved. Tears fell from his own cheeks as he released the responsibilities he had worked so hard to obtain. Harat placed the sash underneath his garment, as of yet unwilling to reveal Vertook's wishes. He walked quietly through the crowd as if nothing out of the ordinary had occurred, and Vertook breathed a mighty sigh of relief; he had chosen well.

* * *

Not far from where Vertook stood, Chase, Strom, and Osbourne gathered.

"When she said to dig, I wasn't expecting . . . I mean . . ." Strom began, but he just trailed off and shrugged.

"I know," Chase said. "I can't believe it either."

"How did she know?" Osbourne asked, looking at the fountain. "How does she do these things?"

"I don't know," Chase said. "I don't understand any of it, and I really want to. This whole thing just keeps getting bigger, and I don't know where it'll stop." He knew he should try to be more positive for the sake of the others, but he couldn't help but speak what was on his mind. "I just don't want to see Cat get hurt. You know how she is."

"The first time I ever met her," Osbourne said, "she was all dirty and scraped up from catching one of our pigs that got loose. The pig was nearly as big as she was, but she carried him all the way across the field to bring him to us. Looked like she took a tumble or two on her way too. She cried 'cause she thought he was hurt."

"I met her at Master Jarvis's lessons," Strom said. "She always looked sad and fragile after her mom died." His words were met with silence heavy with emotion.

"I know I've said this before," Osbourne said without looking up, "but I'm really sorry about your mom and Catrin's mom and Strom's dad. I wish they didn't die."

Chase kicked the sand in front of him. He chastised himself for letting a tear gather in his eye. The pain should be forgotten, he thought, those wounds long since healed, but they were not. When he noticed Strom struggling with pain of his own, it made him feel no better.

Osbourne shifted his weight from foot to foot in the uncomfortable silence. "What do we do now?" He asked, his voice betraying his anxiety.

Chase put a hand over his growling stomach, "I think we should try to track down some food."

Chapter 18

Of all the varied life forms on the planet Godsland, the pyre-orchid is the most curious, only blooming in the wake of forest fires.
--Sister Munion, Cathuran monk

* * *

Catrin opened her eyes for a moment, adjusted the pillow beneath her head, and pulled soft blankets over her shoulders. The morning air was cool, and she closed her eyes to drift back to sleep when voices awakened her. When she became fully aware, she noticed her surroundings. She lay on a light, fluffy bed with a similarly made pillow, which she guessed were both stuffed with down.

A small tent, made of sheer material, shaded her. The breeze passed through the fabric, but bugs could not. It was artfully made and was doubtless the finest the Arghast had to offer. Still dressed in the clothes she'd lived in for days, she was in desperate need of a good bath. Pushing back the tent flap, she walked out into a bright glare that momentarily blinded her, and she heard the sudden murmur of many hushed voices. When her vision cleared, she found all of the Arghast watching her intently. She was not sure what they expected, but their stares were intense and disconcerting. It took some time for her to decide what to say to the assembled crowd, and what came from her mouth was the plain truth.

"If I could trouble someone to help me, I am quite hungry. Is there any food left from the morning meal?" she asked almost timidly. The activity resulting from her request was astounding, and it seemed they all felt compelled to try to help. Some men scrambled to set up a small table; others made a comfortable seat for her from several large cushions, and still others erected a makeshift sunshade made of the same material as her tent.

She sat at the table and waited. People began to approach her with a lavish array of foods. Women were now part of the group, some in typical female clothing and others dressed like the men. Catrin had seen no women the day before and was surprised to see them now. The crowd was now nearly double the number she recalled. Men and women offered fruits, meats, breads, and one elderly man brought her more of the drink she remembered Vertook had given her. Catrin recognized him from his castigation of the tribal leaders, but he gave her a kindly smile.

"What is this drink?"

"Desert mist," he responded with a wink. "How to make is secret, something only spoke in private. We speak alone soon, yes?"

"Yes, of course, and thank you." She paused to take a sip of the desert mist. "What are you called, sir?" she asked.

"Called Aged Goat by most," he said with a toothless grin, "but true name is Mika. You call me Mika. Yes?"

"Indeed, Mika, I will," she responded warmly, and Mika retreated through the masses. Catrin had never been served in such a way, and she found it disquieting; it felt wrong to accept their generosity, to be selfish and indulgent, but it seemed just as wrong to refuse their gifts.

Her hunger sated, she wanted a nap, but more than that she desperately wanted to get clean. As if someone were reading her mind, several women approached Catrin with soft towels and scented soaps. One motioned for her to follow and walked toward the towering fountain Catrin had created. She was delighted to see a pond forming outward from the fountain, and she hoped it would continue to grow. She envisioned a lush oasis nestled in the valley, full of life and vigor--a jewel in the desert.

Two women unfolded a large, thick cloth, which they held up for privacy. Catrin took soap that smelled of peppermint then undressed and dipped her toes into the water. It was bitterly cold, and the frigid spray made her shiver, but she was thankful for the opportunity to get clean. The shallow water at the edge was not quite as cold, and she used it to wash herself. The soap created a rich, aromatic lather, and Catrin lavished in the fragrance as she washed off the grime of many days.

When she emerged from the pool, the same woman who had led her to the pond brought her a soft towel. She dried herself and looked for her clothes, but they were not where she had left them. Another woman approached with clothes similar to Catrin's. She knew that it had taken them much thought and effort to find these for her, and she felt almost unworthy. She put on the borrowed clothes, and they were a fair fit. The shirtsleeves were a little long, but she rolled them up, insisting that it was just the way she liked her sleeves.

There was more food and drink when she returned from her bathing, and Benjin and the boys were there too. In the flurry of the morning, she had not thought of them, and she was relieved to see they were fine--just dirty. The women offered the towels and soap to them, and they wasted no time in getting to the fountain.

The leaders had congregated nearby, looking subdued and clearly waiting for her to speak first. With her hunger satiated and her friends attended to, Catrin turned her attention to them.

"Leaders of the Arghast tribes, will you sit with me?" Slowly the men began to come forward and seat themselves on the ground around her. As Catrin lowered herself to the ground, several rushed to get her a cushion, but she declined with a smile. "I've not come here to rule you or to be worshipped by you. I'm a simple girl, not a goddess or a queen. I don't place myself above you. Speak freely and know your worth."

There was confusion in the crowd, and Vertook approached Catrin. He repeated what she said in his own words and she nodded. With Vertook translating, Catrin continued, trying to find simple words to express complex things. "I praise your leaders for their devotion to truth, for they did not blindly accept my claims or the words of Nat Dersinger. They chose to make me prove myself, just as I would have done. I've now proven my power to you, and we need to reach an understanding. We must put aside any mistakes we've made and forgive others for hurting us," she said, pausing. Murmurs passed through the crowd as Vertook translated. When she addressed them again, she spoke louder.

"Will the tribes of Arghast protect the Herald of Istra?" she asked. The people raised their voices in a high, ululating

194

cry and shook their fists above their heads before Vertook even spoke. Catrin raised her hands to them, requesting silence. She spoke again.

"Tribes of Arghast! Embrace your duty and take pride in what you have already done. You answered the Call of the Herald, and your valor will not be forgotten. You have pledged yourselves to the Herald, and she calls you to battle. How do you answer?" Their cries echoed off the mountains and reverberated along the peaks.

"The Godfist is under attack. Invaders have come to destroy us. The Godfist needs a defender, and the Herald of Istra calls on the tribes of Arghast because they are strong, they are fierce, and they will prevail!" she said, the words spilling forth from her heart. Vertook translated her words with as much emotion as she had expressed, and then he started the crowd shouting "Catrin" in unison. The chanting grew louder and louder. She raised her arms, and the crowd hushed.

"I thank you for your bravery and honor. Take great pride in yourselves and your mighty nation. I will meet with your leaders, and we will make our plans. Many blessings to you all!" As the crowd dispersed, Catrin returned to her seat.

"You very gracious, Lady Catrin. We honor and support you. We have many gifts to give upon you, and we have sorrow for doubting of you," Vertook said then took a deep breath. He continued hesitantly. "I been asked again to speak for all Arghast. Others not understand your talk as much."

"Please speak how you feel, Vertook, and so will I," she said, smiling. Turning to the men closest to her, she said, "Please tell me your names and the names of your people."

The leaders smiled and nodded, and each introduced himself: Harat introduced himself as the chief of the Viper clan. Catrin cast a confused glance at Vertook, who had previously claimed to be chief of the Viper clan, but he said nothing. Halmsa was chief of the Wind clan, Irvil of the Sun clan, Malluke of the Horse clan, Spenwar of the Scorpion clan, and Cheslo of the Cactus clan.

"I am honored to know the names of the revered leaders of the Arghast. As you have received me, I pledge to protect you with all of my strength. But now I have to ask

195

for your help. I must leave the Godfist on a boat, and the enemy soldiers will try to stop me." She knew she could be risking the entire Arghast nation by involving them in a war, but she did not know what to do but follow her instincts and hope they were right.

"I need some time with my Guardians," she said, and as Vertook started to stand, she asked, "Vertook, would you please stay here and plan our escape? We can meet again later."

"Vertook is glad to do that," was his reply, and he turned to the group and began to talk with the leaders.

"Greetings, Lady Catrin," Nat said as he walked toward her. He wore clean clothes, and his hair was not as wild as usual.

"Hello, Nat, and please call me Catrin, like you always have."

"As you wish, Catrin. I'm sorry I couldn't deliver this dire news sooner, but it wasn't possible with what's been going on," he said. "I'm afraid that by some deception, your destination is known to the Zjhon. I don't know how they found out, but we'll need to be extra careful about who we talk to about our plans."

"How did you come to know the Zjhon knew where I was going?"

"It wasn't just one thing, you see. Much of the Zjhon fleet left the harbor, sailing east toward the cove, but ships were also reported off the northern coast. Before I escaped Harborton, Miss Mariss got news the cove had been raided and one of the pirate ships captured. It was enough. The news came from the ship that escaped, and those on board suggested a new place to meet you. We need to get you there as soon as possible. Every day they remain in hiding is risky." It seemed like a thin hope to Catrin, surrounded by the Zjhon, and she felt trapped.

"Before I leave, there is a most unpleasant task I am obligated to perform," he said and took an object from within his robe unlike anything Catrin had ever seen before. An ivory tube, it was about as long as her forearm and decorated with fanciful carvings that were enhanced with gold and gemstones. The ends were topped with gold caps in the shape of a man and woman embracing--the symbol of the Zjhon empire. Catrin reached out slowly, unsure she wanted to accept it.

"This is the other reason I think we've been betrayed. This contains a message and was delivered to Miss Mariss through the channels of the Vestrana. Somehow the Zjhon have infiltrated the Vestrana, and we have no idea whom to trust. I'll leave you so you can read the message, but we must speak again soon. There are many things we should discuss," he said as he walked away.

Catrin felt a new burden on her shoulders. She feared what was written inside, afraid the words might find some way to hurt her and those around her. She walked to where Benjin stood. He looked refreshed after his bath and was pulling his hair into a braid as she approached.

"A storm is coming," he said, rubbing his shoulder, but when he saw the look on Catrin's face, he waited for the bad news. She handed him the tube and told him how it had been delivered. Benjin was stunned and hesitated to take it-- perhaps for the same reasons Catrin was loath to hold it, both fearing what it might contain.

"Please, read it for me. I don't have the courage."

"Perhaps that would be wise. They could have rigged it with a trap," Benjin said. He carefully removed the golden cap. It fell away, and nothing leaped from the tube. He pulled the rolled parchment from the tube, placed it on the ground, and examined it closely before picking it up. He unrolled it and read aloud.

Salutations to the Herald of Istra from His Eminence, Archmaster Emsin Kelsig Belegra, spiritual leader and chief evangelist of the Holy Church of Zjhon.

The Zjhon nation has extended its warmest greetings, and you have evaded my emissaries and ignored our requests for talks of peace. You must not care that lives will be lost.

I do not know why you wish ill toward the Zjhon nation, but we only seek your salvation. Our request for talks of peace still stands, despite your refusals. If you present yourself to any of my emissaries, they will bring you directly to me, unharmed. Your companions are also welcome.

197

If you persist in your attempted flight from the Godfist, we will interpret it as a hostile action against the Zjhon nation. For your own sake, do not seek to flee or to invade the Greatland. My emissaries will remain on the Godfist until you have presented yourself to me personally. This matter must be settled between you and me. It would be a pity if your countrymen and mine suffered needlessly as a result of your selfishness. I beg you to put away your ego and do what you know is right.

I trust you will choose your path wisely.

Most gracious regards,

Archmaster Belegra, humble servant of the Gods

"I don't know which part is the most offensive," Catrin began. "I've never heard so many thinly veiled threats and insults. Why would they wish to provoke me in such a way? What does he mean, I have refused their offers for talks of peace? No one has made any such offer. He makes it sound as if their invasion is my fault!"

"Please stay calm, li'l miss. They wrote those things to provoke you, hoping you would do something hasty and foolish. It's a common tactic in warfare: taunt your opponent and instill doubt and fear in him whenever possible. There's not much in that letter we didn't already know. Try not to fret over it."

But she could not put the message out of her mind. "I'm going to take some time to meditate. Perhaps I'll find some inspiration," she said as she went into her tent. Her own clothes were by her bed, cleaned and folded. The solitude of the tent and the feeling of changing back into her old clothes comforted her, as if they helped her hold onto that which was Catrin. Her thoughts were scattered, and she tried to focus and meditate on each one. She pondered the archmaster's words and Benjin's reaction to them, but she thought there had to be some undercurrent she was not seeing. She found no answers.

The sound of many people shouting yanked her from her thoughts. Shadows ran past her tent, and the commotion continued to grow louder. Benjin reached her as she was emerging from her tent.

"What's going on?" she yelled above the noise.

"I don't know. When I heard all the commotion, I came here to make sure you were safe. Let's find Vertook." They scanned the sea of confusion for Vertook, but it was difficult to identify anyone in the morass, and it took a while to locate him. Benjin spotted him wading through the mob and heading for Catrin. He shouted and waved his arms, but they could not hear his words, and they waited anxiously for him to get clear of the throng. He rushed toward them, and the chaos he left behind seemed to take on a purpose as horses were saddled. That meant the Arghast were preparing to ride, and Catrin's anxiety was intense when she heard Vertook's words.

"Many soldiers coming from all around us."

Chapter 19

Belief systems are fragile things. How will you react when your reality suddenly ceases to exist?
--Ain Giest, Sleepless One

* * *

"You ride with me," Vertook said, giving Catrin no choice but to follow him to his horse. They would all ride on horses with the other men, whose saddles contained a second set of passenger flaps that held soft leather stirrups. The flaps provided little cushion, but they had a large ridge around the back that would help keep them in place when they were riding at speed.

Before Catrin could get her boots into the stirrups firmly, Vertook issued a battle cry and the horse leaped into a full gallop. Catrin grabbed at the leather straps that hung from the sides of the saddle and held on with white knuckles, struggling to get her boots in the stirrups. Once her boots were firmly planted, she settled into the rhythm of the horse's powerful stride. Vertook's eyes showed his pleasure that the Herald had such fine riding skills.

The riders sent clouds of dust into the wind, and Catrin squinted to keep sand from her eyes. Vertook reached into his saddlebag and produced a headgear for Catrin--this time one with eye slits. She felt a little unsteady as they rode, but it was much better than sand in her eyes.

Cheslo and the others rode in tight formation with Vertook, and Catrin saw her companions donning headgears as well. Like a flash flood, they rolled toward the valley entrance in a headlong rush, lest they become trapped.

The mouth of the valley was narrow, and the horsemen funneled together, close enough for Catrin to touch the rider beside her, and as they passed through the narrow opening, they smashed together, nearly unhorsing her.

Clear of the valley, tribesmen surrounded their leaders in a tight, diamond-shaped formation. Vertook directed them straight toward the line of Zjhon soldiers approaching from the north. The wind whipped, and visibility dropped to near zero. The Zjhon were obscured by a veil of dust and were barely visible along the horizon. Despite greater numbers, the Zjhon attack seemed ill advised; they were still distant and spread thin, but Catrin supposed their hands had been forced when the Arghast intercepted their prey. Had the Arghast been less vigilant, she would have been trapped.

She turned her head to see who was behind her, but she could see little through the headgear and the dust that roiled up behind them. As she gazed higher, she could still see the top of the towering fountain, and she was amazed to see a pair of eagles floating on the thermals in the mist surrounding it. They swooped and dived through the water, and Catrin felt a moment of vindication and joy.

The Arghast remained true to the straight path they had chosen, and the enemy forces seemed to be gauging their purpose. As the Zjhon formed into a more dense and organized force, Catrin shouted to Vertook, telling him to take evasive action, but he continued on his direct course.

Looking at the dense formation of Arghast surrounding her, she wondered if Vertook planned to ride straight through the gathering Zjhon. The closer they came to the Zjhon, the more prepared the enemy appeared, looking ready to stand fast against the approaching onslaught. Many soldiers dismounted and held long pikes to protect against the charge, but by concentrating in one area, they committed themselves to holding that ground.

Vertook raised a reverberating cry, and riders charged in every direction, forcing the Zjhon to abandon the ground they held. Catrin held on tight as Vertook turned his mount sharply and headed east. The Arghast horses were winded, but so were those carrying the Zjhon. The Zjhon horses had not been desert bred and were on unfamiliar turf.

Catrin looked around desperately for her Guardians, but the headgears and the dust made it nearly impossible to identify anyone. Vertook's gambit provided a temporary advantage, but hordes of Zjhon reinforcements began to flood the desert, swarming around isolated pockets of the Arghast. One of the tribal leaders rode in close, and Catrin heard Nat shouting and pointing northeast.

"To the cliffs! Must get Catrin to the cliffs!"

Vertook nodded and angled them in the direction Nat indicated. No matter which direction they chose, they would have to break through the Zjhon at some point, and Vertook veered for the largest gap in their lines. In the same instant, Nat cried out in warning. Catrin snapped her gaze to where he pointed, and Vertook cursed when he spotted a formation of soldiers closing in from the north.

These men and their horses wore protective gear, making them much better prepared for desert fighting. The horses showed a bit of lather but did not appear as winded as the horse beneath Catrin. Vertook shouted and turned east, pushing their mount to the limit. Catrin was humbled by the dedication and courage of the Arghast horses, who gave all they had. Feeling such affection and gratitude for the mount that was so valiantly bearing her and Vertook, she placed her hand on the horse's croup behind the saddle, and unaware, her emotions--love, peace, and energy--flowed from her hand into the horse. As she touched him, her hand grew hot, and a tingling pulsated in her palm. The horse seemed to respond to her gentle touch and was rejuvenated. It leaped ahead of the horses surrounding it.

Vertook slowed his mount to let the others make up the ground he had gained. The approaching Zjhon formed into a tight wedge and closed at great speed, making Catrin wonder if this was where the fighting would truly begin. It was terrifying and she could not envision it.

The tension in the air was palpable, and she could hear little above the muted thunder of hooves pounding the sand. No one spoke, shouted, or cried out. It was eerie and unnerving, and Catrin could feel the hair on her arms and neck stand on end. The approaching Zjhon were mostly armed with swords, but a few carried bows. The Arghast were armed with wooden spears, and they looked puny beside the cold iron.

Vertook desperately sought to evade the menacing wedge, but it continued to grow closer. The low din was shattered when the Zjhon overtook them, cries of man and horse ringing above the muted thunder, accompanied by metal striking hardened wood. Catrin ducked under a sword as it whistled by her head and was still off balance when a soldier slammed his mount into hers. She was nearly knocked from the saddle by the impact and leaned out perilously to one side as Vertook smashed the soldier across the face with the butt of his spear.

As she straightened in the saddle, Catrin caught a glimpse of Cheslo and Benjin. She screamed as she saw them collide, at full speed, with a Zjhon soldier. She watched in horror as all three went down, and she was unable to distinguish anything in the chaos. The Zjhon were trying to divide the Arghast to deal with them individually, and they were doing an alarmingly good job of it. Vertook and Catrin were forced away from the others and found themselves surrounded by Zjhon.

* * *

Riding behind a man whose name he did not know and whose dialect he did not seem to speak, Chase watched Benjin go down. He thought he saw Catrin nearby. A Zjhon soldier was bearing down on Benjin, and at the same time, at least a dozen were going after Catrin. Time seemed to slow as Chase was torn by a decision that must be made in an instant; there was no time for debate or second thoughts. He yanked on the shoulder of the man in front of him, pointing and screaming, and by the mercy of the gods, the tribal leader turned his horse toward where Benjin had fallen. Chase cursed and climbed to one side of the horse. Putting his right leg in the left stirrup, he coiled his muscles like a snake about to strike. An instant before a Zjhon blade would take Benjin's life, Chase jumped.

* * *

Osbourne cried out as one of his boots slipped from the stirrup, only Spenwar's firm grip kept him from tumbling to the sand. Riders came from all directions, and it was difficult to tell friend from foe, but when a horse materialized from the dust bearing two riders, he knew it was one of his friends. Strom roared as they passed, throwing what looked like a pear at an oncoming Zjhon horse. The fruit struck the horse in the forehead, startling the animal while it was at a full gallop. The horse and its helpless rider veered sideways and crashed into another Zjhon soldier.

Osbourne would have cheered the victory, but more riders came, and he followed Strom's lead. He opened one of the pouches along the saddle and found soft cheeses wrapped in broad, supple leaves. Knowing they would have no need for food if they did not first escape, he took half of them and began throwing them at approaching Zjhon riders. Though he was aiming for the horses' eyes, he often missed, but one bundle of cheese struck a Zjhon soldier in the face and exploded on impact.

The blinded soldier dropped his reins and tried to clear the cheese from his eyes, but the cheese clung to his skin and lashes, and sand began to collect on it, making matters worse. Unprepared when his horse suddenly veered around a fallen rider, the soldier flew from the saddle and plowed face-first into the sand. Osbourne let out a brief cheer just before a Zjhon horse struck them broadside and at full speed. As the world tumbled around him, Osbourne gave thanks for all that life had given him.

* * *

Activity to Catrin's right caught her attention, and she turned to see what was happening. The Arghast had adapted quickly and were using the Zjhon's ramming technique against them. She watched, horrified, as the Arghast crashed recklessly into the Zjhon. One horse caught her attention as it bowled over an unsuspecting Zjhon soldier, its second passenger taking down the Zjhon with his staff. Nat howled, wide eyed, like a man possessed as he searched for a new foe.

Catrin recognized Irvil of the Sun clan, who rode before Nat. Irvil attacked with a fury, driving his horse into the Zjhon, thrashing them with his spears, and yelling exultantly whenever Nat landed a blow. They cleared a hole in the Zjhon line just large enough for them to break free. Vertook and Irvil urged their horses on, and somehow the marvelous beasts found their wind. They surged ahead of the pursuing

Zjhon and thundered toward the rocky borderland where a sparse forest skirted the cliffs.

Vertook let Irvil and Nat lead since only Nat knew their destination. Catrin could see several Zjhon closing in from behind. She feared their swords, but the men armed with bows terrified her more. Her back exposed, she felt naked and vulnerable and continued to watch for arrows, but the archers were out of bow range and had loosed none, which only increased her terror. Skilled archers would not waste arrows on bad shots, and these men seemed prepared to wait.

As the land sloped upward, stunted trees grew thick, stinging with their branches, and loose rock shifted under hooves. The trail became as much an adversary as the Zjhon, and the nearly spent horses struggled with the terrain.

A sharp crack sounded from behind, followed by sickening thud, and as Catrin spun around, she saw a horse go down, its leg shattered. The flailing animal tumbled down the rocks, taking two others and their riders with it. Irvil struggled to outrun the remaining Zjhon, following a winding path that was barely more than a game trail. Low-hanging branches assaulted them, and brambles clung, biting deep. Catrin counted four Zjhon remaining, and she shouted to Irvil, urging him on, but he was hard pressed, and despite his best efforts, the Zjhon were making better time. All they could do was press on as relentlessly as they could.

Irvil barked a warning, and Vertook veered away from a hornets' nest so large it covered the tree that hosted it. Catrin watched as the Zjhon grew closer to the nest; then, in one fluid motion, she drew her knives and launched them at the nest.

Her old belt knife with the broken tip flew wide, striking only bark, but in the next instant, her Zjhon blade struck home, exploding the nest into a cloud of paper and enraged hornets. Moving like an angry specter with a shared life, the mass descended on the Zjhon with unmitigated fury.

Cries of man and horse split the air, and Catrin watched, awed but horrified by what she had done. Two horses went down and the rest panicked. Some of the hornets overtook Catrin and Vertook, and their horses surged ahead with

205

renewed energy born of pain. Vertook had to duck under many branches, and Catrin was nearly unhorsed by leaves that raked her face and a branch that struck her in the forehead.

The Zjhon fell farther and farther behind, and Irvil took full advantage of the situation. He pushed his mount through brush and brambles, and the noble animal lowered his head and pressed on, ignoring his scrapes and many bleeding cuts. Catrin kept a watchful eye on the woods behind them, seeing soldiers moving between the trees, but they were still a good distance back and moving more slowly.

The forest thinned and gave way to a rocky incline, beyond which loomed the bluffs--the absolute edge of Catrin's world. Sorely winded, the horses were clearly in no condition to carry them across such terrain. Vertook and Irvil spoke quietly and, in a moment, seemed to agree on a difficult decision. First, they dismounted; then they helped their passengers to the ground.

Vertook and Irvil then did what would have seemed unthinkable in other circumstances: they commanded their horses to go on without them, but it was entirely contrary to the animals' nature, and they stood their ground, confused and agitated. The men persisted, and Catrin watched in anguish as Vertook chased his horse away with a flick of a switch. The bond shared by the Arghast and their horses was like mated souls, and it grieved Catrin to witness the scene. The image of these animals, going against their very natures, retreating through the trees--their ears pinned back and their tails tucked--was burned into her senses, and she knew she would never forget it.

Nat took the lead and scrambled up the rocks to look over the edge. He scanned the water, pulled a piece of polished metal from his robe, and signaled wildly. Sounds of pursuit grew closer, and Nat searched the water desperately. Then Irvil grabbed him and spun him to the right. A bright signal, not far east of where they stood, was coming from small boats secluded under the shadow of the cliff. Elated, Nat rushed east along the cliffs. Catrin still feared the soldiers would catch them, and Vertook and Irvil stayed as far from the edge as they could.

Suddenly soldiers emerged from the trees, and Catrin saw one of them nock an arrow. Nat ran to a large rock that jutted out over the water. Catrin and Vertook rushed to join him. When they looked down at the small boats below, the height terrified Catrin, and she turned to retreat. Before she could take a step, however, Irvil cried out and rushed toward the approaching soldiers. He held his ground against a man wielding a sword, but Catrin saw the archer draw and loose his arrow in one smooth motion. She knew where it would strike even as the archer's fingertips slid from the bowstring. Tears filled her eyes as she turned back to the cliff. Vertook stood at her side, looking grim and determined. As one, they prepared to meet their deaths, but as they turned to make their final stand, Nat spoke softly.

"I'm very sorry to have to do this," he said, and Catrin knew what was about to happen as she felt his hand on the small of her back. She screamed as he pushed her over the edge.

* * *

Dust and the smell of blood choked Strom as he pulled himself from under the horse that had given its life to save his. Luck had been with him, and he was uninjured. The same could not be said for Malluke, who was under the horse, dead. As Strom stood, his head spun, and the world around him was a blur. After a moment of shock, he recalled the danger and took a sword from the nearby body of a soldier. Before he could even test his swing, a shadowy rider materialized within a cloud of dust and bore down on him with speed.

Stepping back and bracing himself, Strom prepared to take a desperate swing, but then he saw it was Chase. Leaning down from his saddle, Chase reached out and grabbed Strom as he passed, barely slowing. Strom grabbed on and leaped up in the saddle behind Chase, and he was glad to see that Chase had stolen a Zjhon horse. At least it had a bridle and reins.

"Where are the others?" Strom shouted.

"I don't know. Let's go find them," Chase replied as he drove their mount to greater speed.

Chapter 20

There is no greater act of faith than to put your life in the hands of a stranger.
--Guntar Berga, soldier

* * *

The wind buffeted Catrin about mercilessly as she fell after Nat pushed her off the cliff. The air was sucked from her lungs, and she was unable to control her limbs. She flailed wildly to right herself then tucked herself into a ball, preparing to absorb the impact.

The waves rushed toward her with impossible speed, and she struck the water feet first. The impact forced the last of the air from her lungs, and her momentum drove her far beneath the waves. Terrified, she fought to reach the distant surface. Hampered by her clothing, she didn't think she would make it. Her lungs burned for air, and only willpower kept her from parting her lips to inhale water.

Above her, light reflected off the surface, dancing, taunting her, just out of reach. Her body demanded breath, and she gulped, repulsed by the salty taste and burning in her throat. Her body went into spasm and thrashed with little effect. Something hard struck her, but she barely felt it. Darkness was settling on her as rough hands yanked her from the water.

When the darkness faded, she found herself in the belly of a small boat. A man was beating on her chest and blowing air into her lungs with his mouth. Her body convulsed, and he turned her onto her side so she could empty her lungs and stomach. The small boat tossed violently, compounding her disorientation.

As she tried to right herself, the men in the boat continued to row vigorously. Her stomach betrayed her again, and she clung to the gunwale, feeling sea spray on her face. The wind was cold, and noticing her shivering, one of the men draped a blanket across her back. She wrapped herself tightly, but still she shivered violently and her teeth chattered.

As she regained control of herself, she saw there were four men huddled in the small craft, rowing as if their lives depended on it. Several other boats floated nearby, and they all struggled against the current. The men were oddly garbed and had darkly tanned skin. Catrin had never seen men adorn themselves with jewelry, but these wore rings on their fingers and some had earrings. She had seen tattoos, but none like the complex patterns that ran up one man's arms, looking like a live painting.

None spoke, though, not even to one another, and Catrin huddled in silence, not trusting her voice to speak. Cold rock jutted from the water, looming over them, and Catrin feared the waves would batter them against the imposing cliffs. As she watched, the men turned the boat sideways to the bluffs and rowed into the shadows. As they entered the gloom, an opening materialized before them, previously hidden in the darkness. Cool, musty air barely stirred, and as they rounded a bend, they were bathed in soft torchlight. The violence of the thrashing waters subsided completely.

Their rowing was now confined to keeping the craft in the center of a natural channel that flowed into a large cave. It was lined with jagged rock, and firelight danced on the water ahead. Around a bend floated a ship in a cavern just barely large enough to contain it. The ship didn't look quite right, and Catrin realized it was missing its mainmast.

Above them, on a rock shelf, a fire burned and at least a dozen people milled about, but when they saw the boats return, they ran up the gangplank of the ship, tossed down lines, and secured them to large iron rings on the boat's rails. The men above used a windlass and a series of large pulleys to haul the heavy boats up to the point where they were level with the deck. It was only then she realized there were three boats in addition to her own that must have been waiting for her and her companions below the cliffs. When each boat was empty of people, they hauled it onto the deck and turned it on its side. It took a dozen men to lift the boat to the hooks where it normally hung, but they quickly secured it and dropped the lines down for the next boat.

In relatively short order, all the men were aboard, and the boats were stowed. Catrin found Nat and was amazed to see he still held his staff. It took her longer to locate Vertook, but she eventually saw him huddled in a corner, his head cradled in his hands.

"Are you hurt?"

"No," he said, shaking his head slowly and slightly. "I did not know there could be so much water, or that it could be so"--he struggled for the word--"tall."

She nodded her understanding, touched him on the shoulder, and walked back to the railing. This ship did not move as violently as the small boat had, but it still moved constantly, and Catrin found it disquieting. As she leaned on the railing, trying to move with the movement of the boat and compose herself, a young man presented himself. A skinny lad with bright red hair and freckles, he was the only sailor she had seen without a dark tan.

"Hullo, miss, I'm Bryn. Cap'n wants to see you right away. I can take you to 'im if you'll just follow me."

Catrin nodded and followed him to one of the doorways leading into the deckhouse. As she stepped through the hatch, she immediately felt confined and closed in. She bumped into the walls as she stumbled and had to catch herself to keep from falling. The ship's motions were subtle, but they wreaked havoc on her sense of balance.

Bryn led her down the corridor to a door with no identifying marks. He tapped lightly, opened the door, and motioned for her to enter. The floor of the cabin was lower than the deck, and Catrin looked down as she stepped inside, a motion that proved to be a mistake. As soon as she lowered her head, dizziness overwhelmed her and her stomach heaved.

Desperate to escape the cabin before she lost control, she shoved Bryn aside and ran headlong to the railing where she expelled the remains of her stomach contents; she didn't think there'd be any more after her revival in the small boat, but there was. Bryn came to her side and offered her water and a towel.

"Thank you," Catrin said after a tentative drink. "I'm sorry I pushed you."

"Not to worry. I understand. I was sick for days when I first boarded the *Slippery Eel*," he said with a wink. The cool air soothed her, and she slowly began to feel better. She breathed in deeply then realized Nat and another man had joined them. When she turned toward them, both men stepped forward.

The man next to Nat looked different from the others. His hair was light brown, and he was slight of build. His nose hooked oddly, as if it had been broken more than once. He wore no jewelry, had no tattoos, and his age was difficult to gauge, but Catrin guessed he was in his middle years. Had she been asked, she would have thought him to be a farmer or fishermen, but certainly not a pirate.

"Lady Catrin, I'm Kenward Trell, captain of the *Slippery Eel*, and I welcome you aboard," he said, going to one knee. "Please accept my apologies for not recognizing your discomfort. I've brought you a bit of herb to calm your stomach, and it should also help with the headaches." The herb mixture tasted vile and nearly made her retch, but she had confidence in folk medicine and she focused on keeping it down as she waited for relief.

"You should feel better in a little while," the captain said. "For now, we can talk where you are comfortable."

"Thank you, Captain Trell. Your men saved our lives, and we will be forever grateful."

"Please, Lady Catrin, call me Kenward. Captain Trell was my father's name, and I've never answered to it," he said with a grin.

"Thank you, Kenward, and I am just Catrin."

"I'm disappointed Benjin is not with us yet, but a man as stubborn as he is could never come to harm. I'm sure he'll be along soon," Kenward said. "Your passage fees have been paid by Miss Mariss, though I'd have done it for free had she only asked," he said, winking. "I'll only be taking you part of the way; the *Eel* is stout, but the journey across the Dark Sea is best made in a larger ship. I'll get you as far as the Falcon Isles, where you'll board a larger ship."

"I've never heard of the Falcon Isles."

"Most haven't. It's a string of little islands inhabited mostly by primitive tribes, but they also serve as trading ports and hideouts for pirates, mercenaries, and other misfits--like me." He winked again.

"How do we know there will be a ship there for us?"

"Have no worries. My family has a large ship at port there right now, and they are waiting for the *Eel* to deliver goods before they sail for the Greatland. Your passage has been arranged for on that ship. You've probably heard the folklore about pirates, but we're just free sailors who bow to no government, and we trade goods with other, like-minded groups and individuals. They call us pirates, and we use it to our advantage; it makes us seem more frightening." He chuckled. "That label helps us in many ways. We're in a tight spot now, no arguing that--the cliffs on one side and the reef on the other, not to mention the obstacles in between. We'll need half a day to reach a sizable gap in the reef, but when we're clear, we have open seas to the Falcon Isles.

"Our biggest problem is that the Zjhon know we're trying to escape, even if they don't know for sure where we are. They've probably guessed we're within the reefs and will most likely have the gaps guarded. I doubt they'll bring tall ships inside the ring, for their drafts are much too deep. And let me tell ya that we had quite a time getting the *Eel* in here ourselves, but she's a sneaky wench. The *Eel's* faster and more maneuverable than the Zjhon ships, so we'll just have to weave our way through them.

"The cabin past mine is reserved for you, and there are dry clothes in the chest. If your gut is still sour, feel free to sleep on the deck," he said. Their conversation had taken her mind from her upset stomach, which, now that she thought about it, was feeling much better. Her body seemed to have adjusted to the movements of the ship. Getting dry seemed like a good idea. She thanked him and excused herself. As she walked toward her quarters, Vertook approached Kenward.

"How can such a big thing stay on top water when a man falls under?" he asked Kenward.

"It's all about buoyancy, my friend. Let me show you . . ."

Their voices faded as she walked past the captain's quarters to her own and stepped inside. It was just large

213

enough to hold a hammock, chair, and a small chest. A narrow shelf was built into one wall, and on it was a small lamp, burning low.

Catrin took off her damp clothes and sifted through the chest for something near her size. She found pants that were close enough. She had to pull the belt strings tight to keep them up, but they were comfortable, and she found a baggy shirt made of light material.

A knock at her door interrupted her thinking about how to get into the sleeping hammock.

"Who is it?" Catrin asked.

"Nat," came the response.

"Come in."

"I'm so sorry I pushed you off the cliff, Catrin. It was the only way to save you. I wanted us to go farther east where we could have climbed down slowly. But the soldiers were too close behind us; we would have made easy targets. The bowmen would have done us all in, and I didn't want Irvil's sacrifice to be for naught. I did what I had to do, as much as I didn't want to do it," he said.

"You really frightened me, and you terrified Vertook!"

"I know it. Vertook is quite wroth with me, and I fear he will not be so forgiving. He hasn't spoken to me since we boarded the ship, and he has been shooting me some nasty looks. Would you explain things to him for me, please?"

In that moment, Catrin realized Vertook, who was from a different culture, might want to take revenge to protect her as well as his honor. Although being pushed over the cliff may have been the only way to save her life, Vertook might not see it that way.

"Certainly. I'll talk to Vertook, but right now, I'm simply exhausted and really need to sleep." Another knock came at the door, and Nat slipped out as Bryn stepped in, carrying a mug of soup.

"Hullo again. I thought you might like something to eat," he said. "It's compliments of Grubb, our cook. He says that'll cure what ails ya."

"You are all very kind."

"It's still hot," he warned before she tasted it. It was a hearty broth with chunks of vegetable, and Catrin knew it was the kind of sustenance she needed.

"Would you like me to get your clothes laundered for you?" he asked pointing to the pile of clothing she had dropped on the floor.

"That would be kind of you. Are you sure you have the time?"

"You're my main responsibility for most of this trip," he said. "Cap'n wants me to make sure you're comfortable and that you have everything you need."

She watched him as he folded her dirty clothes over his arm and backed out of the cabin door.

"G'night, miss. If you need anything, be sure to holler out. There's always someone on watch. Right now, you'd best get some sleep. Tomorrow'll be a long day," he said as he closed the door.

Their journey would begin at first light, and Catrin was too exhausted to stay awake and worry, but her dreams were visions of blood and fire.

Chapter 21

Stars are the souls of old sailors. They plot the skies and guide the
wayward home.
--Aerestes, Captain of the *Landfinder*

* * *

Dawn found the *Slippery Eel* deserving of her name. The crew scrambled, and the passengers huddled in the deckhouse, trying to stay out of the way. Maneuvering the ship with incredible skill, the crew prepared to guide the *Eel* through the cavern entrance, which was just barely wide enough for the ship to pass, and wood occasionally strained against rock. Using oars and poles, they worked in concert to guide the ship around the many obstacles, but some were unavoidable, and the ship listed and jerked underfoot.

"Have no worries; the *Eel* can withstand those little bumps and a lot more. We've taken no damage," Kenward assured them as they rounded the last bend, the horizon beyond. Waves battered the coastline; swirling vortices formed around unseen rock formations, and Catrin feared they would be crushed on the rocks. Kenward barked orders, and the crew responded with alacrity, but the men seemed stretched to their limits, and there was frenzied activity on the weather deck.

The ship rolled and turned sharply as they cleared the entrance, caught in a dangerous current, and the waves drove the ship dangerously close to the rocks. Kenward orchestrated the movements of his crew decisively with instincts born of many years.

As the *Eel* glided into deeper water, there was an audible, collective sigh of relief, but the mood and tension on the ship did not lighten completely. There were still obstacles in the narrow channel, and they could not afford to take damage.

Sailors began their practiced routine of unlashing long sections of mast from racks along the deckhouse, while others retrieved massive iron sleeves. They used rope, pulleys, and a windlass to raise the broad bottom section into place and guided it into a huge iron ring amidships. It slid nearly half of its length into the hull. Once the base was settled in its mounting hardware, the crew secured it with spikes, iron bars, and threaded bolts of Kenward's design.

The crew continued to raise sections of the mast, joining them with the sleeves. When the sails and rigging were assembled and ready to be raised, Bryn climbed the bowsprit to attach several lines, and Catrin admired his bravery. Before long, the ship was moving under a small amount of sail.

With her homeland sliding by, Catrin's thoughts turned to all those she had lost and left behind. Tears filled her eyes as she thought of her father and Benjin. Equally distressing were worries over the safety of Chase, Strom, and Osbourne, her faithful companions. They had stayed by her side and risked their lives for her, and now she was abandoning them. Unable to bear the pain, she wiped her tears and concentrated on what lay ahead.

As they sailed into deeper waters, the wind gusted, churning the water to a choppy froth, and the western horizon was lost to view, despite the rising sun. Kenward surveyed the skies and the seas.

"I'd hoped for wind to give us speed, but this weather may be too much for us. We cannot turn back now, though. The water will only get rougher, and we would be hard pressed to enter the cavern again. I'm afraid we must face the weather and the Zjhon on this day. May the gods shine their light upon us," he said solemnly. "We've a strong ship and a seasoned crew, and we've been through tighter spots than this."

All on board kept a watchful eye on the horizon, looking for signs of enemy ships and gauging the weather. Catrin wondered if anyone else felt the intensity of the energy, as if the air were charged. Her carved fish sparkled in the light as she drew it from her shirt, and it looked nearly flawless. She left it out, exposed directly to the light. Breathing in the energy, she felt it flow through her, tingling and vibrating. Her head leaned back, she inhaled deeply, relishing the power as it pulsed around her. Part of her mind warned her against indulgence, but the ecstasy overwhelmed

217

her. Never before had she felt the energy so strongly. It washed over her in massive waves, much the same as the waves' relentless assault on the cliffs.

The energy made her body feel intensely alive, and she wanted desperately to use it. The warning voice in the back of her mind would no longer be denied, and she suddenly realized she heard little besides the wind, water, and rigging. She opened her eyes slowly, returning to the here and now and feeling the loss as she let the energy out of herself. When she focused on her surroundings again, she felt an uncomfortable silence, but it was broken when someone urgently announced enemy ships in sight. The crew sprang into action. Kenward commanded them by hand signals and guided the ship close to the cliffs to hide in the shadows. Everyone remained silent, and the tension grew exponentially as time passed.

Zjhon ships were still visible in the distance, but they neither closed the gap nor appeared to be getting any farther away. Catrin felt in her gut that they had already been seen and were heading into another trap. The feeling persisted, and soon the Zjhon ships moved closer.

"Break ahead!" the lookout called from the crow's nest, and they all looked in the direction he was pointing, knowing they needed to get free of the confining reef and reach the open seas. "Enemy ships charging the break, sir! They're going to beat us there!" he rang out a moment later.

"Prepare for contact!" Kenward commanded. The crew moved with the swiftness of experience. They armed themselves, secured lines, and erected a protective enclosure around the helm. The captain climbed the rigging and joined the lookout, and when he climbed down, he was issuing a steady stream of curses.

"You'd best get to your cabin, Catrin. We may be boarded, and there'll most likely be fighting on deck. Please remove yourself from harm," he pleaded.

"While those around me risk their lives, I will not run and hide, Kenward. I am neither weak nor afraid."

"Do you know how to use one of these?" he asked, drawing his sword.

"I'm better with a bow, but I can wield a sword when I must."

Kenward nodded and sent Bryn after a short sword and a bow. Bryn handed Catrin the sword in its leather scabbard. She drew it out to inspect it. The heavy blade was awkward in her hand, and she sheathed it, hoping she wouldn't have to use it. The bow was larger than she was accustomed to, but she could draw it. Slinging the quiver over her shoulder, she turned her attention to the Zjhon.

As they drew closer to the gap in the reef, Catrin noticed an unusual apparatus on the bow of a Zjhon ship, but she didn't know what it was. The Zjhon ships stayed back, away from the breach, but they were close enough to close the distance quickly, especially with the high winds to drive them.

"Bloody mother of a ballista! Those common som'bits," Kenward ranted.

Catrin had never heard of a ballista, but when she looked again at the ship, she was appalled. The ballista resembled a crossbow, only much larger--far larger than any weapon she had ever imagined. A supply of huge bolts, which were the trunks of small trees, lay beside it. She didn't know if the *Slippery Eel* could survive any hits from such a massive weapon, and she dreaded the impact and aftermath if any struck their mark.

"We're going to have to rush 'em and get the other ships between us and the ballista. We'll be vulnerable for a time, but I'm going to try to make that time as short as possible. That thing'll make a loud noise when they fire it, so be ready to take cover when you hear it," Kenward said. "We're going to shoot the gap at full speed, and then we'll head straight for those two ships. Be ready to repel boarding attempts; you all know the drill. For you newcomers: If it comes from the other ship, kill it. If it attacks you, kill it. And remember to cover my back."

"I will be proud to fight beside skilled and honorable men," Vertook shouted, and a cheer rose up from everyone on deck.

Though the break looked plenty wide enough from afar, it sloped down gradually on each side, leaving only a narrow channel. Going through it at full speed seemed folly, and the crew and passengers shared a nearly palpable anxiety. The gap rushed toward them, faster than seemed possible.

The way looked clear, but still they braced themselves as the ship entered the channel. Dark water closed around them, and the *Eel* slowed and spun, scraping along the reef. The vessel creaked and groaned, struggling to break free, but the impact left it perpendicular to the reef, the waves threatening to drive the ship atop it. Kenward was busy shouting commands, but he stopped suddenly at the sound of an awesome thrum.

"Take cover!" he shouted. The ballista bolt arched across the sky and struck the mainsail with a dreadful tearing sound. Kenward shouted more orders, and the crew rushed back into action. Bryn sprinted by with a long needle between his teeth and a ball of heavy string in hand. He scrambled up the rigging to the tear, which was steadily growing larger, but he got ahead of the ripping and continued to mend it, at times holding onto nothing but the sail itself.

Again the ballista thrummed, and Bryn stopped stitching just in time to brace himself. This bolt struck the sail higher, tearing another large hole, but after piercing the sail, it glanced off the mast and whipped around violently. Bryn didn't see the blow coming and was struck in the back of the head. He went limp, and Kenward yelled for a net to catch him.

Tangled in the stitching, Bryn's arm was all that kept him from falling. When he opened his eyes, he gasped as he realized his predicament. His movements were sluggish and awkward as he regained his grip on the rigging.

"I'll be fine," he said, but then he braced himself as the ballista fired again. The ship dipped low amid the growing waves, and the shot flew harmlessly over the bow, the rough seas and high winds saving them from being struck. Despite his injury, Bryn persisted, and he slowly and deliberately climbed to the other tear and began stitching.

While the attention of the crew had been focused on the ballista ship, the Zjhon had taken full advantage. Another ship was headed toward them on the starboard side at ramming speed. The *Eel* spun slowly away from the approaching ship.

As the Zjhon ship came within bow range, Catrin nocked an arrow and drew. Looking down her shaft, she located a target. He was young and wore a look of determination and fear. There was no hatred in his eyes, only duty. She hesitated and closed her eyes, but in her mind's eye, she saw a Zjhon shaft strike down Irvil of the Sun clan. As quick as thought, she rotated and found a new target: the man giving orders. Her fingers slipped from the string and the arrow sped through the air.

The man Catrin assumed was the captain of the Zjhon ship shouted one last order before he dropped over the side, her shaft protruding from his chest. Still the ship came and struck a glancing blow that sent the ships careening away from one another.

The Zjhon ship was much larger than the *Slippery Eel*, and it rode higher in the water. Sailors leaped from the height to the decks of the *Eel*. Many landed without injury, but some were knocked unconscious when they hit the deck, and others missed the ship completely and plunged into the raging depths.

One sailor landed not far from where Catrin stood, and she drew her short sword. The man smirked, seeing an easy victim, and he waved his sword menacingly. He approached slowly at first then suddenly sprung at her. Catrin was ready for his attack. She dropped to the deck, kicked him hard in the groin, and prepared to swing at his ankles. As he reeled from her kick, though, the anger on his face changed to utter surprise when Bryn swung down from the rigging and kicked him squarely in the chest. The sailor dropped over the railing without another sound, but Bryn lost his grip while fully extended and fell, faceup, landing hard. He looked up at Catrin, moaned, then passed out.

When he did not wake, Catrin dragged him to the deckhouse and into the first cabin. She tried to comfort him before leaving, feeling that she should stay by his side but not knowing what else to do for him. When she returned to the deck, most of the fighting was over. Nat and a crewman forced a final tenacious sailor over the railing and looked for anyone else left to fight. Kenward issued roll call, and eight men failed to report, including Bryn.

"Bryn was hurt in the fight. He banged his head twice and was knocked out. I took him to the first cabin." Kenward was overjoyed to learn Bryn was still with them, and he hugged her, kissed her on the forehead, and rushed to the deckhouse. Catrin joined the cheers when a crewman was pulled from the water. Six men lost were far too many, but it was much better than seven or eight.

The man at the helm earned his keep, swiftly putting distance between them and the Zjhon ships, all the while keeping a Zjhon ship between them and the ballista ship. As they sped northwest, aiming for open seas, they trimmed the sails to take full advantage of the wind while the Zjhon ships lumbered in sluggish pursuit. The gap steadily grew, and the crew became less tense, but as the northwestern tip of the Godfist came into view, their spirits dropped.

"Sails ahead, sir! I count a dozen northwest and three northeast! Zjhon outpost to the northeast and more ships on the horizon, sir!" called the lookout. The Zjhon had constructed a huge lift system for raising men and supplies to the mountain valley high above the sea. Luckily, it appeared mostly abandoned, and only three ships were moored in the harbor. Catrin began to feel much as she had when escaping from the desert--trapped--and the noose was tightening.

Kenward changed course, angling between the ships approaching from the makeshift docks and those still out to sea. Ominous storm clouds darkened the western horizon, casting a depressing pall over the crew. Webs of lightning illuminated the clouds, and as the sound of thunder grew closer to the lightning, the wind intensified.

The crew of the *Slippery Eel* pushed her to her limits, using more sail than was advisable in high winds, and the ship groaned in protest as it tore through the massive waves. Even with the speed advantage, it became obvious they would not be able to evade all the Zjhon ships. Whether the ships were part of a massive trap or were simply returning to harbor to wait out the storm didn't matter. It looked as if the

Slippery Eel would be trapped between the Zjhon ships and the Godfist.

Huge, growing swells crashed over the rails and forced everyone on deck to hold on to something. Many fled for the deckhouse, but Catrin fought her way to where Kenward had rooted himself near the helm.

"I don't know which I fear the most," he admitted. "The storm alone could put an end to us, and there are far too many Zjhon ships to avoid. Every option appears to be suicide, and I cannot decide which death I prefer."

Catrin knew in that moment that it was time for her to test her powers again. "Make for the center of the Pinook harbor," she said. Kenward raised an eyebrow and considered her a moment, seemingly trying to decide if she knew what she was talking about.

"The center of the harbor? Are you certain about that?" he asked.

"I am as certain as I've ever been about anything. There is no path that would not likely lead to our deaths except this one. Is there anyone with another plan?" she asked. "Make for the center of the harbor," she repeated after an uncomfortable silence. "When we arrive, drop anchor and prepare to ride out the storm."

Kenward seemed convinced by the force of her convictions, gave a simple nod, and the crew did what they knew to do without another order.

Darkness fell earlier than usual as storm clouds blotted out much of the remaining light and bands of horizontal rain pelted the crew. The winds forced them to lower part of their sails, and yet they still managed to maintain their speed. The seas were impossibly high. When in the troughs, Catrin could see nothing but walls of water on either side of the ship, and it looked as though they would be engulfed and sunk at any moment.

The *Slippery Eel* entered the Pinook harbor in relative darkness and made for the deeps. Many Zjhon ships were already in the harbor, though most had dropped anchor in preparation for the approaching storm. Many were still making for the harbor and could effectively block their only route of escape. Catrin knew they had reached the point of no return, and as she looked at the crew, all eyes were on her. Holding her amulet tightly, she prayed . . .

* * *

Staring at the familiar knots in the richly grained wood of his cabin walls, Kenward wondered if this was the last day he would spend on the *Slippery Eel*. Memories of his first ship, the *Kraken's Claw*, flooded his mind with every sight and sound of her sinking. Wringing his hands, he prayed this was not another mistake.

Catrin seemed sincere in her convictions, but escape from the harbor would be nearly impossible. Only the intervention of the gods could save him this time, and he could only hope they had not lost patience with him. Though he was not usually a religious or superstitious man, he found himself walking to the rails and tossing a gold coin into the dark waters, an offering to the sea.

Having done what he could do, Kenward returned to his cabin, hoping it was enough.

Chapter 22

The most awesome powers are those not wielded.
--Enoch Giest, the First One

* * *

The journey to the center of the harbor ahead appeared endless to the crew of the *Slippery Eel*. The Zjhon ships already in port were secured for the storm, and they remained where they were anchored. It seemed no one noticed the smaller pirate ship, and nothing barred their path. Even if they had seen her, it would have taken hours for the large ships to pull up their many anchors and raise and set their sails. The Zjhon ships following them into the harbor were so busy contending with the storm that they had to concentrate on survival rather than pursuit.

Catrin, alone for a moment, let her mind turn to a myriad of thoughts and emotions that she attempted to process. She didn't know if her friends were safe, and she felt a pang of loneliness and loss when she thought of them. When she thought of her father and her uncle Jensen, her heart nearly broke.

Her thoughts flashed to memories of the animals on the farm: the horses, cats, and all her cherished companions. She hoped Salty and the other horses were in green pastures, and that Millie and the other cats had found good hunting. Tears slid down her cheeks, but she stifled her grieving, knowing she would need to focus her energy on survival.

She did not want to destroy the Zjhon or their nation, but she could not allow them to continue their siege on the Godfist, and it was clear they would take over her homeland even if she escaped. No words would deter them; they would persist until forced to leave. She wanted to end the siege without the slaughter of men she realized were only doing their duty. That thought struck Catrin like a hammer blow: these men were not evil or her enemy; they were acting on orders. Archmaster Belegra was not evil either. He truly believed that what he did was good and right and protected his nation. Even if he was wrong, he was simply as fallible

225

and flawed as any other person. The actions of the Zjhon were precipitated by prophecies and religious beliefs that spanned thousands of years. It was as if what they did was foreordained and inescapable.

The Zjhon believed the Herald of Istra would descend on them and attempt to destroy them. When she tried to look at things from their perspective, Catrin realized they perceived her as the embodiment of some ancient evil, as the reincarnation of a legendary adversary, and that it was their duty to protect their families and their nation from imminent destruction.

She figured most of the Zjhon would seek high ground once they secured their ships. Rage burned in her belly when she imagined soldiers waiting out the storm at her family's farm. She felt an intense sense of personal violation but pushed it aside. Such self-indulgence would have to wait.

In a universe filled with possibilities, she knew some solution must exist. Battle with the Zjhon seemed inevitable, but she could see no way to defeat such a superior force even with all the people of the Godfist. The Zjhon ships provided them food and mobility, and those things would allow them to starve out those trapped in the cold caves and the Masterhouse. The ships were the key; without them, the Zjhon would be stranded and lucky to survive the winter.

Food was limited on the Godfist, the land barely supporting the current population, and the fields were untended due to the siege. The Masterhouse and the cold caves each had large stores of food and water, and though their food supplies were limited, they had proportionally more than the Zjhon would if deprived of their ships.

Destroying a fleet was not something Catrin would have ever thought herself capable of, but she had to consider the events that led to this moment: She thought of the explosion that saved her from Peten's staff and the storm that ravaged the greatoaks. She remembered her actions on the plateau and the staggering effects of her power. Her abilities were undeniable. The striking of the artesian well proved her ability to accomplish previously unthinkable things when she used Istra's power.

The storm, bearing down on the harbor, drove enormous swells toward land, and ships strained against their anchors. Catrin considered the storm, which was the biggest threat and possibly her greatest source of power. Whenever she reached for the comet, the energy seemed to form a spinning vortex, and she had the same sense of spiraling energy from the massive storm.

Stepping back, she tried to look at her world objectively and to shed her preconceptions. The comet and other heavenly bodies gave evidence of unimaginable size and distance. The shapes in the sky had one common factor: they were all spherical. The Godsland was a sphere, Catrin realized, and it, too, was spinning. She reveled in her intuitive realizations as if shedding overly tight skin.

The sphere, she realized, was the primal shape of the universe. As she extended her senses toward the storm, she felt the atmosphere spinning. It was a vertical column of air, sheared by the rotation of the planet itself, just as her tendrils of energy had been sheared. Insight and understanding, albeit limited, gave Catrin an added measure of confidence. She realized the mechanics of this universe could be used to her advantage.

Waves continued to batter the *Slippery Eel,* the winds making it difficult for the crew to work. The motion of the ship became increasingly violent, threatening to send Catrin over the railing. Nearly everyone else had gone belowdecks, and they were taking turns cranking the bilge pumps. Massive swells forced the bow under water, and the ship took on water as fast as the crew could pump it out.

Catrin had to stay on deck to carry out her plan, and she would need to remain standing. Grabbing a coil of rope from near the helm, she looped it around herself and the mainmast, creating a crude harness that she hoped would keep her in place.

Alarmed shouts from the crew interrupted her thoughts, those remaining on deck pointing wildly out to sea. Catrin saw only a wall of water at first, but when they crested the next wave, she saw two Zjhon ships headed straight for them. She guessed they were among the ships that had been pursuing them, and they seemed intent on finishing the job they had started. The two ships were dangerously close to one another, and Catrin was shocked to realize they were actually chained together.

Men leaped from one ship to the other; some made the jump, but many fell to their deaths. Other men scrambled across the massive chain that hung between the ships, but the chain would suddenly go slack then, just as suddenly, snap taut again as the ships moved closer together and farther apart on the waves. Catrin watched in horror as men were thrown into the air.

Their actions made no sense to her at first, but then she came to a harsh realization: they were evacuating one ship because it was on a suicide mission. She guessed they would leave a few men onboard to control it to make sure it rammed the *Eel*. A direct hit at their current speed could very well sink both ships, but the Zjhon had ships to spare.

Activity on the deck of the *Eel* became intense as men scrambled to mobilize the ship. They might not be able to evade the approaching ship, but they wanted to get the anchors raised so the other ship might only push them out of the way.

No more men attempted to abandon the suicide ship, and the chain was released during a brief slackening. The mostly unmanned ship continued to bear down on the *Slippery Eel* while the other turned aside sharply.

As the *Eel*'s crew hastily secured the anchors and ran for cover, Catrin braced herself and reconsidered the wisdom of tying herself to the mast, but there was no time left to escape. The Zjhon ship rode atop a huge wave, towering above the *Slippery Eel*, and it appeared to Catrin as if the ship suddenly dropped from the sky. The initial impact rocked the *Eel*, and Catrin's head smacked against the mast, leaving her stunned.

Seemingly unstoppable, the Zjhon ship slammed into the aft side of the deckhouse, easily pushing it out of the way. The supple wood flexed and groaned, barely withstanding the incredible force. The *Slippery Eel* rolled under the massive weight, and Catrin heard wood snapping just before she struck the frigid water.

Struggling against the ropes she herself had tied, she grew frantic, having been under water for what seemed a very long time. The ship rose suddenly and righted itself, tossed by another wave. Catrin hung limply against the ropes and tried to get her breath. Above the sounds of the storm, she could clearly hear Vertook praying as he worked the bilge pump like a man possessed.

Shrieking winds left no doubt that the massive storm had arrived and was engulfing the harbor. Catrin knew she had missed her chance to act before the full force of the storm struck, even as she knew she was drawing energy from it. Tied to the mast, she had to endure the high winds and brutal, stinging rain.

The crewmen were all focused on their tasks of trying to drop the anchors again, but they were hampered by the buffeting wind and waves. They looked as though they had suffered injuries--probably from the violent motions of the ship--and they moved slowly and deliberately. Some were bleeding heavily and appeared to be in pain but persisted in trying to do their jobs.

The ship rose high into the wind, which pushed a huge swell toward shore. The massive wall of water rushed on, inexorably, with an awful roaring sound accompanied by deafening cracks and snaps. Many of the Zjhon ships were torn from their moorings, and as Catrin watched, they began to float aimlessly, some crushed against the rocks, others smashed to bits against other ships.

The anchors of the *Slippery Eel* dug into the harbor floor once again, and the ship groaned as it faced the storm. The swells grew so massive that the ship was nearly pulled under by the weight of her own anchors as she crested the tallest waves. A huge piece of sail and rigging hit Catrin, and she couldn't tell which ship it had come from. She was uninjured, except for a gash across her forehead. Blood began to run into her eyes, clouding her vision, and she used the tail of her shirt to wipe the blood away.

Hours passed, but the storm continued, unabated. Then the winds suddenly died and the sky cleared. A surreal calm set in as the eye of the cyclone moved over the harbor. Catrin looked up into the night sky and was astonished to see five comets amid the stars, three of which were little more than small dots with tails, but the other two were large and bright.

The crewmen moved around the deck quietly, trying to take advantage of the brief respite. They all knew the way these storms behaved and that the other side of the storm was yet to come and would likely be worse. Using large hunks of rope, soaked in tar, they temporarily patched the holes in the damaged hull.

"Catrin, please come belowdecks. You could be killed out here," Kenward said as he passed her.

"I'll be fine here. Are there any clean bandages?" she asked. Kenward retrieved one for her and applied it to her wound.

"How is the crew holding up?" she asked.

He sighed. "They've taken some pretty hard licks, but they have to keep working despite their injuries. They are good, strong men, and they'll heal quickly. Bryn's awake and complaining a lot, so I'd say he'll be fine as well."

"Thank you, Kenward. I have to tell you that what I am about to try will be risky, but I must try to save us," she said.

"I have faith in you," he said simply.

As she turned to face the harbor, she saw men scrambling to take advantage of the short lull to try to prevent further damage to their ships. She drew a deep breath and opened herself to the intense energy surrounding her.

"Armies of the Zjhon nation, behold!" she said in her most powerful voice, which was amplified by the power running through her. "You bear witness to the Call of the Herald, and she calls you not to war, but to peace."

She paused then continued. "You came here to defend yourselves against one who had no intentions of destroying you, and by your very actions, you have brought about your own fears. I bear no ill will toward any of you, but I cannot allow you to lay siege to my homeland." She paused again as her words hung in the air. "Without your ships, you will have no food. You will have to choose between peace and death. You'll not survive a winter on the Godfist without the help of her inhabitants.

"I declare the armies of the Zjhon disbanded. All of you are now citizens of the Godfist, whether you wish it or not, and I'll not wage war with you," she said, pausing again for her final statement. "The Zjhon ships, however, are forfeited, and I will destroy them. If you wish to see the dawn, abandon your ships now." Her words hung in the air, echoing in the distance.

Without another word, she reached toward the largest and brightest comet in the sky. The cyclone's eye wall was rapidly approaching, and she had to act. Power and pleasure washed over her as energy flowed through her tingling body. Tendrils of energy reached toward the comet, the spinning of the planet causing them to shear and spin. A massive vortex of energy and swirling colors formed in the air above her.

Wind thrashed and churned the water around the ship, and Catrin expanded her vortex to envelop the ship and keep it within the relative calm of the center. Her senses heightened, she could feel the immense energy pent up in the storm. The clouds were highly charged and seemed to be searching for a place to release their abundant energy. When she cast her senses over the ship, she perceived a massive negative charge, and the result was as if the clouds and the ship reached toward one another, seeking balance. She could almost see a strand of negative energy reaching from the mast to the sky, and she shuddered as she realized one was also extending from her own head.

Casting about the harbor, she found a web of negative filaments rising from the Zjhon ships as well. Targeting the closest one, she reached out to its largest thread of negative energy, which rose from the mainmast. Her connection to the ship created an almost visible link between them, a thread of gossamer stretching into the night. She fed negative energy to the Zjhon ship, and the tendril grew more distinct and extended higher into the sky. The clouds reached down with their positive charge, yearning for ground.

A bolt of lightning suddenly completed the arc with a furious discharge. Up close, it resembled a plummeting fireball with a life of its own, and it struck the Zjhon ship with a fury, engulfing it in flames. The lightning was not spent, though, and it leaped along Catrin's thread of energy, racing toward her. She broke her link with the ship, and the lightning split apart, dissipating. Balls of fire cast waves of intense heat over her, only to fizzle and disappear before they reached her. All of this occurred within a fraction of an instant.

Her energy vortex raged on, unabated, and the eye wall was nearly on them. As the winds pounded against her power, they were forced aside and sheared off, causing them to spin wildly. The intense rotation spawned monstrous waterspouts that thrashed violently through the harbor, tossing ships about like children's toys. Several waterspouts became tornadoes as they left the water and moved over dry land.

Catrin sought more Zjhon ships, but the high winds and rain had returned with the other side of the cyclone's wall and obscured her vision. Determined, she reached out to them with her power alone, casting her energy over the water, feeling her way to the ships as if her power were an extension of her fingers. When she sensed the wooden sides, she knew she had found a target.

Her energy cast about the ship and located the mainmast. She attached a thread and fed it negative energy. Within a short time, lightning pounded her target and illuminated the spectacle for all to see. She released the link more quickly this time, but the bolt of lightning still came perilously close to reaching her, daring her to try again. Massive hail fell from the skies, pounding the ships mercilessly, and Catrin tried to target ships that were less damaged. Soon, the entire harbor appeared to be afire, and despite the driving rain, the fires spread and intensified.

Catrin noticed a nearby ship, which was largely undamaged, and reached out to it, calling the lightning to do her will. Too late she realized the *Slippery Eel* had also built up a massive negative charge. Looking up she saw a fireball racing along a jagged course. It slammed into the mainmast, and she was helpless to protect herself as it descended on her. It struck with a force greater than anything she had ever imagined, and the ropes securing her were vaporized, along with much of her hair and clothing. She fell to the deck, stunned and smoking, her energy vortex collapsing. Darkness overwhelmed her.

* * *

When Catrin opened her eyes, she was lying faceup on the heaving deck. Disoriented, she had difficulty focusing her thoughts. She was about to pull herself back to the mast when a bizarre phenomenon occurred: hundreds of fish, large and small, rained from the sky. It was a dangerous spectacle, and Catrin was struck in the leg by an enormous jellyfish. The gelatinous creature exploded on impact, and its stinging tentacles caused intense pain. Reaching the mast, she wrapped her arms and legs around its base and held on. Flames danced amid the rigging, but the fire was quickly extinguished.

Exhaustion overcame Catrin, her mind and body screamed for rest, but if she relented, she knew all aboard the *Slippery Eel* would surely perish in the powerful storm. Forcing herself to concentrate, she worked to reestablish her protective energy vortex. When she reached for the comet, though, the exertion was just too much in her weakened state. Struggling to hang on to the mast and remain conscious, she closed her eyes and squeezed herself tight around the mast.

The carved fish dug into her chest where it still hung on its leather thong. She had forgotten about it, and it gave her enough hope to try again. She pulled the carving from her shirt and lifted the thong over her head. Placing the small fish in her palm, she wrapped the thong around her fingers. With the carving firmly secured, she tried again to create a vortex.

The carving grew warm in her hand as she drew on it, and she reached into the night sky. Heavy water vapor in the air thrashed her vortex wildly as it tried to form. Catrin poured herself into the vortex. Straining with everything within her, she fed the vortex with every emotion she contained. Fear, anger, resentment, joy, and love all went into the shimmering funnel. It fluctuated and wobbled around her, liquid veins of color dancing across its surface, but it finally established itself and became organized.

As the vortex grew, chaos ensued throughout the harbor as more waterspouts were spawned, and lightning picked its own targets. The vortex provided some protection from the storm, but not all dangers would be so easily held at bay. Catrin was nearly knocked loose from the mast when another ship crashed into them. It had broken loose from its moorings and was now being tossed around the harbor. It rammed against the *Eel* several times before finally breaking free, sent spinning toward shore by the driving winds.

The carved fish had grown hot in her hand, but she continued to draw on the energy reserves it provided, determined to protect the ship and its men from further damage. It was obvious the ship was wounded because she had begun to list to one side, but Catrin could hear the crew still working the bilges, and she prayed the *Eel* would remain afloat.

The relentless storm pounded them for what seemed an eternity, putting Catrin's endurance to the test. She lost feeling in her limbs, and her mind grew fuzzy; she could no longer remember why she needed the vortex so badly, but some part of her held on tenaciously. Only when she felt a hand settle on her shoulder did she become aware of her surroundings again. The dawn had come, the storm passed, and still she held on to the dwindling vortex.

Once fully convinced she no longer needed it, she released the energy and slumped forward. Her body was leaden, and her heart seemed weary of beating. The hand was still on her shoulder, and she looked up to find Nat looking at her with extreme concern. He had risked himself by reaching through her vortex to touch her.

"Are you well?" he asked as he wrapped her in a thick blanket.

"I don't think so."

"What did this to you," he asked.

"Lightning," she responded, unable to elaborate.

As her senses returned, she felt intense pain in her right hand, and she opened it slowly. The leather thong was still twined around her fingers, but as her hand opened, the fish carving crumbled into dust. Instinctively she knew she had lost something far more important than a simple carving or even a mighty tool. She'd destroyed something precious and irreplaceable. The flesh of her palm was covered with tiny blisters, and when she concentrated on it, the pain was overwhelming. She would have collapsed on the spot, but she saw the rest of the crew hurriedly preparing for their departure. The crew repaired what damage they could, and the *Slippery Eel* soon began limping toward the open seas.

"I want to go back. I want to go home," Catrin said.

"Do you think they will welcome you? Do you think peace can so easily be achieved?" Nat asked, shaking his head. "I think not. Your countrymen have already declared you a witch and were ready to turn you over to the Zjhon. And what of the Zjhon? You may have declared them citizens of the Godfist, but you also sentenced them to a hard winter here. You stole from them their only way home." He placed his hand on her shoulder to soften the blow of his words.

"No, Catrin. You cannot go home now. I see dark days ahead on the Godfist, and I fully expect there to be unrest, if not civil war. But even if none of this were true, I would still urge you to seek out knowledge that cannot be found here. I know little of your power, but I know one thing for certain: if you do not find a way to better control your gifts, then they will be the instruments of your destruction."

In the silence that followed, Kenward shifted uncomfortably and waited for Catrin to respond, but she did not. "Do you want me to take you home?" he asked, earning a glare from Nat.

"I do," she responded softly, her eyes downcast. "But I cannot go back. Nat is right. I must go to the Greatland and seek out the Cathurans. I must learn to control my power. It's what Benjin wanted. It's what my father would want."

Kenward nodded and returned to his work. Nat put his hands on Catrin's shoulders and turned her to face him. "I know this is hard for you, and I know it's not what you desire, but you do what is right."

Catrin walked to the bow of the ship in silence. She took one last look at her homeland, knowing she might never see it again. Only when the Godfist had dwindled in the distance did she pull herself from the heart-wrenching sight and shuffle to her cabin.

Just as she was entering the deckhouse, one of the crew shouted in alarm. In the distance, the *Slippery Eel*'s sister ship appeared on the horizon. The Zjhon had captured the *Stealthy Shark* during the raid on the pirate's cove, and no doubt they now planned to use her to their advantage. The *Shark* appeared to have less damage than the *Eel* and was moving swiftly toward them.

Catrin's will and energy were spent. She climbed into the hammock and tried to think of a way to evade the ship, but her muddled thoughts were indistinct, and she fell exhausted into a deep sleep.

Epilogue

Premon Dalls crouched in the drainage ditch, waiting for the Zjhon patrol to pass. Acrid smoke still hung heavy in the air, stinging his eyes and irritating his throat, making him fear he would soon be coughing. Debris from the storm littered the ditch, and he pulled as much as he could over him, trying to make himself invisible.

He assumed these men were still loyal to General Dempsy since they still marched in formation and there was no one he recognized in the group. The defectors were with the followers of Wendel Volker since the Masters refused to accept any of them. With tensions rising between the Masters and the rebels, as Wendel's followers were called, the mysterious presence of the tribes of Arghast only increased the uncertainty of the situation. How they had come to be allied with the rebels was still a mystery.

Spying on the rebels had yielded little new information, but Premon was determined to use every morsel to his advantage. His plain looks had been a handicap when he was an ambitious young man struggling to gain status, but now his appearance was a benefit. Few took notice of him, and even fewer knew his name.

Getting back to the Masterhouse was proving to be more difficult than ever before, as the Zjhon patrolled constantly, seemingly intent on maintaining control over the docks and shipyards. This was not an entirely bad thing, for when the Zjhon repaired their ships and left the Godfist, he would be free.

For the moment, though, he was content to wait.

* * *

While it was still dark, Premon hauled himself out from the mud and trash and crept to the foul-smelling sewer grate he'd told Peten Ross about. Looking around to make sure no one was nearby, he removed the broken bar from the grate and set it inside. Even with the bar removed, he had to squeeze through, and he was bruised and scratched by the time he got down into the sewer. He replaced the broken bar

237

and picked up the torches and flint he'd stashed there several days before. The stench was overwhelming, and he struggled to breathe.

By the time he reached the drain that led to the upper halls of the Masterhouse, his sense of smell was gone, and the powerful odor no longer bothered him. The steep climb to the upper halls was an even worse part of the journey, but he suffered through it, thinking of the future. A place of power awaited him, and it would all be worth it.

Using one of the many service tunnels to gain access to the Masterhouse, Premon made his way to the appointed place without being seen. Once within the darkened room, which was little more than a closet, he waited.

He was sleeping when Master Edling finally arrived, and Premon struggled to pull himself from his stupor.

"Don't you ever bathe?" Master Edling asked, covering his nose and mouth with his hand.

"Stealth has its price," Premon said, shrugging.

"What have you found out?"

Premon thought for a moment before he replied. "The rebels plan to take back the farmlands and the highlands and leave Harborton to you."

"How very kind of them."

"I've heard talk of settling the Zjhon defectors in the upper Pinook and Chinawpa valleys. It seems they're willing to give away our lands to the enemy," Premon continued.

Master Edling appeared lost in his own ruminations, and Premon pressed on, hoping to gain any advantage he could. "General Dempsy's men have already repaired one warship, and they are scavenging materials to repair more. From what I've heard, they plan to pursue the Volker girl once they have three seaworthy ships. The deserters will be left behind."

Master Edling watched Premon but showed no reaction.

"There is one other thing," Premon continued, his lips curling into a sneer. "Wendel Volker sleeps in an unguarded room near one of the shafts that allow fresh air into the cold caves."

"Does he now?" Master Edling said, raising his eyes to meet Premon's. "It would be a pity if he were to die in his sleep, especially with no one to inherit his lands."

Premon could not keep the smile from his lips. "Indeed," he said, a plan already forming in his mind. Acres of farmland were far from enough to satisfy him, but it was a beginning.

About the Author

Born in Salem, New Jersey, Brian spent much of his childhood on the family farm, where his family raised and trained Standardbred racehorses. Brian lives with his wife, Tracey, in the foothills of the Blue Ridge Mountains.

For more information, visit http://BrianRathbone.com

Be sure to grab your copies of books two and three of *The Dawning of Power* trilogy, *Inherited Danger* and *Dragon Ore.*

If you enjoyed this book, please consider leaving a review, rating, or even just "liking" this book on your retailer of choice. Thank you!